# NO FEAR

BOOKS BY CASEY KELLEHER

THE LUCY MURPHY SERIES
*No Escape*
*No Fear*

THE BYRNE FAMILY TRILOGY
*The Betrayed*
*The Broken*
*The Forgotten*

OTHER BOOKS BY CASEY KELLEHER
*Mine*
*The Taken*
*The Promise*
*Rotten to the Core*
*Rise and Fall*
*Heartless*
*Bad Blood*

# NO FEAR

## CASEY KELLEHER

bookouture

Published by Bookouture in 2020

An imprint of Storyfire Ltd.
Carmelite House
50 Victoria Embankment
London EC4Y 0DZ

www.bookouture.com

ISBN: 978-1-80019-016-0
eBook ISBN: 978-1-80019-015-3

*For Sumaira*
*A true, brave, kick-arse warrior x*

# PROLOGUE

Her eyes flickered open, adjusting immediately to the darkness, as she lay deadly still, paralysed with fear, unable to move or speak. She focused on the wall in front of her, trying to make sense of what had woken her. But deep down, she already knew.

Her heart drummed wildly inside her chest. A charge of danger pulsated like electricity in the air all around her. He was here again. She could sense him. His eyes burning into the back of her as he watched her, willing her to wake. He wanted to scare her. He wanted to terrify her. She forced her eyes shut again, hoping to push him out from the dark recesses of her mind. To regain her power and to stop him from crawling deeper underneath her skin. She willed herself to look. To turn and face him. To confront her demons head on. Because he wasn't real. This was just her mind playing tricks on her again. This was all inside her head. Wasn't it?

But the more she tried to convince herself that he wasn't really here, the less she believed it. She forced herself to turn. A surge of adrenaline rushed through her body as she sensed the real danger she was in, as her eyes rested on the dark shadowy silhouette in the corner of the room.

He wasn't just a figment of her imagination. He was real. And he'd come for her.

# CHAPTER ONE

'It's last orders, Gerard,' Jimmy Shelton said, trying to put on a brave face as he poured Gerard Jennings another pint and hoped that, with a fair warning and one last large drink in his hand, Gerard wouldn't create a scene like he had last time. Jimmy lived in fear of upsetting the man.

All he wanted to do was earn an honest living, but there wasn't much chance of that with the likes of Gerard Jennings frequenting his pub on such a regular occurrence. Gerard and his men often took over the Red Fox, especially Gerard, who was always so loud and raucous. He was blatant in how he intimidated the other customers so that they'd end up with the place to themselves and he could indulge himself as much as he wanted with copious amounts of booze and drugs.

The last time Jimmy had tried to broach Gerard's unruly behaviour and the fact that he was losing him customers, Gerard had grabbed him by his throat and pinned him up against the wall in front of everyone at the bar. He'd squeezed Jimmy's windpipe with so much force that Jimmy had been certain he'd been just seconds away from losing consciousness, and it had taken three of Gerard's men to wrench the man off him.

Gerard acted like he owned the place and if he wasn't ready to call it a night, he'd have no qualms about forcing Jimmy to keep the place open, before he and his men proceeded to work their way through every bottle on the optics, just to teach Jimmy a lesson. Still, this was his home and his business and despite the obvious repercussions, Jimmy had to at least try and stand up for himself. Even if his attempts to do so did fall on deaf ears, just as they did now.

'Is that so, Jimmy?' Gerard said with a sly grin, catching the tremble in Jimmy's hand as he handed him the glass. 'You've got a set of brass balls on you after what happened here last time, I'll give you that.' Gerard was purposely winding the man up. 'I mean, they're tiny balls, but brass balls all the same.'

Picking up his pint, Gerard downed the entire drink in just seconds, before setting the glass back down on top of the bar, as if proving a point.

'But I'll tell you when we're done here. Stick another one in there. And bring it over to me.'

Jimmy nodded dutifully. He saw how bloodshot Gerard's eyes were, the man's pupils swollen like black saucers, his glare emotionless. He watched as Gerard staggered back to the table of his men and sat back down. Jimmy knew better than to argue with the man further when he was like this. Gerard was on one tonight, high as a kite on cocaine and alcohol, and Jimmy knew, without doubt, there was trouble brewing.

He had a feeling that Gerard's men, sitting around the table with him, could sense it too. He could see the looks that passed between them all. How they were all acutely aware that Gerard's dark, twisted mood was building inside of him, ready to erupt at any minute. No one wanted to be the one who set the man off from the edge. Jimmy walked across the pub and placed a fresh pint in front of Gerard, glad that he was too preoccupied to give him any more grief, distracted as he was by the line of coke on the table in front of him.

'Cheers,' Paul Denman said, his tone almost apologetic, and Jimmy could tell by Paul's face that he wasn't overly happy with Gerard's behaviour tonight either.

As Jimmy stared around the pub, he was aware of how quickly most of the locals had cleared out since this lot turned up. Apart from the odd loner dotted about, they were the only ones left in here.

'As I was saying…' Paul continued now that Gerard was back at the table. Though he was starting to think that the man was only here in body, and not in spirit. Gerard's logic and brain would have been obliterated by the amount of gear he'd shoved up his nose already tonight. It wasn't the best time for this discussion to take place, but Paul didn't have much choice. Gerard needed to be given a fair warning that they were heading for a complete shit show, otherwise they'd all be dragged down, Paul included. 'I've started moving all the gear and I've told all our boys to stop doing runs and sit on the stuff that they've got left. We all just need to lie low and wait this out until the heat's off us.'

'Not this again, Paul, for fuck's sake! I told you earlier. You are overreacting. We don't need to move shit and we don't need to lay low. They've got nothing on us,' Gerard said with a certainty that Paul didn't share.

'Gerard! They busted the cuckoo house that Jax Priestly was using, remember? Jax was stabbed to death by the tenant and the place got raided by the police? This ringing any bells?' Paul shook his head, furious that Gerard wasn't taking the situation more seriously. 'They seized thousands of pounds worth of money and drugs, not to mention weapons and mobile phones. It's only a matter of time before they start tracing things back to us, Gerard. That's if they haven't already. I'm telling you now, we need to be careful.' He knew how pig-headed his boss could be when his mind was made up. The problem with Gerard was that he was beginning to believe his own bullshit. He was starting to really think that he was untouchable. Above the law. When the truth was, believing that you were invincible was a dangerous place to be.

'There is no trail. I told you, nothing can lead back to us. We used burner phones and we only ever deal in cash. The police haven't got a fucking clue who or what they are dealing with here. They are too busy running around after the hood-rats like that Jax kid to have any inkling who's running things further up the chain.'

Gerard took a mouthful of his beer.

'Anyway, who cares? Who gives a fuck about the likes of Jax Priestly?' Gerard dared anyone around the table to say different. They all clearly knew the score. 'No one, that's who. The kid was nothing more than a commodity, a means to an end. Fuck me, I had the new kid, Jamie Nash, running the next deal line for me before that Jax's body was even put in the ground.' Gerard shrugged. 'That's what we do. We ain't here to babysit the fuckers. If they are stupid enough to get themselves stabbed up, that's their problem. We're here to make money and how are we going to do that if everyone's sitting around on their arses selling jack?!'

Paul nodded, recognising the defiance in Gerard's tone. He knew where this was going. They'd sit here and argue about this all night, because Gerard would never admit that he was wrong.

'Gerard, you know that you can trust what I say. When have I ever let you down?' Paul said, playing on their almost thirty-year friendship in the hope that somehow he could get through to his mate and the man would listen to what Paul was trying to tell him. 'This isn't just about the police, Gerard, we've got bigger problems than that. I've heard a rumour from the top that some of the bosses in Manchester are not happy with the current state of affairs around here either. They're not happy that the police have closed in on one of their most lucrative county line links…' Paul paused, knowing that the next bit of information wouldn't go down well. 'They're concerned that you're not running things the way that they want their business to be conducted, Gerard. That you're not being discreet.'

Paul held Gerard's gaze then, trying not to look down at the cocaine-covered table top. Gerard might be high as a kite, but he was anything but stupid. He didn't need it spelling out to him. But what he did need right now was a huge reality check. Otherwise they'd all be taken down, Paul included.

'I heard that they're sending someone to keep an eye on us, Gerard. To suss out the situation, and report back to them.'

He had Gerard's attention now. He could see it in the man's steely glare as his brain finally clicked in and he realised the severity of the situation. That they weren't just having to watch themselves when it came to the police. The bosses higher up in the firm had eyes on them too.

'So, what do you want to do?' Gerard asked.

'I've told everyone to sit tight. No one sells so much as a bag of gear on our watch. I've pulled everyone out of the trap houses around Wandsworth and Battersea. No one runs any lines. No one does any deals. Everyone just needs to keep a low profile and wait for the order to come from you. When it's time,' Paul said, clever enough to know that in order to keep Gerard on side he had to make it clear that Gerard was very much still in control. Even if it was Paul doing all the legwork behind the scene. That was how their operation had always worked. Gerard was the face of their business. He was the man everyone feared.

'The only thing that I haven't sorted yet is clearing the unit down on Smugglers Way, behind the recycling plant. I wanted to run it by you first. We need to move all the gear from our new supplier to a safe house before anyone starts sniffing around the place.'

Gerard screwed his face up, irritated now, as he stared at his pint. All enthusiasm for drinking had suddenly left him.

'Laying low will lose us a shit load of money. We can't afford to take that big a hit. Not right now,' he said, his eyes boring into Paul's, and Paul knew exactly what he was referring to.

He and Gerard had often spoken about getting out and that's exactly what they'd intended to do with this latest shipment. This stuff was from a new supplier. They already had a good system in play. Gerard wanted to sell it on his terms, severing ties with the bosses. He wanted to go it alone, just him and Paul. Why should they be the ones who had to keep getting their hands dirty and doing all the ground work from some ponce back in Manchester who held all the cards?

'Now more than ever, especially if we're going to go through with this and cut ourselves loose from the bosses and start out on our own.' Paul said, his eyes flashing with a warning. 'The heat is on us big time, Gerard. We need to be vigilant. And we need to stay smart and more than anything we need to stay ten steps ahead of those fuckers at every point of the game; otherwise we'll end up losing everything. Everything we've worked for up until now.'

Gerard nodded. Finally, compliance. Paul smiled. He knew that he had his friend then, that Gerard was finally listening. He'd got there in the end.

'Right, well we better all get some sleep while we can. We'll get down to the unit first light and get everything moved,' Gerard said, getting up from his seat and taking back control just like Paul had been hoping he would.

This was how Gerard worked. He'd heed Paul's words of warning and then make out that their plan of action was his own. That he called the shots. And if it meant that Gerard was toeing the line and listening to him, Paul was prepared to melt into the background, every single time.

'Are you off, lads?' Jimmy Shelton asked, not believing his luck as he watched Gerard and his men all getting up and putting their jackets on, in a bid to leave.

'Here, this should more than cover the tab,' Paul said, nodding in answer and catching the look of relief that spread across the landlord's face, before throwing a roll of notes down on the bar.

'Cheers, Paul,' Jimmy said, grateful then, feeling suddenly lighter as he stood in the middle of the pub and watched the men all leave. He liked Paul. The man seemed fair. It was just a shame that the man's sole purpose in life was to go around cleaning up after the likes of Gerard Jennings.

*

Sitting in the small booth at the back of the Red Fox, where he'd been quietly nursing his pint whilst pretending to be absorbed in the newspaper that was currently spread across the table in front of him, Bobbie Carter peered across the pub, watching as Gerard Jennings, Paul Denman and their men finally left through the main door. He grinned to himself then, shaking his head. Child's play! And to think that he was worried that he'd have his work cut out for him even getting close to Gerard and his men. Gerard was so wired from the gear he'd been snorting that half the pub had probably heard the man's conversation. And Bobbie certainly hadn't appeared on his radar. Not that anyone here had bothered to even look twice at Bobbie since he'd sat down. He had one of those faces. Forgettable, uninteresting. Paired together with his wiry, thin frame and the fact he was average height meant that Bobbie Carter simply blended into the background and didn't pose any kind of a threat to anyone. Traits that served him well, especially in his line of work.

His bosses were right to be concerned about Gerard. If Bobbie hadn't witnessed the severity of Gerard's imminent unravelling first-hand for himself, he'd never have believed it. Bobbie had watched Gerard with fascination tonight. Sensing the air of danger in the room as the man's dark mood descended across the entire pub the minute that Gerard and his men had arrived here this evening. And if Bobbie could get all this information in just one evening as easily as he had, then the rumours about Gerard

Jennings being a liability were true. The man truly believed that his violent reputation alone would protect him and that he'd become untouchable.

Not only that but Bobbie had also learned of a shipment that even his bosses didn't know about. Which was a serious bonus for him. The way he saw it, he had two options now of how he could use this new information. He could tell his bosses about the shipment and earn some brownie points or he could cash in on it himself, and make a real earn on the side. Smiling to himself, he decided on the latter. It was a no-brainer. Finishing the last dregs of his pint, Bobbie Carter got to his feet, ready to take the golden opportunity that Gerard Jennings and his men had kindly served up to him on a platter. He'd make his way down to the unit now, before Gerard and Paul got there in the morning like they'd planned. Why not? After all, he had no reason to fear any retribution from Gerard and his men, because as far as they were concerned he didn't exist. He didn't factor on the men's radar. And by the time they realised they'd been had, Bobbie would be long gone. And once the bosses got word about Gerard Jennings's planning on cutting loose and going it on his own with a new supplier, Gerard Jennings would be long gone too.

# CHAPTER TWO

Driving down the narrow side road, Bobbie Carter pulled up his van by the grass verge that ran down the side of the Wandsworth recycling plant. Eyeing the old, derelict, boarded-up unit to his right, he wondered if he definitely had the right place, though he had it on good authority that Gerard had been using it for years to collect and store his shipments. But then that was what probably made the place such a good front, he figured. No one would suspect it to house such valuable goods. The fact that the unit looked like such a shack was probably a bluff. There weren't any activated alarm systems in place, or any CCTV that Bobbie could see. And there certainly weren't any security men watching over the place. Another testament to the fact that Gerard Jennings really did believe that he was untouchable.

Casting his glance up the road, he searched for somewhere less conspicuous to park. The dark alley that ran down between two buildings further up was perfect. Turning off his engine, Bobbie pulled on his gloves and got out of the van, unable to help but smile to himself as he psyched himself up for what he was about to do, as he walked back down towards the unit.

His eyes fixed on shimmer from the murky waters of the Thames that stretched out across the horizon at the end of the road. The reflection of the dimly lit street lamps that danced across the surface of the dark water, as he walked, looked almost hypnotic in this light. A complete contradiction to the depressing sight the river posed during the day.

So far, the Thames, and London in general, had failed to impress him if he was honest. He preferred Manchester. And he couldn't wait to get back home there. Soon. First he had work to do.

Making his way around the front of the building, he pulled at the front door, tutting loudly to himself as he caught sight of the thick metal chain and padlock that rattled with his movement. He'd never be able to break through it. It would take too long. There must be another way to get inside. He squeezed himself onto the thin strip of grass and edged along the side of the unit, looking for a window, shining his phone's torch down on the overgrown weeds that came up past his knees as he stepped carefully amongst the mass of unevenly piled rocks and rubble. Reaching the first window, Bobbie pressed his face up against the thin glass pane and stared into the darkness, trying to make out what was inside the room. Nothing, as far as he could see. Just a huge vast space. The unit looked empty.

Bobbie wondered if he'd heard the wrong information or if he'd come to the wrong place.

Though to give Gerard his due, even he wouldn't be stupid enough to advertise whatever it was that he was hiding in there. It was probably just well hidden. Bobbie would have to get inside and take a proper look. He'd heard the men. The shipment was definitely here. At this unit. He was certain of it.

He was so close now that he could almost smell the money that there was to be made. Eyeing the single glazed panel, he knew that it would be enough for him to put his fist through and break it if he had to. He could get in that way. First though, he tried his luck pulling at the wooden framework around it, raising his eyes gleefully as he felt the entire panel slide under the movement of his hand. The window was loose. It would be easier and a lot less messy if he could crank it open with a crowbar or something similar. He could be in and out again in minutes.

He checked his watch. It was almost one a.m. now; he had hours ahead of him until the men were due down here to move the shipment. They'd all be tucked up in their beds right about now. Lost in their drunken slumbers, oblivious to the fact that he was about to royally fuck them all over.

Bobbie had free rein to do as he pleased. He smirked to himself as he made his way back to the van to search for his tools, keeping his phone torch aimed at the ground so that he didn't lose his footing in the darkness, shaking his head in wonderment at how easy this all had been for him. As far as he could see, these London lads really were slow on the uptake and they deserved everything that was coming to them.

The first he knew about the car veering towards him at speed was when he heard the screech of the tyres skid across the concrete. He turned too late to see where the noise was coming from. Though he felt it before he actually saw it: the weight of metal slamming into him, throwing him high into the air, as a wave of almighty agony exploded through him, before he came crashing back down on the solid, rough ground.

He lay there stunned and broken, every part of his body screaming in agony. He tried to lift his head but he couldn't move. All he could do was stare at the car that had come to a halt now, willing the driver to get out and help him. The random thought entered his mind that the car hadn't had any lights on. And the driver wasn't making any attempt to hurry to help him.

Finally he saw the car doors open. Dazed and confused at what was going on, Bobbie watched from his crumpled state on the floor, as a sea of black boots and shoes pounded towards him as if in slow motion. Staring up into the balaclava-clad faces of the gang that loomed over him, Bobbie Carter could feel the shock setting in as his body started to wildly shake with fear.

'You took the bait then, Bobbie!' One of the men laughed, grabbing Bobbie roughly and pulling his twisted, broken body upright before dragging him the few metres over to the car, before shoving him into the backseat.

'What's going on?' Bobbie said as two of the men clambered in, one on either side of him, and started wrapping his limbs tightly with thick, black gaffer tape. Not that Bobbie could make a run for it even if he wanted to. The pain that shot up both legs was so acute that he thought he was going to pass out. The car slamming into him had broken them, he was sure. Though he already knew the answer to that as he fixed his stare on the man in the driving seat. The man who had grabbed him and marched him to the car. It suddenly dawned on him then as he took in the man's almighty build. Paul Denman, or Big Paul as he was known. His huge frame was wider than the seat he sat on.

'All right, Bobbie mate!' Paul finally spoke, tilting the rear-view mirror so that he could get a better look at the fear that now radiated from Bobbie's terrified face. 'Fancy seeing you here, eh? In the middle of the night, all on your tod.'

Bobbie realised then that he'd been set up. That it was he who had been so stupid to blindly believe everything that he'd heard at the pub. Everything that they'd purposely fed him. He recalled now the smallest flicker of eye contact that he'd shared with Big Paul earlier in the evening. So fleeting that when Paul had looked away just seconds later, and carried on talking without missing so much as a beat, Bobbie had been convinced that Paul hadn't registered him, or who he was. But he had been wrong.

Just a second's steely look. That's all it had taken for the man to be on to him.

He thought back to how Big Paul had made a point of shutting the night down shortly after that. After giving all that spiel about an extra shipment that no one knew about at the unit. Even Gerard, in his drunken state had seemingly played along. Not so stupid after all it seemed. Only it was too late for Bobbie Carter to do anything other than realise that now. He was royally screwed. His only saving grace was that it didn't look as if Gerard was here. Maybe Paul would take some mercy on him.

'We weren't sure if you were here on business or on pleasure, Bobbie, when we spotted you sitting there earlier on your tod in the corner. Drinking everything in. Thirsty motherfucker, ain't you?' Paul said, letting the man know that he knew all about him. And confirming his suspicions that this lot had set him up. 'But we were expecting you, mate. As you heard, a little birdy had already given us the heads-up that the bosses were sending someone down to keep an eye on us. And that little birdy had already given me a nudge that it was you, you snidey little cunt. Oh, and Gerard sends his apologies for not being here to see the look on your face when you realised what a prize prick you are.'

Paul paused for a few seconds as he started up the engine, purposely wanting to give Bobbie some false hope that at least he'd escaped the wrath of Gerard.

'Don't worry, though. He'll have his chance to see you when we deliver you to him personally in just a bit. He said to tell you that you might be here on business, but the pleasure is most definitely going to be all his!'

# CHAPTER THREE

'Seriously Debs, I'm not lying when I say that Micky is completely useless. I'll put money on the fact that he's probably sprawled out on the sofa right now, watching the bloody footy and waiting for me to come home so that I can cook him dinner. The stupid sod doesn't realise that he's got two more-than-capable hands on the end of those dangly arms of his. I blame his mother. She did everything for him. Still would, given half the bleeding chance.'

Debra Jennings couldn't help but laugh then as Kiera Woodburn rolled her eyes dramatically.

Kiera was for ever griping about Micky and his mother, who both regularly drove Kiera round the twist with their antics. As far as Debra could see, Micky wasn't a bad guy. A bit boring and lazy, though she'd never admit that to Kiera. But the man wouldn't hurt a fly. If anything, he needed to have his guard up with Kiera. The woman was continuously on the warpath about something he had or hadn't yet done. And Debra knew that Kiera told her all her funny stories in a bid to cheer her up. She was only messing half the time, trying to put a smile on Debra's face when she was feeling down. Which was most of the time lately.

The Griffin Estate wasn't the easiest of places to live and bring up a family, that was true. But having Kiera living in the flat next door was probably one of the place's only perks, if Debra was brutally honest. The woman was an absolute tonic and exactly what Debra had needed tonight, especially seeing as Gerard seemed to be out every night working these days, and doing Christ knows what else afterwards. He had crawled in drunk in the early hours of this morning and had been gone again at the crack of dawn to tend to some urgent business. Debra had heard him talking on the phone before he'd left about needing to deal with someone. Whatever he was up to, it didn't sound good and Debra knew she was better off not knowing. If it wasn't for Kiera, Debra would probably spend most of her evenings holed up here in the flat on her own, while the boys were asleep in their beds. It was a lonely life sometimes.

'You not drinking that! You've hardly touched it. Christ, I've lapped you three times now,' Kiera said, nodding at Debra's untouched glass, as she topped up her own for the third time since she'd arrived at Debra's less than an hour ago.

'I'm going to be paralytic and you've barely had a mouthful,' Kiera said, draining the last of the bottle as if to prove her point.

'Oh, I'm just not in the mood for it that's all. I've got another one of my migraines again,' Debra said, diverting her eyes so that Kiera couldn't tell she was lying. But in doing so, she instantly gave herself away.

'Oh my god,' Kiera screeched, eyeing her best friend now as if she'd just sussed it all out. This new uniform look of late that Debra was always seen in: baggy jumpers and leggings. Hardly Debra's usual glamorous style. Kiera hadn't thought much of it to be honest. She'd taken Debra's word for it the last few weeks when her friend had said that she was suffering from huge migraines and feeling really peaky and run-down. But that wasn't the entire truth. Kiera hadn't managed to piece it together until now though.

'You're bloody pregnant again, aren't you?' Kiera guessed excitedly.

'Shh! I don't want the boys to hear,' Debra said, shaking her head and placing a finger on her lips. She winced as Kiera screeched loudly, her excitement heightened by the amount of wine she'd knocked back. She cast a worried look out through the kitchen door and towards the lounge, listening for any signs that Mason and Logan, or Kiera's daughter Maisie had overheard their conversation, and relaxing slightly when she heard them all chuckle in time to whatever TV programme they were currently engrossed in. They were oblivious to her news.

'I haven't told anyone yet. Not even Gerard,' Debra explained.

'Why on earth not? Oh my God, how far along are you?'

'Three months.'

'This is amazing news! What if you have a little girl this time? I've got loads of stuff of Maisie's that I can pass down to you. I mean it's not as if we need it,' Kiera said matter-of-factly. 'I mean, we barely even do it anymore anyway, so chances of Maisie getting a brother or sister any time soon are practically zero.' Then seeing that Debra looked uncomfortable, Kiera narrowed her eyes.

'Are you not excited about it?'

'Yeah, I am. I guess. But, you know!' Debra said, deliberately trying her hardest to play down her concerns. 'I already have my work cut out with the two boys. Mason's settled in primary school now and Logan's just gone into nursery. I guess I hadn't really thought about throwing another kiddie into the mix.'

Reading between the lines, Kiera nodded. What Debra really meant was that she already had her work cut out from being married to that bully of a husband of hers. Debra didn't often say too much about her and Gerard's relationship, but she knew she didn't have to. The walls between the flats were thin, and Kiera heard everything that went on between them.

She'd seen the bruises first-hand too. Though, of course, Debra had never admitted to her how she'd really got them, and Kiera had always just played along with her excuses, not letting on that she knew her husband was a woman-beating piece of shit.

She could only respect the fact that when Debra was ready to talk about it, she would. And it looked like that time was now.

'You're not sure if you want to go through with having the baby?'

'It's not the baby… it's… I don't know,' Debra said, hesitantly, finally allowing herself to open up about how she'd been feeling the past few weeks. 'I look at Mason and Logan, and how could I not want the baby,' she said with tears in her eyes, as Kiera reached out her hand and gave her a supportive squeeze across the table. 'But I want more for it than this. I want more for Mason and Logan than this.' She held her arms out, indicating her life. Stuck between these four walls, day in, day out, with Gerard permanently calling the shots. It wasn't the life or the marriage that she'd signed up for, but Debra knew now that there was no walking away for her. She was in too deep. Gerard Jennings wasn't the kind of man you could ever simply walk away from.

'You know what, Debs, you're a credit to those two boys in there. You're a great mum. And if you do decide to have this baby, you'll be fine, Debra. You'll cope. No matter what happens. You've done it before and you'll do it again.'

'But what if it's not enough?' Debra shot her friend a fleeting smile, wishing that she shared the same optimism.

'What do you think Gerard will say, when you tell him?'

'Oh, you know Gerard. He'll be happy as a pig in shit. The more the merrier because he doesn't get involved with the day-to-day stuff. He just likes to harp on about having his own little army to work in the business with him one day.' Debra shook her head, clenching her fists in anger, because she knew that Gerard meant it. That he'd want to drag her beautiful, clever, sensitive boys into his murky, dark world as soon as they were old enough and, by then, she'd probably have no influence over either of them to stop it. 'Can you even imagine my little Mason and Logan getting involved in all that shit? Working with him? Being anything like him?'

Debra clenched her jaw, trying to control her breathing. She took a few seconds to compose herself before she continued.

'This child will just be another pawn for him to use against me. Another thing for him to dangle over my head and tie me to him even further.'

Kiera eyed Debra curiously over the top of her glass, surprised at Debra's honest yet disturbing confession. It didn't take a genius to work out that Debra hadn't been happy with Gerard for a long time now, but it was the first time that Debra had so openly spoken about it to her.

'I want the baby, but I want to leave him, Kiera. Only, I don't know how.'

'There are ways, Debra. There are charities and organisations set up that can help you. You and the boys. They can find a safe place for you all, far away from here and you can start again, on your own,' Kiera said, trying her hardest to sound convincing. But she could tell by Debra's face that her friend didn't believe her for a second. And why should she? Kiera didn't for one minute either.

'You and I both know that he'd never let me leave,' Debra said sadly. 'He'd find me. You know he would. I'd spend my life looking over my shoulder waiting for him to turn up and hurt me and the boys. Because that's what he'd do. He told me. He'd kill them both to get at me. This one too.' Debra was whispering now, her hand slipping down to her stomach, cupping it subconsciously as she spoke.

'There must be something. I can help, I can make some enquires. You're not on your own.'

Debra shook her head.

'Promise me you won't get involved. You can't tell a soul what I've just told you.' She fought back her tears. Tears wouldn't gain anything. What she needed right now was to be strong and to keep her head together, so that she could work out a way to get out.

'Of course, Debra. Whatever you say. I promise you, I won't say a word.' Kiera saw the genuine fear in her friend's eyes then, now that she'd finally spoken about the abuse she'd endured.

'I mean it, Kiera, I don't want you getting involved in this mess,' Debra said resolutely. The tensions between her husband and best friend were already at an all-time high. The pair of them couldn't stand one another. 'I just need some more time. To work out what my options are.'

Kiera knew her friend wanted this baby. That wasn't why she was keeping it a secret. She wanted to protect it. To give it a life far away from here. Far away from Gerard.

'Mum's the word,' Kiera said with a wink, before downing the last dregs of her wine from her glass. 'I may as well finish your one off too, if it's only going to waste!'

Debra couldn't help but smile then. Kiera always had a way of lightening the mood.

'I'd be lost without you, do you know that, Kiera?!' Debra said honestly, thinking how bored she'd be most nights without her best mate to keep her company after she'd put the boys down to bed.

'Mum!' Mason shouted, running into the kitchen and grabbing hold of his mother's jumper with urgency. 'Logan just tipped his orange juice in Dad's fish tank!'

'Oh, great,' Debra said, shaking her head as she ran into the lounge and saw the plastic beaker floating on top of the water. 'Your dad will not be happy, Logan! You'll end up killing the fish at this rate.' She instantly regretted her choice of words as three-year-old Logan started bawling hysterically at the thought of not only the fish all dying, but upsetting Gerard too. They all knew how precious he was over his tropical fish collection.

'I didn't mean to do it, but Maisie told me to. She said they were th-th-thirsty and they wanted a dr-dr-drink.' The child sobbed loudly.

'Maisie!' Kiera said, grabbing her own child by the arm. 'Why'd you say that to Logan? You know not to do that! He's only three. You can't be telling him to do things like that.'

'I didn't, Mummy. He's lying.' Maisie sulked, trying to get herself out of trouble before catching Mason's glare.

'No he's not a liar. You did tell him, I heard you,' Mason piped up.

'Didn't!' Maisie screeched.

'Did!'

'What's all this bloody noise?' A voice boomed from the lounge doorway, startling the room into sudden silence. Turning his nose up at the sight of his drunk next-door neighbour and her brat of a kid standing in the middle of the lounge, Gerard glared at Debra who was leaning over the fish tank, her sleeve rolled up as she tried to catch some of the fish in a plastic beaker. 'Why are all the kids still up? And who's done something to my fish?'

'I didn't hear you come in,' Debra said, her eyes going to the red smear of blood on Gerard's once white, crisp shirt. Catching her gaze, Gerard pulled his jacket tightly around him, before eyeing Kiera with disdain and noting that she'd seen it too. Though he knew that Kiera wasn't stupid enough to need a warning to keep her mouth shut. The last thing rent-a-gob Kiera needed to do was go around talking about his business to anyone with ears on the estate, because it would get back to him in a heartbeat. And there were reprisals for that kind of talk around here.

'Me and Maisie were just about to go,' Kiera said, locking eyes with the man and sensing by his steely glare that she wasn't welcome here. Not tonight. Not ever really. She only made a point of coming over when she knew the man wasn't home. Which luckily for her and Debra was pretty often.

'Good! The boys should be in bed,' Gerard said, making no disguise of the fact that he couldn't stand Kiera. His eyes boring into hers as he tried to intimidate her. As far as he was concerned the woman was nothing more than a gobby cow, always around his house involving herself in his and Debra's business. Trying to put ideas in Debra's head about him.

'It was my fault for keeping her chatting.' Catching her friend's wavering glance, Kiera played along as she knew was expected, pretending that nothing untoward was happening here. That the sight of Gerard standing there covered in what could only be someone else's blood was completely normal.

'Debra said she needed to put the kids down ages ago! Didn't you, Debra?'

Kiera eyed her friend, as she put the plastic cup down and gave up her attempt at trying to catch the fish so that she could change the water and give the thing a fighting chance at survival. Debra looked frightened now, her face paled to a sickly white. Picking up Logan with one arm, she draped the other protectively across Mason's shoulders.

'I'll knock first thing in the morning, Debra! We can do the school run together,' Kiera added, staring at her friend as she slipped Maisie's coat on. All the while she could sense Gerard's eyes burning into the back of her head. Hoping that the fact that she would be seeing her friend in less than twelve hours' time would be enough to deter Gerard from his usual woman-beating ways. The man might be feared by most, but Kiera wasn't scared of him one bit.

She reckoned that was one of the things that Gerard hated about her the most. She was, however, scared of what he might do to Debra, when she left.

Kiera wanted to stay. She wanted to make sure that Debra was going to be okay. But she knew that she couldn't let on about any of the things that Debra had told her. She had no choice but to take Maisie and leave. Otherwise she'd only make things worse for Debra.

'Come on, Maisie darling. Let's get you home,' she said, squeezing through the small gap in the doorway that Gerard stood purposely blocking. Another intimidation tactic, no doubt. Shaking her head as she passed him, Kiera looked back at her mate, catching the tiny smile of feigned reassurance she gave her; only the gesture didn't quite meet the woman's eyes. All Kiera could see in them was fear. And Kiera could tell by Gerard's mood the second that those kids were tucked up in bed, the woman was going to have to deal with his wrath. And no doubt Kiera would be forced to listen to it all through the thin walls of the flat.

# CHAPTER FOUR

'Holder's keen. He's beaten us to it,' DS Morgan said, nodding over to where their colleague stood, already at the crime scene as he and DC Lucy Murphy got out of the car and made their way down the boggy grass verge that ran along this narrow stretch of Wandle River.

'It's not pretty, Sarge!' DC Holder warned, greeting his two fellow officers as the forensic team finished securing the area before making a start on gathering the evidence. 'The body was recovered by the River Police less than forty-five minutes ago. The divers pulled him out. He's in a right old state.'

'Jesus!' DS Morgan said, staring down at the victim sprawled out on the grass bank, his naked body bloated from being in the water. His head was caved at one side, making him look deformed and alien like. Even the horrendous swelling of the man's corpse couldn't hide the numerous injuries that had been inflicted on him.

'What have we got then?'

'The victim is male and roughly in his late twenties. No ID as yet. He has suffered extensive injuries, and while the pathologist has suggested that a number of the significant ones may have been inflicted after he entered the water, he has confirmed that a number of the injuries were made beforehand. Of course, we're going to need to wait for the full autopsy until we know the complete extent of his horrific injuries and his exact cause of death. But I think it's safe to say, we can definitely rule out suicide.'

DS Morgan nodded in agreement. Most of the bodies recovered from the Thames were the result of accidental drowning or suicides, but that clearly wasn't the case today. This had been called in as a murder.

Nothing could be ruled out at this stage until they had all the facts confirmed. But CID wouldn't have been put on the job unless there was reason to believe that this was a murder investigation, and Holder was keen to point out his findings so far.

'This part of the river is shallow and fast-flowing, Sarge. And the marine unit suspect that his body was swept down the Thames with the tide and somehow managed to end up here.' Holder pointed to where two of the divers had made their way back into the shallow waters, to where the body was found. 'He was discovered floating just there, his body lodged up against that fallen tree. That kept him from being pulled back out there again, I reckon.'

'Sounds likely,' DS Morgan said, casting his eye to the point of water further up where the fast-flowing waters of the River Wandle joined the Thames. 'The river is tidal in these parts. He's most probably been struck by a few boats.'

'There're obvious signs of torture, Sarge,' Holder said, pointing to the red ligature marks around the victim's exposed wrists and ankles, which suggested that the man had been bound and tied up somewhere. 'There're also deep lacerations to his torso – my guess would be knife wounds – as well as a number of large bruises and burn marks. His head had been caved in by a blunt object of some sort. But again, the pathologist did say that it looks like the blunt force was inflicted repeatedly. So he suspects that it wasn't a one off.'

'A hammer perhaps?' DC Lucy Murphy cut in, the sight of the man's lips, tinged blue, and the vacant look of his extinguished eyes instantly setting her anxiety off.

'Yeah, I'd hazard a guess that it was a hammer too,' Holder said, bleakly, nodding down to where the body lay.

'Jesus. Who would do something like this? He looks almost unrecognisable, barely even human.' Willing herself not to close her eyes and show her two fellow officers any kind of weakness, Lucy turned her gaze down the narrow stretch of river, towards the new development of apartments.

'Were there any witnesses?' she asked, trying to compose herself as she eyed the small clusters of residents all standing watching the gruesome discovery from their balconies. Trying to focus on anything other than the sickening sight of the dead body at her feet. 'It's still early. The early morning commute hasn't started yet. Who found him?'

'A dog walker spotted him face down in the water. It's a cliché, I know. The old fella is traumatised. He waited at the riverside until the River Police had pulled the body from the water. But it's doubtful anyone around here would have seen or heard anything. The body could have entered the water anywhere along the river. We don't know his entry point,' Holder said, knowing that unless there was a witness, it would be near on impossible to determine. So far they had very little to go on.

'And you say we don't have an ID as yet?' DS Morgan said, sensing Lucy's discomfort, as she looked back down at the body and physically flinched as her eyes registered the gory sight of the impacted fractures of the man's jagged bones protruding through the flesh of both his legs.

'Not yet,' Holder confirmed.

'Okay, let's make that a priority. Let's find out who this man is and wait for the official post-mortem to be carried out so we know the exact cause of death and the full extent of his injuries,' DS Morgan said. He had no doubt in his mind that this man had suffered greatly in the hands of someone who wanted to inflict a world of pain onto him. Thankfully it was rare in this job to come across such gruesome, extensive injuries.

'Are you all right?' DS Morgan said, noting how pale and quiet Lucy had become.

Lucy nodded. 'Sorry, Sarge, I think it's something I ate,' she said, having no choice but to admit that she wasn't feeling well. If she didn't get away from the man's corpse soon, she was certain that she would throw up. And she'd never live it down if she did. Especially with Holder here gawping at her.

'Go back to the car and update control,' DS Morgan said, wanting to give Lucy an excuse to get away from the crime scene for a few seconds, and compose herself. Lucy nodded, grateful for her sergeant's dismissal.

'It's grim, eh Sarge? None of us ever get used to it,' Holder said, obliviously, as the two men watched as Lucy got into the driver's seat of the car and busied herself talking to Control.

'I think it would be a sad day for us all if we ever did, Holder.' DS Morgan nodded in agreement.

The job was hard. Some days harder than most. No matter how many dead bodies you were forced to deal with, it never prepared you for seeing the next one. It really didn't ever get any easier.

If twenty-five years' experience had taught him anything, it was that.

# CHAPTER FIVE

She was back there again. Back cowering inside the wardrobe, her eye fixed on the narrow gap.

Thud. Thud. Thud. Squeezing her eyes shut, as she winced at the sight of all that blood. Splattered up the walls, a pool of it dripping down from the bed. It was all over him too. The monster. And her mother wouldn't stop screaming, lying there in the middle of the bed, begging and pleading with the man to stop hurting her. Only he didn't stop and the sound was terrifying. She had to stay quiet, stay hidden, but all she wanted was for the horrendous noise to stop. For the man to go away so she could run to her mummy and make everything okay. But when the brutal attack suddenly stopped a few minutes later, she was met with something far scarier. A deathly silence.

She peered out through the gap in the door, her eye focusing on the double bed. Her mum wasn't moving now. She wasn't making a sound. Her lifeless body sprawled out, her skin and dressing gown covered in blood. She wanted to get away. To jump out of the wardrobe and run. Only she couldn't move, because then the man would see her. Then he'd realise that she was here, watching the whole time. He'd catch her.

Pushing herself down into the pile of clothes that surrounded her, she tried to make herself smaller, grimacing as she realised that she'd wet herself, her pants squelching as she moved. The wardrobe creaked loudly. Her heartbeat quickened as she stared out to see if he'd heard her too.

He was standing in the middle of the room, deadly still, his clothes covered in her mother's blood. He looked straight at her. Straight at the wardrobe where she was sitting.

Biting down on a coat sleeve that she'd stuffed inside her mouth to stifle the scream that threatened deep inside her throat, she saw him walking towards her. Her eyes darted to the knife that was still firmly gripped in his hand, the sharp, steely looking blade covered in thick red blood.

He'd found her. He knew she was there. She wasn't safe any more.

Seconds later the wardrobe doors were wrenched wide open, a beam of blinding light forcing her to open her eyes and look. And she did look. She stared at the man's features and recoiled at the sight of his steely grey eyes and his thin, crooked lips.

His expression twisted and evil.

And then he was gone.

His eyes and face all blurred into one big black mass, making him look unreal. Like some kind of evil cartoon monster. She felt dizzy and sick, as if she was going to pass out.

So frightened that when she opened her mouth to let out the scream that threatened, no sound left her mouth. It was as if her voice was so scared, it had been swallowed deep down inside of her. She tried to scamper away, to escape, pressing herself up against the wood at the back of the wardrobe, violently shaking her head. Only, there was nowhere to go. She was trapped. Cornered. The man reached in, wrapping his fingers tightly around her as he grabbed her. Before pulling her out.

*

Flinging herself forward in the bed, Lucy sat up, grateful for the familiar comforts in the room around her as she tried to slow her quickened heartbeat and her rapid short bursts of breath. Her body was wet and clammy, dripping with perspiration.

Throwing back the covers and wrapping her dressing gown tightly around her, annoyed now, because she knew how this worked. How her mind would go into overdrive. How her anxiety would creep back in. There would be no chance of her getting back to sleep anytime soon. She'd had enough nightmares in her lifetime to know that lying in bed with only her thoughts to torment her wouldn't help. Though this time it had been different. Worse.

All the things she normally told herself after one of her nightmares, *You're safe. You're home. It was just another stupid nightmare,* held no reassurance for her now, because she knew it had been much more than just a bad dream.

She finally remembered.

She'd seen his face.

After all those years of her mind somehow blocking him out, making her feel as if she was slowly going mad, her brain had finally allowed her to go back there, to that terrifying place.

It had only been a fleeting memory, but he was there. Staring right back at her.

She'd seen him.

The psychiatrists she'd seen over the years had said that blocking the memory out was some kind of survival tactic.

And Lucy had often wondered if that was true, because she'd lived most of her life trapped inside her own worst nightmares, and it often felt more like torture than survival. But they'd always warned her that this might happen. That one day, she'd be able to recall the one thing that she tried so hard to block out.

Lucy had started to doubt that completely.

Convinced that there could never be an end. That the memory of him was lost forever. Accepting that she'd never rid herself of the misery of reliving that night, over and over again, and the not-knowing was what caused her the most damage.

Her only consolation was that her nightmares didn't come as often anymore.

Though when they did, they still came with full force, igniting her inner demons and throwing her off kilter for days with deep, dark bouts of depression and panic attacks. And tonight's had shown no mercy. It had felt so real. As if she had been back there again, trapped inside the wardrobe, hiding.

And she'd finally seen him. Or had she?

Maybe her mind was just playing tricks on her?

Because a police officer had found her hiding inside the wardrobe and lifted her out to safety. In the dream, her mother's killer had found her.

Maybe this was just another layer to her torment. Because she thought about him all the time. Who he was, why he'd taken her beautiful mother from her. And the fact that she'd been the only witness, but that she hadn't been able to give the police anything. No ID, no clues, nothing. It made her feel as if her mother's killer not being caught was somehow her fault.

Padding her way down the stairs and into the kitchen, Lucy put the kettle on to make herself a cup of hot, sweet tea, her hands shaking violently as she reached into the cupboard for a cup.

What if it was real, and she had finally remembered?

All she had was a vague description of a man that taunted in her nightmares. Would it be enough, and more importantly would it be worth dredging it all up again, if it meant that she'd not only upset her nan, but she'd also have to come clean to her colleagues about her past?

Taking a sip of the hot, sweet tea, Lucy shuddered, wrapping her hands tightly around the mug as if seeking out any kind of comfort she could find. She knew what had triggered tonight's nightmare. The man, yesterday. Bludgeoned to death down by the river bank.

Sometimes the job really got inside her head, no matter how hard she tried to distance herself from the daily horrors that she had to deal with. She wondered if he'd suffered? If he'd been forced to feel every ounce of pain inflicted upon him before he'd died? Or if it had been quick and brutal.

She shook her head as if to dispel the thoughts that lingered there. Unsure what she should do with them now. One thing she knew for sure was that this job really didn't get any easier and tomorrow was going to be another busy day, as her team tried to piece together what the motive for the murder was, to catch the killer.

She made her way back up the stairs with the mug still in her hand, hoping to get at least another hour of sleep before her alarm went off. Though she couldn't just walk past her nan's room. Instead, she paused, lingering in the doorway, her eyes going to the perfectly made up bed in the corner.

Empty now.

She felt the tears in her eyes then, remembering how as a young child, she'd clamber into her nan's bed in the middle of the night after another of her nightmares. Her nan would always wrap her arms around her tightly and tell her that everything would be okay. She'd make up her silly stories about an old lady called Winnie who was cursed with breathtaking beauty, and all the men wanted to kiss her, which always made Lucy laugh. Then she'd tell her stories about a little girl called Lucy who was really strong and brave.

'But I don't feel very brave, Nan,' she'd whisper back through the darkness.

'Oh, but you are, my girl. We all get scared sometimes, Lucy,' Winnie would say, as she hugged her in close. 'But you know what's the bravest thing of all? That you carry on. You keep going. No matter how frightened, how scared. That's real bravery.'

Lucy closed her eyes and smiled, wishing her nan was here now. Though she could just imagine the woman's face – twenty-five years old and a trainee DC, climbing into bed with her little ol' nan in the middle of the night because she was scared! Winnie probably wouldn't even bat an eyelid.

The older Lucy got, the more she realised that it wasn't true that there was no such thing as ghosts or monsters. They did exist. Only the worst ones lived inside your head.

# CHAPTER SIX

'Winnie, darling, Lucy's here to see you!' Nurse Hamilton called through the door, loud enough so that Winnie Murphy would be able to hear her over her chanting.

'We shall, we shall not be moved. We shall, we shall not be moved.'

'She's protesting! The Treetop One!' Nurse Hamilton smiled at Lucy, trying to make light of the matter as she pushed down the door handle and leaned against the wood with her full body weight, to no avail.

'She's barricaded herself in. We've been trying to talk her out for almost half an hour now. We don't want to force the door open unless we really have to, in case she gets hurt.'

'Shall I try?' Lucy asked. She'd been left with a sense of dread all day, ever since she'd woken in the early hours of the morning from her nightmare, worrying how her nan's first overnight stay at Treetops had gone.

She'd promised her nan that she'd visit her every day, after she finished her shift, if it wasn't too late, and this had been the last thing she'd expected when she'd arrived. She'd thought the nurse was joking when she said that Winnie was on lockdown and causing havoc in the place.

'Go for it. At this point, anything is worth a try,' Nurse Hamilton said, nodding, hoping that the sound of Lucy's voice might just be enough to win Winnie round into at least opening the door.

The woman certainly knew how to make her presence known. Shouting and banging about, she'd alerted most of the other residents of the drama she'd created, spreading unease through the home as the normal evening routine was spectacularly broken. Nurse Hamilton and her staff would be playing catch up all evening because of this. For now, though, Nurse Hamilton's main priority was coaxing Winnie safely from the bedroom.

'Nan?' Lucy said, stepping forward and raising her voice so that Winnie could hear through all the racket. 'It's me, Lucy. I've come to see you like I told you I would.'

'Don't try and fool me. I'm not stupid,' Winnie said, with certainty. 'You're not my Lucy. You're trying to trick me. My Lucy is at work. She's a police officer you know. She's busy catching people like you lot. Criminals. Locking innocent people like me up against our own free will.'

'Nan, they haven't locked you up! You've done that yourself. They're trying to open the door and see if you're all right,' Lucy said, shaking her head in wonderment at what was going on inside her nan's head in order for her to do this. Lucy knew better than anyone that when Winnie got an idea into her head there was no persuading her otherwise. 'Open the door, Nan! It really is me, I promise. I've just finished work...' Lucy paused, remembering the advice the doctors had given her when they'd first diagnosed Winnie's dementia: to give her as much detail and information as possible to help her not feel so confused. Sometimes all it took was a few words to bring her nan some familiarity and help her come back to reality again.

'Vivian's on her way too, Nan. She said she'd sit and have some tea with you when I have to leave,' Lucy said regretfully. She'd called Vivian on the way here, wracked with guilt knowing that she couldn't stay for long this evening.

She had an early start. DS Morgan had insisted on it. Her boss was on the warpath at the moment, and Lucy understood why. Today had been a tough one, they still had next to no new information regarding the body that they'd pulled from the Thames. DS Morgan had summoned the entire team to work solely on the case, around the clock until they had something. 'She said you promised her a game of Scrabble. She seems to think she's going to beat you! She doesn't know how much practice we've both had, huh? Do you remember New Year's Eve, Nan? We sat up half the night battling it out, didn't we? I seem to remember being crowned the ultimate winner though, at the end of the night.'

Lucy waited patiently, her eyes going to meet Nurse Hamilton's as they heard some movement inside the room. There came the sound of dragging furniture before the door handle clicked open.

'You did not bloody win. I did! 2-1 to me,' Winnie said defiantly.

'Oh, Nan!' Lucy laughed then, though the sight of her tiny nan, still dressed in her pale blue floral nightdress, staring at her with a confused look on her face was heartbreaking.

'What's with the welcoming committee?' Winnie said eyeing Nurse Hamilton suspiciously.

'They were trying to get you to open the door, to check you're all right!' Lucy said, narrowing her eyes as she spotted an empty toilet roll woven into Winnie's hair.

'What have you got on your head?'

'Rollers, Lucy! What do you think they are?' Winnie said, narrowing her eyes as if Lucy was stupid. 'I always put my rollers in at night.'

Deciding it wouldn't do Winnie any harm to believe that the loo roll pinned to her hair was a roller, Lucy nodded and smiled, before eyeing up the ransacked room.

'Have you been having a little rearrange of the furniture, Nan?' she asked, noting how the bedding was strewn in a pile in the middle of the floor, and how the mattress had been dragged over towards the door. The armchair that had previously been on the other side of the room next to the window was upturned too, as if Winnie had given up halfway through moving it.

'Oh, she may be small but she is mighty!' Nurse Hamilton muttered playfully, as she entered the room and moved the chair back over by the window, before starting to put the rest of the room back together again.

'There's a tray of dinner waiting for you in the dayroom, Winnie. Maybe Lucy could walk you down and I'll join you both shortly?'

'Yeah, let's do that, Nan? Come on,' Lucy said, gently taking her arm and guiding her towards the dayroom before she could protest.

Spotting the single tray loaded with food still placed on the large dining table, Lucy walked Winnie over to the chair, glad that the other residents had all finished their dinner and there were only a few people about.

'Oh, Lucy! What a lovely surprise this is! I didn't know you were coming to see me today?' Winnie said, her tone suddenly cheerful, as she made a start on her dinner.

'Well, clearly, Nan! It's not the sort of reception I was expecting that's for sure,' Lucy said lightly. It still took her by surprise how quickly her nan's volatile moods could change. But as long as Winnie seemed happier, Lucy wasn't about to complain.

'So, what were you doing, Nan? Why did you barricade yourself in your room like that? I thought you liked it here?' Lucy said, watching as Winnie lifted her fork and took a small mouthful of her meal.

'I do like it here!' Winnie said, swallowing the food down. Her tone was indignant, as if she was wondering why Lucy would think otherwise.

'And you like the nurses?'

Winnie nodded, before wrinkling her nose mischievously.

'Nurse Hamilton is a bit bossy though, isn't she? I think she likes the sound of her own voice a bit too much, personally. But she means well.'

Lucy rolled her eyes then and laughed.

'Well, bossy is good, Nan. Someone needs to keep you in check. And you like staying here, don't you? Hanging out here in the dayroom with all your new friends? I know it's not home, but you'll get used to it eventually,' Lucy said, worried that her nan locking herself away in her room was her way of saying that she wasn't happy. Not that there seemed to be any rhyme or reason to most of Winnie's behaviour these days.

'I like most of the people here, but…' Winnie gazed around the room as if to check who was listening in on their conversation, not continuing until she was satisfied they couldn't be overheard. 'Some of them are not right in the head here, you know!' Lowering her voice, she nodded her head to the far side of the room, to where a short man sat in the armchair in the corner, his eyes fixed on the television, clearly minding his own business.

'Like him. Dirty Bertie!' Winnie said, almost spitting the man's name from her mouth.

'Dirty Bertie? Nan, that can't be the man's real name?'

'Well, it should be!' Winnie nodded with certainty. 'Funny little man he is, with horrible beady eyes. And worse still…' Winnie leaned closer to her granddaughter. 'Last night he was walking around the dayroom asking us all if we've seen…' Winnie paused, glancing at Bertie once more and shaking her head with venom as if she still couldn't believe the audacity of the man, 'his… Balls! BALLS!' Winnie paused for effect, watching Lucy's face intently, waiting for the shock and disgust at what she was hearing to register.

When Lucy didn't react she added, 'You know as in his dangly bits. Testicles, Lucy…'

'I know what balls are, Nan,' Lucy said cautiously, convinced that her nan must be making up one of her stories, though what Winnie was telling her was possible. Many of the patients here suffered with all stages of dementia and were often confused. There had been many times when Winnie had said rude and inappropriate things due to her confusion.

'I'm sure he didn't mean to upset you. He's probably just a bit confused,' Lucy said, trying to disguise the smile that teased her lips.

'Confused? I'll say! The man thinks he's lost his nuts! I mean, you have to have something seriously wrong with you if you can't remember the things that are dangling between your own legs, don't you? Mind, it would have been much worse if he'd been looking for his brain. The old sod would have no luck at finding that! Anyway, it gets worse.' Winnie was almost whispering now. 'The dirty bugger only "accidentally on purpose" wandered into my bloody room last night.' She looked mortified at the thought. 'You should have seen him! There I was, in my bed, I'd just slathered on my face cream and put my rollers in.' Winnie touched the toilet roll tube that she'd tightly wrapped her hair around as if to prove that she was telling the truth. 'Just about to close my eyes, and there he was. Bold as brass. Dirty Bertie, standing in the doorway and taking a good look at me! Why else was he there? He wasn't going to find his balls in my room, was he? No!' Winnie spat, her cheeks turning puce as she spoke.

'That's why I locked myself in my room tonight. To keep that pervert out. I'm not giving him the chance to perv on me again.'

'I'll speak to the nurses, Nan, and make sure he doesn't come to your room again,' Lucy said, not entirely convinced at her nan's story, but making a mental note to mention what her nan had told her to the nurse before she left, just to be on the safe side.

'Oh look, Nan, it's Vivian!' Lucy said, grateful for the distraction as she caught the woman's eye as she walked towards them. She got up from her seat and hugged Vivian tightly to her.

'Hello, Lucy darling. Hi, Winnie, I'm so sorry that I'm late, what have I missed?'

'Dirty Bertie's testicles. That's what you missed, Vivian,' Winnie said bluntly, only too happy to enlighten her old friend.

'Trust me, Vivian, you really don't want to know,' Lucy said, rolling her eyes playfully before putting her jacket back on, glad that Vivian was here to take over.

'Testicles? Ohh, what a shame that I missed those. Delightful conversation to have over your supper, Winnie my darling! Enough to put you off your lasagne.' Vivian nodded towards the half-eaten dish, as her loud laugh filled the room.

'Right, Nan, I've got to get home, I've got a really early start in the morning. I'll leave you with Vivian and I'll see if I can pop back in again tomorrow night, okay?' Lucy kissed her nan on the head.

'Don't you worry. Me and Winnie are going to have a game of Scrabble, aren't we, Winnie?' Vivian beamed, getting the board game out of her big shopping bag, and sitting down next to her friend at the table.

'Thanks, Vivian!' Lucy said, feeling grateful that the woman was spending some time with her nan, when she was so busy having to work.

'You do not need to thank me. You know my lot at home, I'd much rather be hiding out here playing games with Winnie. Trust me.'

On her way out of the home, Lucy stopped at the reception desk to speak to Nurse Hamilton.

'She seems to have calmed down now. But she did mention that another resident – Bertie? – had come to her room last night and that was why she was feeling anxious,' Lucy said, interpreting her nan's version of events the best she could without sounding completely ridiculous. 'Though I know she says a lot of things that, well, aren't strictly true.'

'Oh no, he did try!' Nurse Hamilton said, nodding. 'Though as you know, our residents can't just access another residents' bedroom, but your nan left her door propped open with a chair. We managed to stop him from entering her room. But he did seem very distressed. He was looking for his balls.'

'His balls?' Lucy mouthed in disbelief.

'Yes, he's a golfer, or at least he was until he got ill. His prize possessions are his lucky golf balls that his wife bought for him. He carries them everywhere with him. He couldn't find them last night and for some reason he thought Winnie had taken them.'

'Golf balls?' Lucy said, unable to suppress her smile that this had all been over something so innocent after all. 'Right!'

'Yes. We managed to convince him she didn't have them, and he's also calmed down now. Fingers crossed the whole drama will blow over and be completely forgotten about by now. Though…' Nurse Hamilton opened the desk drawer and held her hand up, holding two white golf balls for Lucy to see, 'I found them stuffed down the cushion of her chair in your nan's room just now. It looks like she had them all along.'

# CHAPTER SEVEN

'Okay, everyone, if you could gather round for our morning briefing. I want to make this quick. We've got a lot of work to get through today,' DS Morgan said, addressing the entire room. CID had a mammoth job ahead of them today, and the priority was the murder investigation into the body that had been pulled from the Thames two days ago. Time was of the essence on these investigations. And it was not on their side.

'As I'm sure most of you are aware, we finally have a name. For those of you not yet up to speed, the victim is a Mr Bobbie Carter, place of residence Manchester, and he's known to work for a criminal firm up there. Only minor criminal offences on his record though, so he'd managed to keep his nose fairly clean. But we suspect that he was in London on business and that he has a possible connection with Gerard Jennings, who as you all know has been on our radar for a while now. Holder, would you care to enlighten the rest of the team?'

'Yes, Sarge,' Holder said, stepping forward, and speaking up now so that everyone could clearly hear him. 'The autopsy shows that Bobbie Carter was already dead when his body entered the water. We believe that he was in the river for less than twelve hours before he was found, and he suffered substantial injuries in the water due to contact with submerged objects such as rocks and debris, possibly boats too. His cause of death was blunt force trauma to the head, which we strongly now suspect was caused by repeated blows to the skull with a hammer. There's no murder weapon as yet. The victim was also severely tortured, his body punctured by a knife and burned in several places by what we believe to have been a blowtorch.'

DS Morgan pinned the graphic photographs detailing the injuries to the board before addressing the room again himself.

'We received an anonymous tip-off late last night that Bobbie Carter was murdered by Gerard Jennings. The caller rang the main number and told the operator. They didn't leave any other information and we didn't get a trace on the caller's ID. So as it stands, this tip-off is all we have to go on and we're yet to find any evidence to make it stand up in court. Though interestingly enough, we have managed to source CCTV footage of Bobbie Carter's last movements the night he was killed.' Morgan walked round to the front of the desk and perched on the edge. 'Bobbie Carter spent almost two hours at the Red Fox pub – the same facility that Gerard and his men also frequented that night.'

'Oh come on! Bit of a coincidence, isn't it? They're all in the same place all evening and then we get a tip-off stating Jennings's name?' another officer said, and a few others joined in in agreement. Morgan had expected as much.

'It is, but as we all know coincidences and suspicions don't stand up in front of a jury. It's not enough to bring Gerard in, I'm afraid. We need hard evidence that directly connects him with the crime, and all the CCTV footage we have so far only proves that the two men were in the same place at the same time several hours before Bobbie was murdered. We all know that's not nearly enough. I checked with the landlord...' Morgan faltered, looking to DC Holder to give him the name.

'A Jimmy Shelton, Sarge,' DC Holder confirmed.

DS Morgan nodded.

'Shelton confirmed that Bobbie had been in the pub and drinking alone all evening. But he'd kept himself to himself, and he'd had no contact with Gerard Jennings or any of his men. They hadn't even made eye contact as far as Shelton was aware. He also told me that Gerard and his men had left first, before Bobbie. And the CCTV confirmed that.'

'That doesn't rule out them meeting up after the pub.'

Morgan was making notes on the board as Holder spoke.

'It doesn't… only that's where our trail runs cold. We lose Bobbie from all CCTV footage about ten minutes later. His van was last seen on Swandon Way heading towards Battersea. We've been searching the area, but so far we've yet to recover it.'

DS Morgan made a note on the board of the make and model of the vehicle along with the registration number.

'So, there you have it, people. In a nutshell,' Morgan said. 'I want you all on this today. We need every lead followed up, and every bit of CCTV footage we've collected analysed again. Let's hope that by the end of today, we can get ourselves nearer to some kind of result.'

# CHAPTER EIGHT

Waking up on the cold kitchen floor, it took Debra a few seconds to remember how she got there. Though the pain that rippled through her as she tried to sit up served as an instant reminder. Her whole body burned with agony. Reaching up, she touched her face, already knowing without having to look in a mirror that Gerard had given her a black eye. As her fingers lightly swept the bulbous swelling that had sealed her eyelid completely shut, an acute pain pulsated across her entire face, making her head throb.

She flashed back to Gerard standing over her and raining down punches and kicks as he took all his frustration out on her. His almighty blows mercilessly kept coming. The last memory she had, had been of Gerard's fist connecting with her face. The force of the blow must have knocked her out. And Gerard must have left her there, blacked out on the kitchen floor.

Listening out for the boys now, she relaxed slightly as she took in the silence, relieved that there was no crying or whimpering. They'd slept through her ordeal, thank God, seemingly undisturbed. The only sound she could hear was Gerard's voice floating over the noise of the gushing water as he sang to himself in the shower, whilst washing off her blood, no doubt. Singing. Without a care in the world.

That was the cold-hearted malice of the man she'd married. Acting now, the same as he always did, as if nothing had happened. As if he'd done nothing wrong, as if he hadn't just attacked her and left her sprawled out on the kitchen floor. She closed her eyes, holding back her tears, angry now.

To him the beatings were nothing more than a release. He'd justify to himself that she deserved it, that she'd crossed the line. And perhaps tonight she had. She should have just dropped it. But instead she'd stupidly questioned him about the blood on his shirt the other night, realising as soon as the words had left her mouth that she'd made a terrible mistake. Only she hadn't been able to shake the sight of him standing there in the doorway, covered in blood, from her mind. Because this time he'd made no effort to conceal the horrors from their boys. He'd stood there brazenly in front of them. And that's what scared Debra more than anything. How lax Gerard was becoming. How he could normalise blood and violence. And she didn't want that for her sons. Debra knew that something big was going on. Something bad.

Because Gerard's moods had become darker and darker the past few days. And tonight he'd finally snapped as soon as the question of whose blood it was left her lips. The only small mercy being that he had allowed her to put Mason and Logan to bed before he'd done his usual and taken his frustrations out on her. Though that was all part of the man's sadistic games too, wasn't it? Because Gerard had worked it out long ago that no matter what he did to her, she wouldn't dare scream out, for fear of upsetting the boys. Debra would never allow Mason and Logan to lay frightened in their beds as they listened to their father beating their mother. She'd never allow them to hear her cries of pain. Instead, she sucked it all up, just like she'd always done, taking every beating that Gerard dished out to her in absolute silence, biting down on her lip every time a groan threatened to involuntarily leave the back of her throat.

She learned a long time ago that it was better not to put up a fight. It was easier just to let Gerard do whatever it was he was going to do to her without riling him up further.

To remain submissive, no matter what, for the sake of her boys. He was getting worse, she thought, unable to stop her tears filling her eyes. She could have banged her head and been lying here dead for all he knew. Gerard could have killed her tonight, and it was probably only a matter of time until he eventually did.

Wincing, she tried to get up slowly from the floor and the pain in her stomach intensified, causing her to double over and clutch the small round of her stomach protectively.

She knew. Even before she looked down and noticed the blood seeping through her leggings. Before the pain in her stomach ripped through her, that Gerard had extinguished the tiny life that had been growing inside of her. She felt dizzy suddenly, weak, as her blood, her baby, slipped from inside of her.

She was slipping, too, slinking back down to the floor, crippled with pain. She had no choice but to break the only rule she'd lived by and to scream out. To call loudly for help and pray that someone heard her before she passed out again. That was her last thought before she gave into the darkness that descended over her. The baby had gone, she knew that instinctively. Now she had to save herself.

# CHAPTER NINE

The loud knocking dragged Kiera from her sleep. Turning onto her side, she eyed Micky through the darkness of the room, tracing the outline of his body as he lay on his back with his mouth gaped wide open, snoring loudly. The noise clearly hadn't disturbed him. She wondered if perhaps she had imagined it. To be fair, Micky was such a sound sleeper he could sleep through an earthquake, she thought, as she heard the knocking sound again, louder this time. It was coming from the front door. Who could be knocking here at this hour of the night? Though she'd lived on the Griffin Estate for long enough to know from experience that trouble can come knocking at any time of the day or night.

She thought about waking Micky and getting him to go to the door, but it would be quicker just to go herself. Otherwise if whoever it was banging didn't stop soon, they'd wake Maisie, and then she'd never be able to get back to sleep. Dragging herself from the warm bed, she pulled her robe around her tightly before making her way to the front door.

'Who is it?' she called out, peering through the spy hole and trying to make out whose shadowy silhouette stood on the other side blocking the view.

'It's me. Gerard. Open the door.'

Kiera bristled at his tone but opened the door slightly, careful to keep her foot up against the PVC panel between them, ready to slam the door shut if she had to. Her earlier suspicions were confirmed: trouble was knocking all right. Whatever reason Gerard was here for, it couldn't be good. 'It's almost midnight, Gerard!?'

'You need to come,' Gerard commanded, his voice quiet but urgent.

'I need to come where, Gerard? Are you okay? What's going on?' Kiera asked, looking at the man as if he was insane, noting how edgy he seemed. More so than usual. His fists were tightly clenched at his sides and he was hovering nervously from one foot to another, which ironically made the six foot something giant look strangely childlike in his stance.

She could see the sweat glimmering on his forehead as he turned his head and scanned both ends of the balcony, as if he was expecting somebody.

'It's the middle of the night. Micky and Maisie are in bed. Asleep. Where I should be. Are you drunk?' Kiera asked, guessing it was more than likely that Gerard was coked up off his face, going by his random visit.

'It's Debra…'

'What's happened, Gerard? Is Debra okay?' Kiera's heart immediately started to hammer inside her chest as she watched Gerard anxiously run his fingers through his hair, his hands shaking as he did so. He shook his head in answer.

'There's no time. You need to come,' Gerard said, not taking no for an answer as he roughly hoisted Kiera by her arm and led her towards the flat next door. Barefoot and only wearing her dressing gown, Kiera didn't bother to protest. If Gerard was demanding her help then something really bad must have happened and her need to know that her friend was okay far outweighed her fear of the man beside her.

'The paramedics are on their way. If they ask what happened, she fell. You haven't seen me. I haven't been here all night, okay?' Gerard said, making no attempt to go inside his flat.

'She fell?' Kiera nodded dumbly, staring at the man in utter confusion as she realised that he wanted her to go in alone. The word 'paramedics' was whirling around her mind. Gerard pushed her into the hallway of his flat and started to rapidly walk away.

'The paramedics? What… why…?' She called out, watching him head towards the stairwell.

It was only then that she heard the sound of loud wailing noises coming from the kitchen. Recognising the voices of Mason and Logan, who were both crying loudly, she braced herself for what she was about to see.

'Boys? Debra? Oh my god, Debra. What happened?' Kiera cried, not wanting to frighten Mason and Logan any more than they already were, but her voice betrayed her the second she laid eyes on her friend, sprawled out on the kitchen floor, unconscious. Her face was swollen, bloody, unrecognisable.

The two boys, dressed in their matching blue pyjamas, were clinging to their unresponsive mother. Kiera instinctively went to them, scooping them up into her arms and letting them snuggle into her as they continued to cry hysterically.

'It's all right, boys,' Kiera said, panicking now as Mason and Logan both looked up at her expectantly. As if she was going to suddenly make everything better and fix their mother.

'It's going to be all right,' Kiera lied. The truth was, she had no idea what to do or say.

She'd gone into shock herself. The sight of her friend so broken and beaten was too much to take in.

Gerard had done this. That bastard. She could feel the red-hot anger surging through her. No wonder Gerard had upped and left so quickly. Dropping to her knees, Kiera quickly checked for a pulse. Debra was alive, that was something. But she was unconscious and badly hurt by the looks of it.

'Paramedics!' A voice called out from the open front door.

'In here,' Kiera shouted, her voice cracking with emotion as the relief flooded through her. She wasn't on her own. Debra had help now. Real help. She was going to be okay.

'It's okay, my darlings, the paramedics are going to make mummy all better again,' Kiera said, catching the eye of the paramedic nearest to her, as she watched them both crouch down next to Debra's body and tend to her friend, checking her pulse just as she had, before looking over her for other injuries.

'What happened?' one of them asked her.

Kiera shook her head. Surely they could see by the state of her that she'd been badly beaten?

But then, remembering Debra's words she knew that information couldn't come from her. Gerard would make her pay if she went against him. And she had Maisie to think about.

'She fell over.' Kiera said, catching the disbelief on the paramedic's face at Gerard's lie she was repeating. She saw him glance around the kitchen looking for an obstacle that may have caused her to trip over, before returning his gaze back to where Debra lay in the middle of the kitchen floor.

Her eye was swollen from where she'd been punched. Her arms were covered in bruises, old ones, too. Debra's exposed flesh showed the remnants of ripened bruises that had turned an ugly shade of purple and black. They didn't believe her, of course they didn't. What did Gerard expect? He'd gone too far tonight. He'd overstepped the line.

'Is there anyone else who lives here?' the paramedic asked lightly, aware that the children were in the room, and that there was clearly something much more sinister going on than he was being told.

'Gerard, her husband. But he hasn't been home all night—'

'Yes, he was home,' Mason cried, still visibly distraught. 'He was shouting at mummy. I heard him. She was crying and he wouldn't stop shouting.'

'Come on, boys, let's get you back to bed yeah?' Kiera said, biting her lip to silence herself. Surely she couldn't do this? She couldn't stand here and lie to protect that man, not after what he'd done to Debra and the kids. 'Come on, darlings, let's get you back to bed and let these lovely paramedics do their jobs. Mummy's going to be just fine. I promise you,' she said, carrying Mason and Logan through to their bedroom in the hope of shielding them from the sight of their poor broken mother, because she could see how distressed they both were. How they would both already be traumatised by tonight's goings-on. Gerard had a lot to answer for.

'Here you go. You can stay together, okay,' Kiera said, placing both boys down on Mason's bed, before switching the bedside lamp on. 'You don't have to go to sleep, you can just sit here. Stay under the covers and keep nice and warm. I'm going to go back and check on Mummy, but I'll only be a few minutes. And I'll make us all some hot chocolate. I'll be right back,' Kiera said with a nod, looking Mason directly in the eye.

Mason nodded back at her. Believing her.

'Can we have a teddy?' Logan asked, his face streaked with tears.

'Of course.' Kiera passed each boy a soft toy from the end of the bed.

'Stay here. Don't get back out of bed. I'll be right back.' Kiera was fighting her own tears now at the heartbreaking sight of the boys both huddled together in the bed, with their tear-streaked faces, clutching their teddies tightly to their chests.

'She's pregnant,' Kiera said, making it to the hallway just in time to see the paramedics carrying Debra on a stretcher through the doorway. 'She's not that far gone. Is she going to be okay? The baby? Will the baby be okay?'

'We're going to get her over to St George's. She'll be in the best hands there. Can you stay with the children?' one of the paramedics asked and Kiera nodded without so much as even thinking about the answer. 'You might want to give her husband a call and notify him. Or another next of kin that you can think of,' the paramedic added.

His eyes met hers and she knew without doubt that he knew the truth of what had happened to Debra tonight. That Kiera had lied. That she'd protected that scumbag of a husband of Debra's.

But she could also see that he knew it was because of fear. Stepping out on to the balcony, Kiera watched as the paramedics made their way to the lift at the stairwell. Numb with shock, she was oblivious to the cold night air. She was oblivious to everything.

Stepping forward in a trance-like state, she stared down over the balcony to the car park where the waiting ambulance was parked, her eyes transfixed by the pulsating blue lights as they flashed hypnotically across the dark night skies. She waited until she saw the paramedics finally reach it, and place the stretcher inside before driving off at speed. Then she went back inside the flat to check on the boys.

She'd have to wake Micky up after all. He'd have to come over and keep an eye on the boys, so that she could get herself down to the hospital. She couldn't just sit here and hope that her friend was going to be okay. Debra needed her now. More than ever.

# CHAPTER TEN

'Gerard?' Jodie Edwards said, jumping from where she was lying on the sofa, about to catch up on an episode of *Love Island*. Though with all probability she would have fallen asleep – she could barely keep her eyes open, but there was no point going to bed, as Jenson was due his next feed any minute. 'I wasn't expecting you.'

She looked hopeful, thinking that Gerard finally wanted to see her and their new baby son. She was starting to think he'd completely lost interest. It hadn't been the best start so far. She hadn't fallen pregnant on purpose, not really. Gerard had never asked her if she was on the pill, and she'd never made him wear anything. So, it was down to both of them when the inevitable had happened and she'd ended up pregnant. And Jenson was the ultimate prize as far as she was concerned.

But since he'd been born, Gerard had shown almost no interest in Jenson at all. He hadn't even turned up to the hospital until hours after Jodie had given birth, full of excuses as to why he'd missed the thousands of calls and texts from her saying that she had gone into labour. He'd left her to do the hardest part completely alone. She'd been so petrified of giving birth all alone in the hospital that she'd even considered calling her parents, but she knew that if she did then she'd only be proving them right. That she'd only be confirming all the things they'd said about Gerard just using her to be true. That seventeen was too young.

Jodie hadn't been able to face their disappointment. As far as she was concerned they'd disowned her, and she was on her own.

And when Gerard had finally turned up, she convinced herself that maybe he really had been busy, maybe he really did care, but again those thoughts were quickly dismissed when he'd held Jenson in his arms for what seemed like barely five minutes, looking awkward and uncomfortable before quickly placing him back down in the hospital cot again and announcing that he couldn't stay. That he had some important business to tend to. She remembered the tears that had filled her eyes later that night when she'd found the huge envelope of money stuffed inside Jenson's changing bag.

As if their new son was some kind of business transaction. The money made her feel cold and cheap, as if Gerard thought that he could just throw some money at her and she would keep her mouth shut about his lack of effort.

Of course, there were things she wanted to buy for Jenson. She wanted her son to have the best of the best. A smart new state of the art buggy with a fancy detachable car seat. Some cute designer outfits and little matching trainers. But more than just the stuff itself she'd wanted her and Gerard to go shopping for their son together. She'd wanted him to show some interest in Jenson's life. But he hadn't, and the past three weeks, she'd been left completely alone to deal with her baby. Stuck within these four walls with no one to help her or give her any advice. Feeling as if she was losing it, going slowly mad, with no idea if she was even caring for her baby right. But one thing she did know was that she loved her son with every part of her being. And Gerard would too, if he just gave Jenson some time.

'You must think I'm a right lazy cow,' she joked, reading that exact expression on Gerard's face as he looked around, turning his nose up at the mess of the place. She felt embarrassed then at the stench of Jenson's stale nappies that lingered in the air from the overflowing bin in the kitchen. If Gerard had given her a bit of notice she could have put them out, or done the dirty dishes that were currently stacked up in the sink.

She felt self-conscious at how she must look, too, unable to remember the last time she'd even managed to have a shower or bothered to brush her hair. What was the point if it was only her here? She was unable to concentrate on anything else right now other than making sure that Jenson was clean and fed and getting as much sleep as possible. He was her only priority.

'He's sound asleep. But trust me, he's been hard work, bless him. Feeds almost on the hour, every hour. And he cries. A lot,' Jodie said, rolling her eyes up and making light of the fact that really she was physically and mentally exhausted. She hadn't slept properly for days and even just breast-feeding Jenson was leaving her drained. And as angry as she was with Gerard for abandoning them both, he was here now. The last thing Jodie wanted to do was put a dampener on that.

'I can wake him if you want to see him? He's due another feed soon, anyway. It might be nice if you held him for a bit.'

'Nah, let the kid sleep. I need somewhere to kip for the night,' Gerard said, bluntly, making no attempt at even pretending he was interested in either of them.

'You've come here to sleep?' Jodie said thinking she had misheard him. 'Of course you have! Why else would you just randomly turn up here?' She realised how dishevelled Gerard looked then: his shirt was all untucked and unbuttoned, as if he'd got dressed in a hurry. She noted how his knuckles looked sore and red too, as if he'd been in a fight. Though she knew not to ask. Because it was none of her business what Gerard did. He'd told her enough times. But Jenson was very much her business. And she wasn't prepared to keep her mouth shut about him.

'You haven't even bothered to ask how your son is!' Jodie spat, furious now that she'd ever been so stupid and naive as to think that Gerard would ever step up and be a decent father to him. 'Don't you give a shit, Gerard? Don't you care about him?' Though she already knew the answer to that. She was incensed that Gerard seemed to just come and go as he pleased, though what choice did she really have? She was beholden to him, wasn't she? He paid her rent and bills.

'Jodie, not now, okay? I've got a fucking headache. The last thing I need is you harping on,' Gerard said with a finality that warned the girl he wasn't in the mood to be pushed. 'I'm stressed to fuck right now, I need to get my head down. So I'll sleep out here, or in the bed. Make up your mind where you and the kid are sleeping, and stay out of my way.' He walked off before Jodie could find her voice again to reply.

And even if she could find her voice, how could she respond to that? To him totally dismissing her as if she was nothing. Worse than that he was dismissing their son, and Jenson deserved better than that. He deserved better than Gerard. Feeling hot tears of anger pour down her cheeks, she got the spare duvet from the airing cupboard and dumped it on the sofa before going into her bedroom and shutting the door.

Lying on her bed, she couldn't keep her tears in. She'd done this to herself. This was all her own stupid fault, for falling for Gerard's hype. She'd seen how everyone on the Griffin Estate feared and respected him. How his notorious reputation proceeded him, and Jodie had wanted to be part of all that so that when she walked down the street people took notice of her too. She'd wanted that life. She'd wanted him. She'd lapped up all his attention and believed that the man actually cared about her when it had all come together and he'd moved her into this flat. She'd believed him when he'd told her that he couldn't get enough of her, and that he'd be round here too, visiting her at all times of the night or day. And that one day, they'd be together as a family.

It had all been lies. She'd been so blinded by the man that she hadn't realised until now that Gerard had just been playing her, manipulating her all along so he could get what he wanted from her. Her parents had been right all along. And now she was stuck with him.

# CHAPTER ELEVEN

Her eyes opened and immediately Debra winced at the brightness of the room, before a voice to her right startled her.

Disorientated, she turned her head.

'Hi, Debra.'

Narrowing her eyes, Debra didn't recognise the woman's friendly looking face as she smiled down at her.

'My name is Nurse Davids, but you can call me Kathy.'

A nurse? Debra registered the woman's uniform.

'You're in hospital. You're going to be just fine now though. You're in good hands.'

It was only then that Debra realised that she was lying in bed, in a cubicle on a hospital ward. The curtains had been pulled around to give her some privacy and Debra was grateful for that, as her hand instinctively moved to her stomach.

'The baby?' She pressed her palm against the flatness that she knew she would find there. There had been no bump, no curve, because she hadn't been that far along in her pregnancy to be showing outwardly yet. But even so, she was acutely aware of the hollowness there now. A void inside of her that made her feel as if a piece of herself was missing suddenly.

'It's gone, isn't it?'

The nurse nodded sadly, knowing that there would be no words of comfort that she could offer the woman.

And Debra didn't need any. She didn't even need the nurse's confirmation, because she already knew that she'd lost her baby.

Closing her eyes once more, she felt strangely calm. There were no tears, no hysterics. No anything. Just a numbness that engulfed her entire being.

'Has my husband been here?' Debra asked the nurse, the softness in her voice quickly replaced with a cold tightness as if she couldn't even bring herself to say his name. Her jaw tensed with anger at just the thought of the man. The man who put her here again. The man who killed their unborn child.

The nurse shook her head. 'No. But the paramedics that brought you in said that you had a bad fall?' The nurse paused, giving Debra the chance to speak up and tell her otherwise. This woman had taken the beating of her life, and the first thing she'd asked when she'd opened her eyes was where was her husband. But not in the usual way that a loved one seeks comfort from their partner – Kathy had seen the genuine fear in the woman's eyes, quickly replaced with relief when she'd confirmed that the man wasn't here. Kathy wasn't stupid. She knew men like Debra's husband. Men that belittled, bullied and beat women, as if to exercise how much power and control they really possessed. She waited patiently for Debra to take her opportunity and speak up for herself, only she could see that Debra wouldn't do that either.

She knew women like Debra too. Women who were so terrified of the repercussions of what would happen to them or their children if they finally spoke up about the abuse that they suffered, that they chose to remain silent. So consumed by fear of going against the bully who inflicted their pain, they unwittingly ended up protecting them instead. And Kathy could see it now, as Debra kept her eyes trained on the crack in the ceiling tile above her. How she refused to talk about the man who put her here.

'Your friend was here though. Kiera. She seems so lovely. She sat by your side for a couple of hours after you were brought in, bless her. I told her to go home and get some sleep, that she'd be better off coming back this morning. She made a call to your husband and let him know how you were.'

Debra nodded, understanding what the nurse was telling her. 'Did she tell him? About the baby?'

The nurse nodded again and Debra bit down on her lip, the pain of her tooth pressing sharply against the flesh, as she embraced the tiny ripple of satisfaction that spread through her, visualising the moment that Gerard was told what he'd done. That she'd been pregnant with his child and Gerard had killed his own flesh and blood that had been growing inside of her. That would have hurt him deeply, Debra knew that for a fact, because Gerard would have wanted another child. Another life to tie her to him for evermore. Another possession to add to his collection. He'd be raging that Debra had kept it from him. And even worse, it would have killed him that it had been Kiera who had been the one to deliver that news to him. Good. She was glad. Let him suffer too, though it wasn't enough. Not nearly.

'She said to let you know when you wake up that the boys are absolutely fine. She and Micky are looking after them and she's going to be back straight after the school run. So you don't have to worry about rushing off anywhere today, Debra, sweetheart. You just concentrate on getting some rest.'

The nurse paused before lowering her voice and continuing, 'And if your husband wants to visit you, and you're not feeling up to seeing him, I can tell him that you're sleeping. That you need your rest,' Kathy said, letting Debra know of her suspicions without having to voice them.

Debra nodded, grateful that the nurse was on her side and that she didn't have to see Gerard. Not yet, at least. Gerard wouldn't turn up here anyway, not after what he did.

That wasn't his style. He'd be hiding away until things had died down a bit. Then he'd come crawling out of the woodwork and come creeping home with his tail between his legs, pretending that he was sorry for what he'd done. The man's apologies were never sincere. They were all just another part of his game to manipulate and control her, and make sure that he still had his power over her.

'We don't have to let anyone in here, Debra,' the nurse said. 'It's up to you who visits you.'

Debra wanted to laugh then. Wishing more than anything that the nurse's words could be true and that she had any kind of real control over her own life. That this lovely nurse had any real powers to stop Gerard from coming in here. The woman was foolish if she thought that she or the hospital security could stop him. Gerard was a law unto himself. But she knew that the nurse obviously only meant well.

'Actually…' the nurse paused, placing her hand lightly on Debra's as if to show her support, 'you do have some other visitors here to see you, if you're up for it?' Debra looked at her, confused. 'There're two police officers waiting out by the nurses' station. I told them that I'd let you know that they were here. It's completely up to you if you talk to them or not. No pressure. But they just want to help you, Debra.'

'No!' Debra said, point-blank. 'I can't speak to the police.' She felt a wave of panic spread through her again as she thought about her babies, Mason and Logan, and all the threats Gerard had made about what would happen to them if she ever dared to talk to anyone about what went on inside their four walls.

'Look, you don't have to say anything to them, if that's what you're worried about. But it might help to hear what they have to say? They might be able to help you. There's no harm in doing that, is there? You won't have done anything wrong by just listening,' the nurse reasoned.

Debra doubted that the police would be able to say anything she'd want to hear. Gerard was public enemy number one as far as they were concerned, and as his wife, she couldn't imagine that they'd hold much sympathy for her. But another part of her wanted to believe that this nurse was right. That maybe it might help her in some way. Because right now she felt so broken, so destitute, that she didn't know what else she could do. And she felt so angry with Gerard for doing this to her.

Each time was getting worse and God knows how much the boys had seen and heard last night.

'At least let them come in for a few minutes, Debra. You have nothing to lose.'

'Five minutes, and that's it.' Debra finally agreed, watching the nurse go and get the officers quickly, before Debra could have second thoughts and change her mind.

Sitting in the small, sterile cubicle of the ward they'd placed her on, she waited with the nurse's last words spinning in her head. *You have nothing to lose.* Placing a hand gently across her stomach she closed her eyes and thought about the life that had once been inside of her, before it was so viciously taken away. The baby that would never be. Mason and Logan's brother or sister. She thought of her two precious boys and knew that this time she had to do something different. This time she needed to find the courage, to be brave enough to speak up and to tell the police what Gerard had done. Because only then could she put an end to this abysmal existence of hers once and for all.

Because the nurse was wrong about one thing: Debra still had so much more to lose.

# CHAPTER TWELVE

'Hi, Debra, we've not met. My name is DS Morgan and this is my colleague, DC Murphy. We're both based in CID at Wandsworth station,' the older of the officers said, smiling at Debra warmly as the two of them made their way inside the cubicle and pulled the curtain back around them to give themselves some privacy. 'We're sorry for what's happened to you, and for your loss.'

Nodding, Debra eyed the two plain-clothed officers dubiously. Going by their titles these were not standard uniformed officers, and she wondered what their real motives for being here were.

'CID doesn't normally deal with domestics?'

'A domestic? Oh, we heard that you took a nasty fall,' DS Morgan said lightly, his expression giving nothing away. He waited patiently in the hope that Debra would tell him the truth about what had happened to her, because the bullshit story that had been fed to the paramedics who had brought Debra in hadn't washed with him or any of the nurses here one bit.

'That's what I meant. I fell.' Debra shrugged, backtracking though she didn't have the energy to put any real conviction behind her words. These officers weren't stupid, and neither were the nurses here. 'Still, don't you lot have enough to keep you busy without adding hospital visits to your list of things to do?' Debra suddenly thought that speaking to these officers, even just hearing them out, was more trouble than it would be worth.

Trying to play for time to compose herself, she slowly eased herself up in the bed, trying to sit, wincing as she shuffled back against the pillows. Only she underestimated how weak she still felt as she struggled to shift her body back far enough on the bed. The pillow slipped down behind her, leaving her leaning awkwardly at an angle.

'Here, please. Let me,' Lucy said, quickly stepping forward and adjusting the pillow, before offering Debra her arm to lean on so that she could use it to manoeuvre backwards.

'How's that?' Lucy said, checking the woman was more comfortable now.

'Thanks…' Debra said gratefully, pausing as she tried to remember the officer's name.

'DC Murphy, but please, call me Lucy. Would you like me to pass you some water?' Lucy said, eyeing the fresh jug and plastic cup that had been left on the bedside tray for Debra.

Again Debra nodded, taking the cup from Lucy and drinking the water down in one.

'You're right, Debra, CID don't normally get involved in cases like this,' DS Morgan continued now that Debra looked more comfortable. 'The paramedics have to call incidents like this in. Especially when the story doesn't add up. And it was brought to my attention that you've had quite a few nasty falls over the past few years, going by your hospital records.' Morgan looked intently at Debra, letting her know that he knew the truth even without her having to voice it.

He knew she was scared, too. That's how men like Gerard Jennings got away with their abuse. By keeping the women in fear of them and what they were capable of. By messing with their heads and making even the strongest of women, like Debra, truly believe that she'd never be free of him. That if she dared to speak up, he'd kill her, or worse, as DS Morgan suspected, knowing that there were children involved, he'd use the kids against her too.

'In the last five years you've been hospitalised four times, suffering a broken nose, a fractured jaw. Broken ribs. A broken arm, a black eye. A missing front tooth. The list goes on…' Morgan took a deep breath, knowing that he was in danger of crossing a line. But Debra Jennings wasn't going to just offer the information they needed willingly. 'You know, Children's Services will need to get involved this time, don't you, Debra?'

Lucy bristled at her sergeant's change of tactics when this woman had already suffered enough stress for one day, though she knew rationally that DS Morgan would only do something like this if he was desperate. The mention of Children's Services getting involved was probably the only way that they'd be able to get through to her.

'Is that some kind of a threat?' Debra said, recognising the comment for what it was, already unsure now if speaking to the officers was such a good idea. She wasn't sure that she could trust them. This might be a trick. What if this lot were on Gerard's payroll too? What if this was a test and whatever she told them would get straight back to him?

'Children's Services can't do anything, because as I told you, I fell. Let them prove otherwise,' Debra said, determined not to rise to the officers' attempt at getting a reaction from her. 'I'm clumsy,' Debra said quietly, repeating Gerard's excuse that he'd used a hundred times before, to anyone who'd listen. She bit her lip, annoyed that she'd ever considered that this lot might be able to help her.

As much as she hated Gerard sometimes, he was right. The police sometimes played dirty too. Especially the bent coppers. The only difference was they wore uniforms and badges and used the guise of enforcing the law to get what they wanted; which was normally to cash in on something more lucrative than their own poorly paid career offered them. Gerard had a few bent coppers on his books and often said that they were the most greedy, manipulative people that he'd worked with. That they were wolves in sheep's clothing and should never be trusted. A part of her had always believed that he'd just said all of that to ensure that she didn't betray him and ever turn to them. But now she had these officers' undivided attention, she wasn't so sure.

'Children's Services were contacted before we arrived here. The paramedics who attended the scene at your home would have had a duty of care to inform them. It's not down to the police, and DS Morgan isn't trying to threaten you, Debra. He's just being honest with you,' Lucy said now, hoping the woman would see that she was telling her the truth. 'He wants to help you. We both want to help you, if you'll let us. Because whatever happened to you, shouldn't have happened.'

Lucy knew that persuading Debra to talk to them wasn't going to be an easy task. Debra had been brainwashed into keeping her silence about the violence that Gerard inflicted on her. According to DS Morgan, any time the police had been called to Debra and Gerard's address over similar incidents in the past, Debra had always refused to make a statement about her husband, choosing to cover up for the man instead, because she believed she didn't have any other choice. Only this time Lucy and DS Morgan had thought it might be different. Debra Jennings had lost her baby due to the vicious assault she'd endured. This time Gerard had gone too far, and the man's actions might be the catalyst that Debra needed for the woman to finally find her courage and tell them the truth about what she'd been suffering. All they needed was for Debra to trust them.

'You lot make me laugh,' Debra said, staring at Lucy and shaking her head, because she'd already weighed up her options here. Even if these two officers did mean well, they couldn't help her. Nobody could.

'Let's just say he did do this to me. What would he get? Three months? Six, if I'm lucky,' Debra said. 'Come on, be serious with me. And what then? If Gerard even got time, he would have me and my sons watched while he was inside. He's got too many connections. He'll want to make sure we don't do a disappearing act on him. I won't be able to go anywhere without being spied on and it reported back to him. I'd be no better off than if he was out. He has trust issues you see.' She laughed then, a dry bitter sound with no humour in it. 'Though God knows why I'm the one that gets accused of all sorts, when the bloke's got the morals of an alley cat.' Debra took a deep breath. 'He has an army of men working for him and he has eyes and ears everywhere. All over London. Even amongst you lot. He's got officers that work for him. How do you think he always manages to stay ten steps ahead? So, if I spoke to you, he would find out in a heartbeat. And do you know what would happen when he got back out?'

'We'd protect you, Debra. We could place you and your boys somewhere he won't find you.'

Debra shook her head disbelievingly. 'He'd make it his life's goal to find us. We'd never be free.' She closed her eyes, forcing back the tears that threatened, before opening them again.

'I'm not scared for me. I don't care about what he'd do to me. I care about Mason and Logan. He'd kill them. He has implied as much. And do you know what, that mad bastard is capable of it too. The boys are just leverage to him. Another way for him to get at me and control me.' Debra was crying, unable to stop the fresh hopeless tears as they cascaded down her face, now she'd finally opened up and shared with the officers the fears that had been engrained so deeply into her.

'Till death do us part. What a stupid cow I was, that day, thinking our wedding vows were romantic. It's the only line that bastard meant. That's the only way I'll ever get away from him: when I'm dead. Until then, he'll always be there, making our lives a misery.' She almost spat the words out, unable to hide the hate she felt for the man she was tied to. She wiped her tears away. She knew that they were pointless. They only made her look weak. And that was one thing she fought so hard on a daily basis not to be.

'You lot have no idea of the things that he's capable of, or the stuff he's involved in.'

'We know more than you think, Debra,' Morgan said softly. Aware that as much as this woman was scared of Gerard Jennings, and wanted to get away from the man, she was still his wife and might report their conversation back to him. But there was something so genuine about what Debra was telling him that he decided to take a risk.

'What if we could get him on other things that he's involved in too?' he said carefully. Debra was right: Gerard most likely wouldn't go down for assaulting her. It would be her word against his, and it was more than likely that by the time it went to trial he would have got to her and she would change her story once more. DS Morgan needed more than that.

He didn't need permission or a statement from the women to bring Gerard down, he could arrest Gerard on his own accord. That wasn't why they were here today.

He'd wanted to sound Debra out, to see where her loyalties to the man that put her here, lay.

'We could put him away for a very long time, Debra. We're talking years. Him and his men.'

The two officers bristled visibly when Debra laughed again. Loudly, almost mockingly. She realised their real motives now.

'And so the penny drops. That's why you are really here. You don't care about me, not really. You don't care that I've just miscarried my baby. You're here for yourselves. So what's the plan? You want information on him? You want me to grass on my own husband? And what, you're happy to use me as bait in the process?'

Debra felt her anger return now.

'You're all the same. You want to use me for your own gain. You know what he's capable of, yet you're happy to gamble with my life. With my children's lives. Get out.'

'It's not like that, Debra.' Lucy tried to explain.

Only Debra had heard enough.

'I said GET OUT!' Debra shouted now, forcing her voice out loudly enough so that the nurse outside could hear her.

Seeing Debra so visibly distressed, the nurse ushered the officers quickly from the cubicle.

Debra sat in the empty cubicle. Staring at the curtains. And never had she felt more alone.

*

'Well that didn't go down so well,' Lucy said as she followed Morgan out to their car in the hospital car park. 'Do you think she'll tell him that we came to see her?'

'I don't think so, no,' Morgan said, annoyed with himself for not being able to get through to the woman. In fact he realised that, if anything, he'd just made things worse. He'd assumed that Debra would be willing to talk to them, to get justice for her treatment by the man, but it wasn't always so black and white. Not when there was real fear involved.

'She's shit scared of the man, and rightly so. Not only is Gerard Jennings notorious for using extreme violence, the man is also mentally unhinged. My guess is that he will stop at nothing to get to anyone who dared to wrong him. And that includes his wife, I'm afraid. But I don't think she'll tell him about our visit, no. There'd be nothing for her to gain by doing so. It would only put Gerard even more on edge, and she wouldn't want that.'

'Do you think we messed up?' Lucy asked, wondering now if their visit to Debra had been the right thing to do after all.

Morgan shook his head. Reaching the car, he got in the driver's seat and waited patiently for Lucy to get in the passenger side before he continued.

'Years ago, I made a promise to a victim of domestic abuse. A young woman, Bethany. Early thirties, she'd been run over by her boyfriend after a night out. Run over and then reversed over.' Morgan fought with the emotion that was evident in his voice. 'The man in question had been drunk and coked up, accusing her of all sorts, of flirting with other men in the nightclub that they'd been in. The accusations were ridiculous considering that she had been with him all night and she was shit scared of him. But then that's what these kinds of men do, they judge their girlfriends by their own cheating standards.' Morgan stared out of the window, watching as a young woman walked past the car pushing a buggy with a young child inside. 'Bethany had a child, too. A little boy. He wasn't even a year old, the poor thing. I told her that we could help her, that we could put him away for good, if she'd just testify. Only she was too terrified of what he'd do to her, what he'd do to her little boy. So after she was admitted from hospital she went back to him…'

Morgan started the engine then, wanting to distract himself with driving so that he could get the rest of the story out and explain to Lucy why this meant so much to him.

'Two weeks later, we found her body in a skip, on the very estate that she lived in. Dumped there, amongst all the rubbish, as if she was nothing. We had no evidence, no proof, but it was that fucker of a boyfriend of hers, I'd lay my life on it. But he got away scot-free. And the worst thing was, he got full custody of their son. Can you imagine how Bethany's family must have felt? Knowing that that monster not only took their daughter and sister from them, but he took their grandchild and nephew from them too.'

'Jesus, that's awful, Sarge,' Lucy said, aghast.

'Awful doesn't even cover it. That kid is just like him now. Running around the estate like a mini-me gangster. Expelled from school. Exposed to only Christ knows. And with no memory at all of his mother either, no doubt. The woman who lost her life, trying to protect him.'

Driving towards the exit of the car park, DS Morgan took a deep breath.

'Debra is wrong. I'm not doing this to just catch Gerard, though I'd be lying if I didn't admit that I want that bastard sent down for a million things. But I don't want to use her. I want to help her get away from that bastard and get her justice. I want to make sure that we don't end up with another dead woman on our hands and two little boys who grow up to be just like their father. Because he's capable of killing her. I know he is.'

Lucy nodded in agreement. Hearing the raw emotion in her boss's voice made her want to reach out and give him a hug.

'But we can't do it for her. She's got to do it herself when she's ready. And I pray to God for her sake that it's some time soon.'

Morgan pressed his foot to the floor then and drove back to the station in complete silence. Lucy got it. She understood more than anything that justice for their victims was the reason that any decent police officer did this job. And, some days, through all the horror and the shit that they had to deal with, that motive was the only thing that kept them going.

# CHAPTER THIRTEEN

'Where am I? Who are you?' Winnie Murphy woke abruptly from her nightmare, stricken with fear.

She pushed up against the bedroom wall in a bid to get away from the strange woman standing over her. 'Get away from me!'

She stared wildly round the tiny room, not recognising the four beige walls, nor the dressing table and the armchair. This wasn't her home. This wasn't her bedroom.

'Where am I?'

'There, there, Winnie. You had a bad dream,' Nurse June Hamilton said in a hushed, soothing whisper as the elderly woman continued to cower on the far side of her bed. 'I found you wandering out in the corridor, didn't I? I was just putting you back to bed.' Seeing Winnie's eyes narrow suspiciously, June continued, 'You're at Treetops Care Home. I'm Nurse Hamilton. June. I've been looking after you, love.'

'Where's Jennifer? Where's Lucy?'

'Lucy's going to visit you later, darling. She comes every day. Vivian might pop by too. Do you fancy a cuppa now you're awake, sweetheart?' Nurse Hamilton said, taking Winnie's reaction completely in her stride, acting calm and unfazed so that Winnie had no choice but to relax.

Winnie slowly gave in and nodded. Part of her just wanted an excuse for the woman to leave the room and give her a few minutes alone so that she could gather her thoughts.

'Two sugars, and a nice brew coming right up.' Nurse Hamilton smiled before leaving the room.

Winnie got out of bed and wrapped her dressing gown tightly around her before taking a seat in the armchair by the window and staring outside at the early morning frosty view. She could just about see the sun peeping out from the clouds on the horizon.

'There you go, Winnie. Strong and sweet. Just like you, my love,' June said, sitting across from the woman now, aware that Winnie was still shaken from the nightmares she'd endured.

'I don't remember being out in the corridor,' Winnie said, her voice small but still indignant.

'It happens, my love. Nightmares or night terrors making us want to get up and run away while we're still half asleep. Is that what you were doing, Winnie? Running away from something?'

June asked the woman softly, hoping that if Winnie could remember her dreams, if she could try and get some understanding of why she was having them, it might ease her terrors slightly.

Patients wandered outside their rooms frequently at night, often because they felt threatened or anxious and June understood why. They just wanted to go somewhere 'safe'. Some of them believed that they could make their way back to their childhood homes. Others merely wanted to get away from something that was scaring them. Night terrors and hallucinations were common with dementia. The disease left no mercy in its wake, not even in sleep.

'Or trying to find somewhere safe?'

Winnie shook her head.

'This wasn't a nightmare. It was real.'

June nodded, thinking that she understood. No doubt they felt real when they were happening.

But that wasn't what Winnie meant.

'I dreamt about Jennifer again. She was screaming for me to help her,' Winnie said sadly, her voice breaking as she spoke her daughter's name. 'Only the door was locked. He'd locked it. And I couldn't get to her. I couldn't help her. So, I was looking for help.'

June eyed the woman, sadly. Winnie's mind wasn't manufacturing things. Her terrors were real. She'd lived through them and they were still taunting her each night. Lucy had told June all about what had happened to her mother, to Winnie's daughter, Jennifer Murphy. How she'd been brutally murdered all those years ago and how Jennifer's death often affected Winnie so acutely on a daily basis that she was crippled with the pain from the loss of her only child. On other days, she was left with no recollection of her daughter dying at all.

'Why is life so cruel? Why am I forced to remember it over and over again? Why is my brain always trying to trick me? I wake sometimes and I don't even know she's gone. I sit here, waiting for her to walk into the room. How is that fair?'

'It's not, my love. And I wish more than anything that I could take away your pain, Winnie my darling,' June said sincerely, knowing that there was nothing she could do or say that could make Winnie feel any better. All she could do was what she was doing right now and just be there for Winnie while she was present. 'I'm always here if you fancy a cup of tea and a chat if you wake again from a bad dream. Or if you can't sleep,' June said, reaching out a hand and placing it on Winnie's.

'Do you want to get back in to bed and see if you can get back to sleep?'

Winnie shook her head and turned away to look out of the window.

'I'll leave you to your sunrise, Winnie.' June stood up and gave Winnie's hand a gentle, supportive squeeze. Winnie nodded dully, staring out of the window and willing the sun to rise higher in the sky as she sipped her tea. The last place she wanted to go was back to bed where her nightmares would take her back to that dreadful time and place.

# CHAPTER FOURTEEN

'Mummy!' Mason screeched excitedly at the sight of Debra and Kiera coming through the front door. He bounded towards her as Logan ran along behind him.

'God, I missed you!' Debra laughed, hugging the boys close to her, feeling tears fill her eyes.

'Careful, boys. Your mum's still in a lot of pain from the fall,' Kiera said, making sure that both boys didn't jump on Debra or pull at her. Debra was doing her best at putting on a brave face now that she was at home with the boys, but it had taken a painstaking twenty minutes to get her to hobble the short distance from the car park to the lifts of their block.

'You all right?' Gerard said, making his presence known as he stood watching the scene from the kitchen, his body language guarded as he leaned up against the sink, his hands cupping a hot mug of tea close to his chest.

Kiera noted the sorry look on his face now that he was faced with Debra for the first time since the assault he'd carried out on her three days previously. And so he should feel sorry, she thought, placing her hand lightly on Debra's arm to give her support.

'Come on, Debs. Let's go and get you sat down, mate. I'll get the kettle on and make you a brew.'

'No, you're all right, Kiera. You've done enough,' Gerard said, his voice tight as he dismissed the woman. She'd done her bit and brought Debra home. She wasn't needed any more. She could leave. Then, remembering that he was going to have to fight his hardest to get back into Debra's good books this time, he changed tack, aware that the tension in the room had become palpable since Debra had entered it. He could feel the hate and anger radiating from her in waves.

'We can't thank you enough, Kiera,' he said, making a point to sound humble and grateful, though she could see that his rare act of kindness was forced and uncomfortable for him.

Gerard wasn't fooling any of them with his act, not even the kids, Kiera suspected. Though for Debra's sake she knew that she didn't have any other choice but to play along. They all did.

'I don't mind, Gerard, honestly. I'm happy to make a cuppa and stay for a bit. Keep Debs company.'

'No, you're good. I'm here. We'll be fine.' Gerard's face was neutral, but it was a command all the same.

Kiera caught the look that Debra shot her and knew that was her cue to leave.

'Well if you need anything at all, ring me, yeah, and I'll be straight over.' Giving Debra a kiss on the cheek, she ruffled Mason's and Logan's hair, before leaving the family to it.

'You want me to give you a hand into the lounge?' Gerard said, stepping forward and offering Debra his arm for support.

Debra immediately flinched. Cursing herself for being so transparent, she shook her head.

'No.' Her voice came out sharper and louder than she'd intended and she registered the shocked look on Gerard's face. It felt good, powerful even, to stand up for herself. Letting the man know that she was beyond angry with him. Because this was the start of it – the act that he always put on. The olive branch. The out-of-character gestures. None of it was for her benefit, she knew that well enough by now.

Seeing her, with her face still swollen and purple, her body battered, the sadness in her eyes from the loss of their unborn child, the man acting as if he was consumed with guilt. And this was all just to make him feel better about his actions. As usual, Gerard was only thinking of himself.

'Mummy are you still sore?' Logan asked, watching his mother hobble into the lounge and ease herself slowly down into the chair, wincing in pain as she did so. 'I don't want you to be sad, Mummy.' Logan's bottom lip started to tremble, as Mason looked at her too. Both her beautiful boys staring at her swollen battered face with an expression of horror at what they saw.

'I feel much better. But yes, I'm still a little bit sore,' Debra said lightly, hoping to play down her pain and injuries.

'We drew you pictures, Mummy, and made you a card. Kiera helped us,' Logan said, grabbing the piece of coloured card that he'd left on the side for when Debra came home.

'Oh that is beautiful. Heart and flowers. My favourites!' Debra said, feeling emotional as she examined the pretty fabric hearts and flowers that the boys had so carefully and lovingly cut out and stuck on the front of the card for her.

'And that's a dinosaur.' Logan pointed proudly. 'Dinosaurs are your favourite, too, aren't they, Mummy?' Logan eyed his brother then, as if they'd both had a disagreement over the matter.

'Of course they are.' Debra nodded, discreetly winking at Mason so that her older son would know that she was just keeping Logan happy and that he had been right all along.

'I'm so happy to see you both. I'm so happy to be home.' She ignored the look on Gerard's face as she brought both her boys in towards her for another cuddle. She could sense there was something wrong with Mason the second she did. Going tense in her arms he held back. Unlike Logan he wasn't going to be so easy to appease.

'Did you fall over, Mummy?' Mason asked now, his voice quiet, but she could hear the challenge in his tone. He was testing her to see if she would be honest with him. Kiera had already told her how she'd found the boys clinging to her in the kitchen. How Mason had told the paramedics that Gerard had been shouting at her, that she'd been crying.

He might only be five years old, but even at this young age, her son wasn't oblivious to his surroundings. And it pained Debra to have to sit here and lie to him, but as she caught Gerard's eyes, she knew that she didn't have much choice. She had to lie to him for all of their sakes. For now anyway.

'Yes. I did. I had a really nasty fall. But don't worry, Mason, it won't happen again. I'll be more careful next time…' She stared at Gerard over Mason's head, challenging him, wanting him to see the damage that he'd done, not only to her, but to their boys. The shock on their faces as they took in the sight of her swollen bruised face, the fear in their voices that it might happen again.

Logan was too young to question anything much about it all, but Mason wasn't so quick to fall for Gerard's story. There was doubt in his eyes, and she saw how he looked from her to Gerard so questioningly. Gerard hadn't been able to fool a five year old, so why would he expect anyone else to believe his story?

'Boys, why don't you both go and get your teddies and we'll put on a film now your mum's home,' Gerard said.

Debra bit her lip. This was another tactic of Gerard's, suddenly playing the doting father because he knew only too well that the way to her heart was through her kids. But she had no intention of falling for the man's act this time.

'Why didn't you tell me about the baby?' Gerard asked as soon as the boys had run from the room.

'Why? If I had what would you have done?' Debra said glaring at the man now as if seeing him for the very first time. All six foot of him looming above her with a sorry expression on his face.

'Would you have avoided my stomach when you kicked and punched me? Concentrated on my face?' Debra spat her words now.

'It would have been different...' Gerard said, and Debra couldn't help but laugh then.

'What, you'd have waited until after I'd had it until you kicked the shit out of me? Like you do regularly regardless of the fact that Mason and Logan are both here in the flat? They hear things, Gerard, they see things.' Debra could feel the swell of a lump in her throat. Even after everything he'd done to her physically, knowing that her kids suffered because of Gerard was what hurt her the most.

'You did me a favour. I don't want to bring any more of your kids into this world,' she said resolutely. She would never normally get away with speaking to Gerard like this and she could see by the twitch of the vein on his temple that he was doing his best not to retaliate to her words. That she'd struck a nerve. But suddenly she no longer cared about whether or not she could shut her mouth and keep her opinions to herself. Gerard attacked her on his terms, whether she'd done something to deserve it or not.

And something had changed in her the past few days, she realised, as she stared right through Gerard now, and wondered what she'd ever really saw in the man in the first place. Because she didn't love him. Not any more, not one bit. In fact she hated him more than anything or anyone.

That's what they said though, wasn't it? That there was a thin line between love and hate. And now that Debra had crossed that line, she knew with certainty that there would be no coming back. She didn't want this life any more. She wanted out.

# CHAPTER FIFTEEN

'For Christ's sake, Mason and Logan, can you keep the bloody racket down,' Gerard bellowed loudly from the kitchen, wrapping his fingers tighter around his glass of Scotch. The sound of his two boys giggling and running around the lounge was beginning to grate on him.

'The boys are only having a laugh, mate. Come on…' Paul said, sitting back and staring at Gerard, recognising that the man was on the brink of losing his temper.

'She's letting them run riot. Thinking that they can do and say whatever they please. Debra needs to be stricter with them. Show them some discipline. They're out of control,' Gerard spat.

Gerard was clearly annoyed with Debra, though thankfully for now he seemed to be staying out of her way.

Paul pursed his mouth. He didn't agree. 'They're good kids, Gerard.' Mason and Logan were only five and three. They were full of life and boisterous and Debra was a great mother; there was nothing that Gerard could say that would ever convince Paul otherwise. He'd seen it first-hand. If anything it was Gerard who was out of control.

Paul had only been at his flat for less than twenty minutes, but already he could see that his friend was close to losing it big time. And that wasn't helped by the fact that in that short space of time, Gerard had already snorted a huge line of coke and necked two large Scotches.

Though, of course, Gerard was oblivious to his double standards. The fact that he'd been the one to put his own wife in hospital this week, yet had the nerve to sit here now complaining about her, just about said it all. Paul needed to try and get through to him somehow.

'Christ, we weren't much older than Mason when we met, Gerard. Do you remember? You had me stealing from the newsagents after school. Filling our pockets with as many sweets as we could shove inside them, and when the old boy who ran the shop caught us, you kicked him in the shins and called him an old bastard, before making us run for our lives.'

'Yeah, only you ended up blabbing everything to your mum that night!' Gerard rolled his eyes.

'I was worried that the police were going to turn up and arrest me.' Paul laughed. 'I got a right hiding when I told her. I was mortified when she dragged me out of bed and marched me back down to the shop to apologise. We couldn't have been more than seven or eight.' Paul laughed again, recalling the memory.

'We were seven. Yeah, I remember.' Gerard laughed then too. They'd been friends for almost thirty years, since primary school. It seemed like a lifetime ago now. But Gerard trusted Paul with his life and Paul felt the same.

'And you got off scot-free if I remember rightly.'

'Only cos my mum didn't give a shit about what I got up to, as long as I was out of her way,' Gerard said, bristling at the memory of his own volatile upbringing. He knew what Paul was getting at. Deep down he knew that Mason and Logan weren't bad kids, and Debra always did her best by them. No matter what else he might think of her.

'You need to chill out, Gerard. You're going to end up losing your head, mate.' Paul nodded down to the empty glass.

Gerard shrugged.

'Tell me about it. Shit, laying low just ain't good for me, Paul. I feel like the four walls are closing in on me. Anyway, fuck all that. Let's talk about something else, yeah? You said you had news?' Gerard said, tapping his fingers against the table, knowing that Paul hadn't just called in today for a chit chat. He must have something for him.

'The Old Bill found Bobbie Carter's body a few days ago.'

'And?' Gerard shrugged. This wasn't worrying to him. Dead bodies turned up all the time. 'They won't be able to find any evidence to link it to me. I was careful,' he said arrogantly.

'Well, that's just it, Gerard. They have linked it to you. One of our boys on the inside tipped me off. He told me they received an anonymous call saying that his murder was down to you.'

Gerard narrowed his eyes, clearly agitated by the news that Paul had just delivered but trying not to show it. 'But only a handful of us knew about it.' Gerard gritted his teeth. He'd made sure that he'd done a thorough job of not leaving any evidence on the man's body when he'd killed him. And the last time any of them had laid eyes on Bobbie Carter's corpse, was when they'd dropped the body into the Thames, hoping that Mother Nature would do the rest and make it even harder for the police to come to any conclusions that might lead back to them.

'Do you think we've got a grass?' Gerard asked, though he knew that was the only viable explanation. How else would the police know?

Paul shrugged. 'I dunno, Gerard, maybe someone saw something? Fuck knows, mate! But it doesn't look good.' Paul was clearly just as pissed off about the entire thing as Gerard was because accusations like this put them all in jeopardy. If Gerard was in the firing line, so was he.

'I take it your man is going to keep digging about? See if he can rat out the grass for us?' Gerard said, raising his brows questioningly; one thing that he couldn't abide were grasses.

Especially amongst your own. Paul nodded. Although he wasn't holding out much hope for that.

'They're placing you under surveillance, Gerard,' Paul said, knowing that this last bit of news could more than likely tip Gerard over the edge because it meant that the police were taking the claims seriously. It meant that the police genuinely believed they had a chance of linking this back to him. And Gerard was paranoid at the best of times. Now he had good cause to be.

'You're going to have to rein it in, Gerard. Big time. Everything's going to have to stop, for a while at least. And I mean everything. We can't afford to risk it. I've already made a start and got some of the lads to shift some of the gear about. But you can't go near any of our buildings. You need to stay put here, as far away from the set-up as possible. Otherwise you'll lead them right back to us.' Paul made the mammoth task that he'd had to deal with the past few days sound much simpler than it actually had been. He'd had to organise that everything be moved from the usual cuckoo houses and drugs dens they frequented all over London almost single-handedly, other than a few of the men that he trusted with his life, because for now, he and Gerard needed to be wary. They couldn't trust anyone and Paul wasn't taking any chances.

'No. We can't just sit on our arses not doing anything. Otherwise the pigs win either way. If we ain't moving anything, then we ain't making any money, Paul. And we need to strike out now on our own, more than ever. This is bullshit. There must be another way?'

'There's not, Gerard. You could end up going down for years if they pin it all on you. This could destroy everything we've worked for. So we need to keep our heads down and our noses clean for a couple of weeks until this all blows over. Let the Old Bill waste their time watching you. They won't find shit on us, if we're not moving anything.'

Paul had known that Gerard would be difficult to convince. The man was all about making money and over the years they'd made a fortune supplying most of the dealers this side of the Thames, from their main supplier up in Manchester. Only even that had gone to shit now that they'd killed and disposed of Bobbie Carter and drawn the attention of the police. And that was nothing compared to what the bosses up North would do once they realised that their man had been taken out of the equation. And Gerard and Paul intended to cut them all out too. But first they needed the police off their backs.

'You said that you wanted to cut out the bosses. That we're going to run this firm our way. Just you and me. The way it should be, so that we could take control back and start pulling in our money, ourselves. Real money. Well, there's no going back now, Gerard. We've played our hand. When word gets back to the bosses that we took Bobbie Carter out, if it hasn't already, they'll receive the message loud and clear that we are out. There's no coming back from this now. So we need to be smart and stay ahead. If we don't give the Old Bill anything, they can't do shit to us. That's more important right now than anything else,' Paul said, shifting forward in his seat and keeping his eyes firmly on Gerard, willing the man to realise that he was talking sense. And he was the only one capable of doing so. Paul was telling him this for his own good. He just hoped Gerard listened to what he was saying.

'If we get ourselves a capture for this, then we lose it all, Gerard. That's the bottom line. So we have to choose. We lose a couple of weeks' worth of profit, or we lose everything we've worked for. We lose the lot.'

Gerard didn't speak. He refilled his glass, before he picked it up and necked the drink down in one, which Paul took as him finally agreeing to his terms. Because ultimately it needed to be Gerard who called the shots. Outwardly anyway. Gerard was the one with the name. He was the ruthless bastard around here. Reckless with it, and the fact that he was capable of pretty much anything made him a liability. People were afraid of that. And it meant that ultimately Gerard had the final word. This was his operation. His baby.

He and Gerard had both set up as small-time dealers almost ten years ago, but it had been Gerard who had caught the attention of the bosses up in Manchester with his ruthless business acumen and the fact that he didn't take any bullshit from anyone. The bosses had personally sought him out. And Gerard had insisted on only working with them if Paul could come on board too. The two men had clawed their way up the rankings ever since. Running county lines this side of the river and making huge amounts of money in the process. They'd built themselves an empire. But as the years had gone on, Gerard had grown greedy and bitter. Not happy with the huge amounts of money they pulled in, because they then had to hand over a large cut of it to their bosses. And to be fair to him, Gerard had a point. Why should they be the ones to take all the risks and do all the dirty work so that they could line the pockets of men who just sat back and reaped the rewards, while keeping only a fraction of the profits for themselves? So it had been agreed: Paul and Gerard were cutting loose. And people would soon be wary of the war that was about to erupt on the streets because of it. Especially where Gerard was concerned, because the man took no prisoners when it came to getting what he wanted.

But what a lot of people didn't realise was that Paul was the real brains behind the operation.

He was Gerard's adviser, his confidant and the man who unfortunately spent a lot of time cleaning up after him. He'd been giving the man his honest and brutal advice since day dot so that the business could be run successfully. Though lately he had had his work cut out for him. Because it felt as if Gerard was going off the rails. He was taking too many risks. Coked up way too often, his behaviour had become even more unpredictable than usual. Christ, putting his own wife in hospital this week had more than proved that. Gerard was starting to believe his own hype and had become convinced that somehow he was invincible. Right now, in order to pull this off, Paul had to make Gerard comply. If they were going to get through this without a capture from the Old Bill, or the big bosses sniffing around and poking their noses in, Paul was going to have to keep a closer eye on his friend.

'It's only a few weeks, Gerard. We just need to sit tight until the heat's off…' Paul said, before breaking off as the kitchen door opened and Debra walked in.

'You all right, Debra?' he said, changing his tone and watching as she nodded in answer. Not bothering to look at him, she busied herself washing up the boys' matching blue beakers before placing them down on the draining board. Her shoulders stooped so that her head hung down in a bid for her short blonde hair to cover her face, but even from here Paul could see the black and purple bruising that had formed over half her face.

'I'm going to take Mason and Logan to the shops with me and pick up a few bits for dinner.' Debra directed her comment at Gerard. Her eyes rested on the bottle of Scotch on the table and the empty glass next to it, as Gerard topped it up. That Gerard had started drinking already today didn't bode well for her at all.

'I'll put a film on for the boys when I get back. Keep them out of your way.'

'Whatever. Just get something for you and the boys. I'm going out later.'

Debra nodded, and Paul could see the wave of relief wash over her expression that she wasn't going to be stuck inside this flat with the man after he'd been drinking and snorting gear all day.

Watching as Debra left the room, Paul shifted uncomfortably on his chair.

'That shit has got to stop too, Gerard, do you hear me?' Paul said now, looking to his friend, unable to hide his anger.

They dealt with a lot of shit in their game and with a lot of dodgy situations and people, and there had been many things over the years that Paul didn't agree with when it came to the way Gerard conducted his business – more so lately if he was honest. And Paul had learned how and when to speak up, and when to say nothing. And this wasn't a time to keep his mouth shut.

Paul let Gerard get away with a lot, too much sometimes, before he reined the man in, but beating up women wasn't something he'd ever condone.

'What were you thinking?' Paul said, his face screwed up in an expression of pure disgust, knowing that there was no reason Gerard could give him that would justify his actions of physically attacking a woman.

'Watch yourself,' Gerard said, ignoring the glare that Paul was giving him, placing the top back on the bottle. Paul knew full well that he wouldn't get the truth out of the man, not now he had a skinful inside him. This is what Gerard always did: he pretended that nothing had happened. That none of this was his problem. Cocooned in his own denial.

'All I'm saying, mate, is that you need to be careful. With Debra too. We're lying low from now on, remember? You can't draw any attention to yourself,' Paul said, aware that he was pushing his luck now, offering Gerard advice on his own family. But Paul also knew that he was the only one who would ever get away with being so frank with the man.

They were as close as brothers, and even if Gerard didn't like what he was hearing, he still listened when Paul spoke. He was slipping lately, though – drinking more and more and shoving coke up his nose as if the stuff was in short supply.

'She's a good girl, Gerard. A good mum. You know that!' Paul persisted. He knew he was close to the line, but he also knew that if he didn't say his piece now, next time Gerard might go too far and he'd be too late. Paul had always liked Debra. She was a diamond of sorts, a rare breed around these parts. Easy-going by nature and never giving Gerard any earache no matter what he did. The man could come and go as he pleased. He could work all the hours, laze around the house on his days off. Yet still she wasn't enough for him.

'What I know is that it's none of your business, Paul, so don't push it, yeah?' Gerard said eventually, his eyes flashing a warning. Paul nodded. Another thing that had served him well over the years had been knowing when to quit. All he could do now was hope that Gerard let his words sink in.

# CHAPTER SIXTEEN

'Mummy? Can we get something nice?' Pulling at Debra's coat sleeve, Mason eyed his mother hopefully as they made their way down one of the food aisles in the shop. 'Cos we've been good boys today, haven't we?'

'You have been the best boys in the whole world,' Debra said, laughing despite herself, always unable to resist the puppy dog eyes Mason threw at her. The boy would grow up to be a complete heartbreaker one day. He'd have every girl who even so much as looked at him wrapped around his little finger, of that she had no doubt. She could barely leave the room without both of the boys clinging to her the past few days. They'd both suffered because of Gerard's actions too. They were both terrified that Debra might get hurt again, and Debra couldn't blame them. The reality was that it was only a matter of time until Gerard lost it again.

'Go on then, take your brother and pick one thing each. I'll just be here, packing everything up at the till, so don't take long,' Debra said, placing the shopping basket full of fruit and vegetables and a few packs of meat down on the counter. Seeing the flash of concern on the shopping assistant's face, at how battered and blackened Debra's own face was, Debra shrugged and shot the woman a tight smile.

'I had a nasty fall,' she said casually, attempting to make the ordeal she'd suffered seem less traumatic than it actually was. 'It looks much worse than it was.'

Debra busied herself placing the items in the carrier bags. She still didn't feel able to face a big supermarket shop. She'd decided to get a few bits from the local shop on the estate parade for once, so she could get back home as quickly as possible. Not only because of the pain she was still in, but because of exactly this: the sympathetic glances and the questioning eyes. Because as much as she claimed that she'd been clumsy and taken a fall, no one would believe it. Still, even if people suspected the truth, most people with any sense knew not to start asking questions or poking their noses in. Not if they wanted to remain intact, anyway.

Placing the last few items from the conveyer belt into the bags, Debra sensed someone close behind her and turned, expecting to see Mason or Logan there, creeping up behind her. But she was met with the same girl she'd spotted earlier. Debra had thought she'd been imagining it, that the girl had been staring at her. She'd assumed at first that she'd just been doing what everyone else was, looking at her face and wondering where she'd got those horrific bruises. But Debra was convinced now that there was something more going on here. Had the girl been following her? Well, there was only one way to find out.

'What a gorgeous baby!' Debra said, looking down into the pram the girl had been pushing, where a gentle crying had now started. She was unsure if this girl was the baby's mother or sister, she looked that young. Though as she watched the girl bend down and place the dummy in the child's mouth before gently cooing at the boy in the way that only a mother can, that question was answered straightaway.

'How old is your little one?' Debra asked, bending down to admire the tiny baby boy, unable to get the thoughts of her own lost baby out of her mind.

'He's almost four weeks; he's probably a bit young for a dummy, but it's the only way that I can get him back off to sleep,' the girl said, her tone flat, almost unfriendly. She seemed shifty now that Debra's attention was on her child, tilting the pushchair slightly away from Debra's gaze as if trying to conceal him from her.

Debra initially found that strange, as most new mothers were so eager to show their babies off to anyone who paid a slight bit of interest.

'He's gorgeous. He looks content now. You're obviously doing a great job.' She hoped that the girl would take the compliment as intended. She wondered if this girl was just being defensive because she was so used to people passing judgement over her for being such a young mum. After all, Debra had wondered if she was old enough to even have a child. She felt guilty, then, for doing exactly that: judging the girl.

'I'm sorry. I didn't mean to sound patronising,' Debra said, offering the girl a smile; but she just bit her lip and continued to look down at the floor, shuffling her feet awkwardly.

'Are you okay?' Debra asked, sensing that she was missing something here. That this awkward, stilted encounter was no accident, and for a second it looked as if the girl might speak. Then as Mason and Logan both came bounding over laden with chocolate bars in their hands, the moment was gone.

'Mummy, Logan said he wants three bars. And he's already opened one and taken a big bite out of it. He's being greedy, isn't he, Mummy? We shouldn't eat the bars until you say. We haven't paid for them yet.'

'Logan!' Debra said, shaking her head. 'I told you that you can only have one each. So take your pick and then go and put the others back. Logan, you'll have to keep the one you opened. Now hurry up, go on. Put the others back. Quickly. I need to pay the lady.

'Boys huh!' Debra added, raising her eyes towards the girl as if to say 'this is what you have still to come'. But there was something about the way that the girl was staring down at Mason and Logan now that stopped Debra in her tracks.

She saw the way the girl didn't seem to be able to take her eyes off the boys, and when she looked back at Debra, she saw how the girl's skin had paled and how she was standing deadly still, rigid almost. She was gripping the buggy so tightly her knuckles were turning white. Placing the boys' bars down on the counter top, Debra took out her purse to pay for the shopping, unable to shake the sickly feeling that was forming in the pit of her stomach.

When the girl finally spoke, Debra realised that she'd anticipated the words before they even left her mouth. She'd already worked out the link.

'You're Gerard Jennings's wife, aren't you?' the girl said, her voice almost a whisper. Her eyes darted around the shop, cagey, as if she was checking that no one else was listening.

'Yeah I am. Why? Do you know him?' It was Debra's turn to sound defensive.

Debra's instincts were right, this wasn't just small talk now. This girl wasn't just talking to her by chance. She had been following her around the shop today, on purpose. Whilst trying to pluck up the courage to speak to her. And going by the girl's nervous demeanour, Debra guessed that she wasn't going to like what she was about to hear as the girl nodded in answer.

Debra looked back down at the tiny baby, as the last piece of the puzzle fell into place. The expensive looking pushchair. The tiny child dressed impeccably from head to toe in expensive designer clothes, his feet displaying a soft pair of the latest fashionable trainers. She drank in his coffee-coloured skin and the thick mass of black hair on his head and realised that it wasn't just the longings for her own lost baby that had made her stomach flip when she'd first set eyes on the child.

It was the familiarity. How similar he looked to Mason and Logan when they were that age. The same colouring. The same hair. She felt the room start to spin.

'Mason! Logan!' she managed to call out, scooping up the bag of shopping and throwing down a couple of twenty pound notes in their place.

'Don't you want your change?' the shop assistant called out as Debra grabbed hold of Logan's hand, and somehow made her way to the doorway.

'Keep it,' she mumbled, not loud enough for the checkout girl to hear. She just needed to get out of this shop. To get out in the air and get some oxygen in her lungs before she passed out. Her legs were trembling now, her heart thumping inside her chest. She didn't dare look back, because she knew without doubt, without the girl having to say a single word, that that little baby was Gerard's son.

# CHAPTER SEVENTEEN

Standing just inside the stairwell of the Griffin Estate, tucked away out of sight behind the door, Lucy cast her gaze along the balcony one last time, her stare fixed on Debra and Gerard's front door, as she silently willed it to open. She'd been hanging around for the best part of an hour already in the hope that either Debra or Gerard would leave that flat at some point this evening, in a bid to try and get Debra on her own so that she could check that the woman was all right.

Ever since she'd seen Debra at the hospital, Lucy hadn't been able to stop thinking about her. She'd seen first-hand how scared Debra was of Gerard, and Lucy knew that the woman had every right to be.

It was strange to think that she'd once lived here, on the same estate as Gerard Jennings as children. She'd been just five years old when she'd left to live with her grandmother and Gerard would have been twice her age, she figured, so she had no memory of ever knowing him.

Though she knew who he was now. Everyone around these parts did. Gerard Jennings was a very dangerous man – suspected murderer, from what her team had already managed to dig up on him. And if anything happened to Debra, Lucy wouldn't be able to live with herself if she didn't at least try one more time to help the woman.

Pushing herself back up against the wall as she saw another resident walk down the balcony towards her, Lucy let out a huge sigh of relief at not being spotted, as the man stepped inside one of the doorways. She should leave. It was a huge risk coming here off duty, and the longer she stuck around, the more chance she had of drawing attention to herself. And the chances were that this was all a waste of time anyway. This might all be for nothing; she might not even see Gerard or Debra tonight. They both might be home for the night.

Talking herself out of her plan then, she realised that it had been a mistake to come here after all. About to walk away, she faltered, her eyes going to the thick pool of bright light that streamed out from the doorway that she'd been watching.

Holding her breath, she watched as Gerard Jennings stepped out on to the balcony. She eyed his huge, intimidatingly large frame as he walked in the opposite direction from her, talking on his mobile phone, oblivious to her standing and watching him. Gerard disappeared out through the double doors into the other stairway.

Not quite believing her luck, Lucy waited for a few minutes just to make sure that the man wasn't coming back anytime soon, then after what felt like an age, she decided that it was now or never. She had to take her chance. Moving fast, Lucy made her way to Debra's front door, tapping gently enough not to wake the children if they were in bed. She scanned the balcony one last time, as a shadowy figure moved behind the glass panel of the door. The door opened.

'You!' Debra Jennings said, a look of shock spreading across her face at the sight of her unexpected visitor, that immediately turned to fear. Stepping out of the doorway, Debra scanned the balcony for any sign of Gerard, looking relieved when there was no sign of him, but still angry with Lucy all the same.

'What the hell are you doing here? He's only just left. If he found me talking to you, you know what he'll do to me,' Debra said, furious that the officer would put her life in danger, knowing full well what Gerard was capable of.

'I watched him go. If he comes back, I'll lie and say that I'm one of the mums from Logan's nursery,' Lucy said, holding out a children's book as if to back up her story. Though her well-rehearsed excuse about returning one of the children's storybooks this late in the evening didn't sound so convincing now that she was met by the look of fury on Debra's face. 'I'm sorry. I just wanted to check that you were okay.'

'You better come in.' Seeing the genuine concern in Lucy's face, Debra nodded in acknowledgment as she stepped back and invited the girl inside, realising that Lucy meant well. The officer was putting her neck on the line too, by turning up like this. Debra wasn't used to anyone giving a toss about her enough to put themselves at risk by checking up on her.

The last thing she needed was any of the neighbours spying on her and feeding back information to Gerard.

'You can't stay, though. He might be back at any minute,' Debra said, keeping her voice down so as not to wake the boys up as she closed the front door behind them. But she didn't move from where they stood in the hallway.

Now Gerard was out, chances were that he'd be gone for the night. Which after spending a day tiptoeing around the man and trying to keep the boys out of Gerard's way while he plied himself with coke and whisky, wasn't such a bad thing. Debra was glad of the respite. Though she wasn't willing to take any chances in case the man came back. Gerard was full of surprises lately. Who knew what went on inside that head of his?

'Are you okay?'

'I'm fine,' Debra said with a shrug, grateful for Lucy's concern, though a part of her still wasn't completely convinced that she could trust her.

'I just wanted you to know that we meant what we said when we saw you at the hospital. We can help you, Debra,' Lucy said, believing that they really could. Sensing the desperation of the woman, she pushed on. 'I've made some enquires and there are places you can go, places he won't be able to find you. You can be rehoused, away from here. There's charities that do exactly this, helping women who flee from abusive relationships. I can help you, if you'll let me.'

Debra pursed her mouth then and shook her head.

'You really haven't got a clue, have you? No offence, Lucy. But you're a bit naïve, aren't you, considering you're a copper,' Debra said, unable to help herself as she took in the girl's concerned look, standing there looking all perfect with her long dark hair twisted into a neat plait down one side of her head. The minuscule amount of make-up on her face, which didn't need it, because she already had a warm rosy glow to her complexion. Conscious of the contrast of her own bruised face in comparison, Debra felt acutely aware then of just how worlds apart their lives both were.

'How old are you?' Debra guessed that they were about the same age. 'Twenty-three, twenty-four?'

'I'm twenty-five.' Lucy was on the defensive now that Debra was intent on picking her apart. She was ready for the comment about her being too young for the job, which seemed to be the opinion of many lately.

Only Debra didn't go on to say that.

'I thought as much. You're the same age as me.' She looked down at the doormat before looking back up, and holding Lucy's stare. 'Amazing, isn't it, how people's lives can be so different? I bet you haven't seen a day's hardship in your tiny, sheltered life, have you? Not first-hand anyway. I bet you can't even imagine how most of us mere mortals have been forced to live. So, please do not come around here acting like a do-gooder and making claims that you can fix my life, when you have no idea what it's like for the rest of us, out here just trying to survive.'

'It would pay you not to assume, Debra. You don't know anything about me,' Lucy said, bristling at being so misunderstood; she had only wanted to help and she certainly wasn't going to let Debra talk down to her.

'Go on then?' Debra challenged her. 'What's your story?'

About to respond, Lucy faltered, quickly changing her mind.

'That's what I thought. You lot make me laugh. This is just a job to you, isn't it? Telling victims that you'll catch the criminals. It's empty promises and good intentions, I get it. You're trying to make people keep the faith, only there isn't much faith out there anymore. And the reality is, people like Gerard will always get away with their crimes. They'll always get off scot-free. Because you don't always catch them, do you? The drug dealers and murderers?'

'We try our hardest…' Lucy said, indignantly, trying not to show that Debra had just hit a nerve.

'But trying isn't good enough, is it? Trying and failing gets people like me killed. You have no idea about the life I live. The life most of your victims live. Because you live in a bubble, sweetheart. And while I get that your intentions are good, and you mean well, you haven't got a clue about my life. You couldn't possibly even begin to imagine. I think you better leave!'

'You're wrong. I've lived that life too,' Lucy shot back, unable to hold her temper now, riled at being dismissed, when all she'd wanted to do was try and offer Debra some help. 'I used to live here, on the Griffin Estate. I was born here and stayed here until I was five years old. Until my mother was brutally murdered. She was stabbed, thirty-four times in total, while I had no choice but to watch. So don't tell me that I don't know this life, or that I don't know real fear and pain. Because I do. And if I say I'm going to help you, then that's not just my intention. That's a fact.'

The two women fell silent then, as Lucy shifted uncomfortably on her feet, realising too late that she'd messed up, big time. Registering the shock on Debra Jennings's face at her sudden outburst, she knew that she'd said too much.

'I'm sorry. I just wanted to help. I just wanted you to understand…'

Lucy felt her chest constrict. Scared that she was going to suffer the onslaught of a panic attack in front of Debra following her confession, Lucy opened the door. She needed to get the hell out of there. Fast.

'I'm sorry… I need to go.'

Making her way back along the balcony without so much as looking back, Lucy cursed herself for losing her cool and acting so unprofessionally. Because Debra Jennings was right. She shouldn't have come here tonight. She'd only ended up making the situation a million times worse.

# CHAPTER EIGHTEEN

Staring across to where the small grey Moses basket sat in the corner of the bedroom, Jodie listened out for her baby. But, unusually, tonight Jenson seemed to be sleeping soundly. She could hear the slow, steady rise and fall of Jenson's breath as he slept peacefully. Silently she willed the child to start crying so that at least she would have the excuse she needed to go to him and give him his night feed. Anything so that she didn't have to lie here in Gerard's arms while he pawed at her and groped her roughly, eager for a second round.

'Chill out, Jodie! He's fine! He's out for the count,' Gerard said pulling her back down in the bed beside him.

'God, is it me or is it hot in here?' Jodie lied, and shifted slightly away from the man, being careful to keep herself covered as she wrapped the thin sheet tightly around her naked body. Gerard didn't need any encouragement. The man had seemed insatiable tonight. Turning up unannounced like he used to and demanding sex from her. And it wasn't as if Jodie had any say in the matter. What Gerard asked for, the man always got.

Glad that he seemed to be getting the message now, though, Jodie breathed a discreet sigh of relief as she watched him pick up his phone and start scrolling through his messages, momentarily distracted. The irony wasn't lost on her one bit that the very man that she'd been pining for for months now, was finally here, in her bed, yet all she wanted was for him to leave.

Because as she'd found out to her dismay in the four weeks since her son had been born, Gerard had no real interest in their child. He'd come here for her, leaving her feel nothing more than dirty and used. He hadn't even asked her how Jenson was tonight. All he'd wanted was sex. Wincing to herself as she sat up in the bed, she could feel the pain down between her legs where Gerard had taken her roughly, despite her pleading with him to be gentle. Her health visitor had told her that it would be better to wait for at least six weeks. Her body was still healing from the birth. She'd repeated the advice to Gerard, only he hadn't cared about any of that. He'd taken her regardless. He always found a way of persuading her, grinding her down until she knew that she had no choice but to lie there and give in. Sometimes it was just easier to let the man have his way.

And when she'd seen Gerard's wife in the shop on the estate earlier, she hadn't been able to help herself but want to get close to her, to try and work out what she had that Jodie didn't have. Jodie had seen her from afar before. Gerard didn't know, but Jodie had sometimes watched them both. Gerard playing happy families with his pretty wife, with her sharp blonde bob and the naturally striking beauty. But today Jodie had got so close that she'd also seen the bruises on the woman's face.

Marks that had been left by Gerard no doubt. Jodie had suffered them too over the course of their relationship, when Gerard had grabbed her roughly and shoved her up against a wall by her throat during arguments, or when she dared to speak her true feelings and try and make any demands of him. The truth was Jodie felt different about Gerard now.

Ever since she'd seen Debra today, the woman was all she could think about, and she was consumed with guilt and remorse for ever wanting to physically break up Gerard's family. Because that was what Jodie had wanted once: for Gerard to leave his wife and kids and come and live with her. She hadn't cared about hurting Debra's feelings, all she'd thought about was herself. But now she was a mother too, her feelings had changed. She was angry for the way that Gerard treated her, for the way he treated his wife and most of all for the way that he treated Jenson as if he was completely irrelevant. As if his little life didn't matter.

And when she saw Debra earlier, Jodie hadn't meant to get so close. She'd just wanted to watch her for a while. To satisfy her own curiosity about the woman. All she'd done for the past four weeks was sit on her own inside this flat and look after a tiny baby. She must have been losing it. Because when Debra Jennings turned around and smiled at her, and said something nice to her about Jenson, it was all Jodie could do not to cry. She hadn't expected the woman to be nice.

Her first thought when Gerard had turned up here tonight had been that maybe Debra had gone home and caused merry hell for Gerard. Because Jodie had seen the realisation on the woman's face as she'd stared down at Jenson that he was Gerard's son, and then she hadn't been able to get out of the shop quickly enough. She had no idea about Jenson. Not a clue.

Only Debra couldn't have mentioned their chance encounter to Gerard, because otherwise Gerard's surprise visit wouldn't have been a friendly one. He certainly wouldn't be here now, lying in her bed, pawing at her. And part of her wondered if Debra hadn't said anything to Gerard for her sake. Girl code, if you like, because they were both all too familiar with the reprisals from upsetting the man.

'Oi!' Gerard said, his words abruptly cutting through Jodie's thoughts. 'Earth to Jodie? Hello?'

'Sorry! I was a million miles away. I'm knackered,' Jodie said, realising that she'd been daydreaming. 'I haven't been sleeping so well. Since Jenson…' she added, hoping that Gerard would take the hint and go home. Or at least take some interest in the boy. She willed herself to be brave and say something. To test the waters and see how Gerard really felt about her.

'I think I saw your wife and kids today. At the shop on the estate. Didn't think that would be the type of place your wife would shop, though? She looks so… I don't know, upmarket,' Jodie said, sensing the tension rise in the room at the first mention of Debra. The way that Gerard was staring at her now was unnerving. But she'd started the conversation so she may as well finish it. All she wanted was for Gerard to show some interest in his child. Jenson may not have been born in wedlock but he was an innocent little child and he deserved the love and adoration of both his parents. Jodie wanted that for her son more than anything. She needed to speak up for him. She was his mother after all.

'Jenson looks a bit like your boys. Mason and Logan, isn't it? They have the same hair colour and eyes. It's weird to think that he has brothers.'

Gerard was on her then. Rolling over on top of her, he clamped his hand over her mouth to shut her up.

'Don't ever let me hear you talk about my wife and kids again do you understand? Their names don't leave your mouth. And if you see them out on the street, you walk the other way. Your kid has got nothing to do with my family. Do you understand?'

Pinned to the bed by the enormous weight on top of her, Jodie nodded regretfully, realising that she'd gone too far, as fresh tears streamed down her face at the strong reaction she'd just provoked from the man. She'd realised just how wrong she'd been about Gerard.

'Good! Now I reckon we've still got some time to kill before the kid wakes up.' Gerard rolled back over, pulling the girl roughly around on top of him, ready for round two, whether Jodie wanted it or not.

And Jodie didn't bother to protest this time. What was the use? Gerard did exactly what he wanted regardless. She just wanted to get it over and done with, and to get Gerard gone.

# CHAPTER NINETEEN

Moving the can of lager that sat in the cup holder between the two front seats into the panel on the passenger side door, hoping to conceal it, Debra cursed as she spilled the liquid all down herself and the floor and quickly wiped herself down. She eyed the glare of blue flashing lights in her rear-view mirror, then she did what she knew was expected of her and pulled the car over, desperately trying to compose herself as the police officer approached the driver side window and peered inside. She decided that attack might be the best form of defence.

'What's this then? Don't tell me! Another one of your routine stops?' Debra said, convinced that the officer would be able to smell the sharp stench of beer she'd spilled a mile off.

'You were driving erratically,' the officer said, eyeing Debra suspiciously.

'Erratically? How?'

'You were swerving, and one of your brake lights is out.'

'A brake light? God, how unlucky can one person be? Last time you pulled me over, you said that I wasn't wearing my seat belt, when I actually was! And the time before that you pulled me over because I was going three miles over the speed limit. Three miles! I'm beginning to think that you lot just have it in for me.' Debra laughed and shook her head incredulously.

'I'm going to need to see your licence, please.'

'As if you don't know who I am! This is harassment, you know,' Debra said, tight-lipped as she rooted through her handbag before passing the document to the officer. 'And you couldn't have picked a more conspicuous place to stop and pull me over, could you? Right outside my son's school. But then that's exactly what you want, isn't it? Maximum inconvenience and exposure. You lot are always trying to make a point. Trying to humiliate myself and my husband in a bid to make our lives as difficult as possible. This is a joke! Seriously, don't you lot have real criminals to catch instead of preying on mothers dropping their kids off at school?'

'Would you mind stepping out of the car, Mrs Jennings,' the officer said, interrupting Debra's rant.

'Why? What have I done?'

'As I explained, you were driving erratically and I have reason to believe that you're under the influence of alcohol.'

Debra frowned. The officer could smell the booze then. Still, she wasn't going to make it easy for him.

'I've just dropped my kids off at school. I wouldn't drink and drive.' Though she knew that she had no choice but to do as she was asked.

Stepping out of the car, Debra ignored the smug look on the officer's face, which only confirmed what she already thought. The man was clearly getting off on the fact that he'd just pulled over Gerard Jennings's wife and had a good enough reason to arrest her. The stupid sod probably thought he'd be hailed a hero back at the station.

'This is bloody ridiculous,' Debra said, aware that a group of mothers with children in Mason's class were all glancing over in her direction now and having a good old nose. She shook her short blonde bob down so it concealed some of her face in the hope of concealing some of the bruising as well as the fact that her cheeks were now burning red. She should be used to all the attention by now. Her family were the talk of the school most days, thanks to the notoriety of her infamous husband and all his dodgy dealings. After all, you didn't marry a man like Gerard Jennings and expect to live a quiet life, did you? And saying that he wasn't popular with most people around these parts would be a complete understatement. For all the fear her husband instilled in everyone around him, Debra knew that beneath that fear, hate festered.

'That's a nasty black eye you've got there,' the officer said, scrutinising her face. 'Been in the wars?' The undertone to his voice suggested that he knew exactly how the injury had been inflicted, and more importantly by whom.

'I walked into a door, didn't I?' Debra said, not bothering to come up with a more convincing excuse. There wasn't any point. They both knew the score. Besides, Debra knew full well this lot couldn't be trusted any more than Gerard could.

'You all enjoying yourselves? Having a good look, are we?' Debra muttered loudly, to the crowd of mums that had congregated across the road. 'Oh well, at least you're giving this lot something decent to gossip about in the playground later.' She turned back to the officer who was now climbing into the driver's seat and leaning across to the passenger side door.

'What are you looking for?' Debra asked nervously as he leant over towards where she'd stashed the can. 'I've already told you, you're wasting your time…'

'This yours, is it?' he said, holding up the half-empty beer can triumphantly. 'I'm going to have to breathalyse you.'

Debra bristled, looking guilty now that she'd been caught out. 'It must have been there from last night. One of Gerard's mates must have left it there.' Debra started to protest, but the police officer wasn't having any of it. 'I've just dropped my two boys off at school. I'm hardly going to do that drunk, am I?'

'You'd be surprised at what goes on, Mrs Jennings.' The officer continued searching the vehicle in case there was any further evidence that he'd failed to find. 'We've found drug paraphernalia inside toddlers' nappies before now. There's a lot of scumbags out there.' The officer finished his search and stepped back out of the car, then looked Debra up and down as if she was exactly that. A known drug dealer's wife, caught on the school run dropping her children off, clearly intoxicated.

'I'm going to place you in the back of my car, and get you to do the breathalyser test…'

'No. I'm not doing a test,' Debra said, refusing to give the onlookers the satisfaction of thinking she was drunk in charge of her children. Let them look. She didn't care what any of them thought of her.

'It's up to you. Either you do the test or we arrest you and you'll be made to do the test back at the station regardless.'

'I'm not doing your stupid test. I haven't been drinking. This is harassment.'

'Well in that case. Debra Jennings, I'm placing you under arrest. You do not have to say anything. But, it may harm your defence if you do not mention when questioned something which you later rely on in court. Anything you say may be given in evidence…'

'You're actually going to arrest me?' Debra said, a look of sheer disbelief on her face now as the officer moved towards her and guided her into the back of the police car. Sinking down on the back passenger seat she stared out the window and bit her lip, as the police officer pulled away, making his way back to Wandsworth station.

Gerard had warned her that the police had them under surveillance and they would be watching their comings and goings for the next few weeks. Word would get back to Gerard about her arrest in just minutes. Debra Jennings was counting on it.

# CHAPTER TWENTY

Opening the front door just enough so he could see out through the slight crack, Jamie Nash nodded at the lad he'd been expecting, before opening the door fully and letting him in.

'Cheers, Jamie. I appreciate it, man. I heard that no one's serving up at the moment. Can't get gear for love nor money,' Steven Hadley said gratefully.

'Yeah I know, mate, the streets are running dry. But don't worry, lad, I've got you covered.' Leading the lad into the lounge, Jamie Nash grinned like a Cheshire cat as he walked over to the cupboard that held his stash. 'Same as usual?' he said, holding up the bag of brown.

Steven Hadley eyed the bag greedily, nodding and holding out the usual amount of money.

'Ah, no, mate! Sorry, I should have said...' Jamie Nash screwed his mouth up, as if he'd made an accidental error. 'The price has gone up. It's double-bubble. Sorry, mate, but it's supply and demand and the demand right now is through the roof.' Shrugging his shoulders, Jamie went to put the gear back where he'd just retrieved it from.

'Nah, Jamie. It's cool. I get it. Here...' Steven said, digging deeper into his pockets and getting the right amount of money before Jamie changed his mind. The price might be extortionate but Steven knew if he didn't pay up some other mug would and he'd be the one still out of gear.

Smiling as he handed the little bag over and took the lad's money, Jamie knew it too.

'If you want some more, remember, not a word to anyone yeah! If anyone finds out that I'm the one getting you this shit, I'll have my hands cut off. And so will you,' Jamie said, acutely aware of the danger he was in, if this little money spinner he had going backfired on him. Though he wasn't convinced that this Steven was gauging the seriousness of the situation. So he figured he'd have to play to the man's fears and weaknesses too. 'And if you open your mouth, I'll have every other Tom, Dick and Harry here trying their luck to get their hands on some stuff. There'll be nothing left for you next time.'

'I won't say a word, mate. Thanks, I appreciate it, mate; cheers, Jamie,' Steven said, his ears pricking up at the mention that this might be his last lot of gear unless he did as Jamie said, and kept his mouth shut.

Jamie could barely conceal his smirk as he let the kid out and shut the door behind him, before folding up the notes and shoving them inside his jeans pocket. That was the fifth customer of the day and he was charging them all double. If business kept up he stood to make a killing. He'd taken a huge risk in creaming gear off the supplies he'd been given over the past few months, cutting the drugs with baking soda or powdered milk, with the intention of making a bit of extra money. Fate had thrown Jamie a golden opportunity. Gerard had called a halt on all supplies being sold, which meant that there was a huge gap in the market now and Jamie stood to make a killing of his own by selling this gear on for twice its value. Three times if the punters realised the watered-down potency of their supply. He was laughing. Though he had no intention of being complacent. If Gerard ever found out, Jamie knew he'd be a dead man walking.

But so far, so good. Gerard hadn't noticed a thing. As notorious as the man's reputation was, Jamie had somehow managed to pull the wool over his eyes. And it was paying off for him now, big time. Jamie didn't have a clue what was going down with Gerard right now, but he guessed that the pigs must be on to him. Why else would the man need to start lying low? And now that Jamie and the rest of Gerard's men had been given the order to stop working, this little sideline of his had become his lifeline. Because he needed to make money, and a shit load of it. He still had his own debts to pay. And the one he had hanging over his head right now wasn't the type of debt that you could just ignore. So it wasn't as if he had any choice but to still sell gear on the sly. But he had to be careful and only sell to the few men he could trust. The ones desperate enough for it that there was no way they'd tell anyone else where they got their supply from, through fear and danger of their own supply quickly running out. So really it was a win-win for him. He stood to make a shit load of money, and there was no middle man.

As long as Gerard didn't find out, there was no way that Jamie could lose.

# CHAPTER TWENTY-ONE

'Since when did CID deal with drink driving cases?' Debra sneered in the direction of DS Morgan and DC Murphy as they both walked into the interview room. The arresting officer, PC Josephs, was still in the room with them, watching. Lapping it all up.

'Jesus Christ, you lot really are on a mission, aren't you?! What is this? Some kind of a set-up? Arresting me on the school run for drink driving? God, I knew you lot were desperate to get to Gerard, but this? This really is the lowest of the low. Wait until my solicitor gets here.'

Catching the look of contempt that PC Josephs threw to DS Morgan, Debra knew that the officer had completely bought her story, hook, line and sinker. He thought he saw her for exactly what she was: the gobby wife of a drug dealer who thought the law wasn't applicable to her. But the PC didn't have a clue what he was dealing with here today, and Debra had no intention of enlightening him.

'We'll take this from here,' DS Morgan said, dismissing PC Josephs, much to his obvious displeasure.

Debra's gamble had paid off. She'd been right to think that as soon as she mentioned the two senior officers by name that PC Josephs would go running back to them and make it known that he'd just been the one to pull Debra in for refusing to do a breathalyser test. And DS Morgan was indeed a smart man. So far he hadn't disappointed.

'Drink driving?' he said, raising his eyebrows questioningly.

'Thank God someone can read between the lines,' Debra said, giving the sergeant a tight smile.

'Hang on…' Lucy looked between her boss and Debra. Until today, Lucy had felt sorry for Debra for being tied to a man like Gerard Jennings and for losing her baby. She hadn't struck Lucy as the kind of woman who would risk her children, drink driving on the school run, though Lucy knew that sometimes people were full of surprises. It really did take all sorts. Still, she couldn't help but feel disappointed. But now she was beginning to think she'd missed something.

'I haven't had a drink. I was pretending.'

'You wanted to get arrested on purpose?' Lucy said, raising her eyebrow, the penny finally dropping.

'He knows that you've got him under surveillance.' Debra shrugged. 'I assumed I would be too. I tipped a can of beer out in the footwell of the car and swerved a few times after I clocked that police officer following in his car behind me. If you want me to prove it, I'll happily do the breathalyser test. I haven't touched a drop. I wouldn't. Not with Mason and Logan in the car with me.'

Morgan nodded. He believed her. He indicated for Lucy to take a seat.

'Why then? Why go to the trouble of getting arrested outside your son's school? I don't understand?' She'd just publicly made herself look as if she was a bad mother. A drunk. The rumours and judgement against this woman at the school would be rife not only in the school but all around the estate too. 'What if the school report you to Children's Services?'

'But I haven't done anything wrong, have I? This was all a misunderstanding. You'll back me up on that, won't you?' Debra said, eyeing the two officers, a tiny tremor of doubt creeping into her head then, that maybe this hadn't been the best plan. 'This was the only way I could make contact with you, without him getting suspicious. The whole estate will be gossiping about me getting nicked on the school run. It probably got back to him before my arse even hit the seat in the back of the police car. But if I'd just walked in here to see you, one of your lot would have informed him just as quickly.'

'One of our lot?' DS Morgan said, raising his eye and shifting uncomfortably in the chair at the accusation. Though it wasn't a real surprise to him. There were always bent coppers, he knew that. The ones that got pulled over to the dark side by making bad choices, or by their own greed. They saw what the criminals made each day, how easy some of them made it look, and they wanted a piece of that. 'You know that for a fact? That one of our lot is on your husband's payroll?'

Debra shook her head. 'No. But I wouldn't put it past him.'

DS Morgan nodded. He had his suspicions about Gerard having men on the inside too. Nobody was lucky enough to get away with as much shit as that man did. Gerard always seemed to be one step ahead of them. Every house they raided, emptied. Every time they were told of a deal, it was a no-show. And the numerous drop off and collection points they'd been tipped off about over the past few weeks had all come to nothing too. It stood to reason the man had someone from the force in his ear. But until they could find concrete evidence of that, all they had was their suspicions.

'So you don't know any names?' DS Morgan said, already knowing the answer before the question left his mouth.

'Like I said,' Debra shrugged, 'he doesn't discuss the ins and outs of the business dealings with me.' Rolling her eyes, she pointed up at her battered face. 'I'm a little lower down the food chain than his work colleagues. He keeps me out of it.'

DS Morgan offered a small smile of understanding, although he couldn't hide the disappointment in his expression at not finding out who the leak was.

Debra pursed her mouth. 'Or at least he thinks he does. I still hear everything. Let's just say he's not exactly discreet about keeping his business quiet when he's around me. I think he just forgets I can hear him; either that or he thinks I'm completely irrelevant. But I hear him sometimes when he's on the phone and when people come to the house. His business associates, if you can call them that. More like dogsbodies and thugs.

'That's why I couldn't just walk in here and speak to you both. Because he'd know in seconds that I'm speaking to you. Someone would let him know. He checks my phone, too. This was the only way.'

Lucy watched as Debra tapped her fingers erratically on the table as she spoke. She could see the woman was genuinely scared of her husband, and after the beating that she'd taken less than a week ago, Lucy could see why. Gerard Jennings was an animal. Ruthless and unhinged. She'd read over Debra's medical report when she and Morgan had visited her at the hospital earlier that week. Sickened at the countless beatings Debra had endured at the hands of her husband.

'It's a bold move on your part, Debra. People can still talk. And this police informant on Gerard's payroll, they could tell him that you're talking to us right now.'

'And say what? That a copper pulled me in for drink driving?'

'So you want Gerard to believe that we've arrested you?'

'He'd believe that. He's paranoid enough. He says that you lot are out for his blood, and he knows that you're watching us around the clock. He'll think you tried setting me up when he finds out you wanted to breathalyse me on the school run. He thinks you guys will stop at nothing to get to him any way you can.' Debra clasped her hands tightly together. She'd played her hand fully. There was no going back now.

'And how do we know that this isn't some kind of set-up too? You coming in here today and claiming you want to help us put Gerard away? What if this was Gerard's way of pulling a double bluff to find out what we've already got on him?' Morgan said, testing the waters to see just how serious Debra was about handing her husband over to them. 'There must be something you can give us, something so that we know that you're telling the truth and you really want to help us put him away.'

Debra nodded compliantly. 'The night that he attacked me... He did it because I stupidly questioned him about the state he'd been in a few nights beforehand. When he'd come home with blood on his shirt. I should have just left it, I shouldn't have brought it up again, but I couldn't shake the feeling that something really bad had happened. Gerard had been in a really bad mood ever since and as soon as I mentioned it again, he started arguing with me about my mate Kiera being in the flat that night, saying that she was a gossip and that he didn't trust her.' Debra closed her eyes for a few seconds. Ever since the attack had happened she'd been trying to block it out, but she knew that she needed to be honest with the detective now.

'It was insane. Him standing there, in our home, completely disregarding the fact that just a few nights earlier he'd been covered in blood – and there was so much blood – and yet he's shouting at me for having my friend over.' She shook her head, still not able to get her head around how deluded Gerard had become. 'It was if he'd lost sense of all reality! And I just got angry. I lost it. I screamed back at him. I said that if he didn't come home covered in someone else's blood, no one would have anything to gossip about. And that it needed to stop, whatever it was he was involved in. He couldn't come back to our home in that state. The boys might see...'

Morgan made a mental note of the date that they'd visited Debra in hospital. If Gerard had been covered in blood a few days before that, then the dates also matched with when they'd pulled Bobbie Carter's body from the river.

'Do you know whose blood it was? Did he say a name?'

Debra shook her head.

'Do you remember what Gerard had been wearing? Do you know what he did with his clothes?'

'I'm not sure. I don't recall seeing them since I've been back. He might have got rid of them.' She shrugged, knowing that what she had wasn't much, but right now it was all she had. 'The next thing I know I was bleeding on the kitchen floor. I was in so much pain, and I must have passed out, because when I woke I was at the hospital. I didn't see Gerard for three days. Like I said, he doesn't tell me anything. But I am around him enough to overhear things and I know that there's something pretty big going on at the moment. He's losing his head. He's going to slip up.'

Morgan thought that Debra was probably right. He also knew that her word alone wasn't enough. They needed some names, dates and places so that they could catch the man in the act. If they were going to put Gerard away for good, then they needed solid evidence. They couldn't risk pulling him in with anything less.

'When you came to my house last night, when you said you wanted to help me, you meant it, didn't you?' Debra said, turning her attention to Lucy now.

'You went to her house?' DS Morgan asked disapprovingly.

'I'm sorry, Sarge, I shouldn't have gone. I realised that while I was there...'

'No, you shouldn't have,' DS Morgan snapped tightly, pursing his mouth as if to purposely stop the conversation and shooting

Lucy a warning look that they'd be continuing this little chat another time. Out of Debra's earshot.

'She didn't mean any harm,' Debra butted in, hoping that she hadn't just landed Lucy in trouble with her sergeant. That hadn't been her intention. 'It's only, well, you were straight with me. All that stuff you said about living on the Griffin Estate, and your mum. Being murdered. Maybe you really do get it.'

It was Lucy's turn to shift uncomfortably in her chair then. She could feel DS Morgan's eyes on her. Burning into her, yet she couldn't bring herself to look at him now. Not now her secret was out there. Christ knows what he must be thinking. Luckily for her, Debra seemed oblivious to the tension in the room and carried on talking.

'And I thought about what you said, about being able to help me. That you can get me away from him. I want me and my boys to be safe. But I need more than just to get away.'

'So what is it exactly that you want from us, Debra?' Morgan said, clearing his throat. 'If you don't want us to help relocate you?'

'If I press charges for a broken arm or a broken nose what do you reckon he'll get? A slap on the wrist? Maybe a few weeks away? Women like me don't get to just walk away and start again somewhere new. He'll find me, we'll never be safe. And where would that leave me and my boys? Always looking over our shoulders as we live in fear,' Debra said sitting forward in her chair. 'I want out, and I want out for good. I need to know that if you get him, when he goes down, he's going down for life.'

'You want to help us to take Gerard down? You want to be an informer?' Morgan knew that he should proceed with caution with this matter, but his gut reaction was to believe what Debra was saying. He could see in her eyes that she meant every word.

'No. I can't do that. He'd get suspicious if I try and run back to you with information. He'd find out.'

'So how are you going to help us put him away if you can't get any information back to us?'

'What if I had someone on the inside with me? Someone that Gerard wouldn't suspect?'

She jerked her head towards where Lucy sat, and Lucy paled as she already predicted the next words out of Debra's mouth.

'Someone like her.'

# CHAPTER TWENTY-TWO

'I'm sorry, Sarge!' Lucy said feeling shamefaced as Morgan followed her back into his office.

'I know what you're going to say. I shouldn't have gone around to see her. It was completely unprofessional of me and I jeopardised everything by doing so. I know that. And I shouldn't have told her about my past. It just came out. I'm so sorry.'

Closing the door behind them to give them some privacy, Morgan perched on the edge of the desk, watching as Lucy paced the small room, clearly still reeling from her actions. He wanted to give Lucy her time to talk now that she'd finally shared her secret with him.

'I never wanted you to find out like this. I'm sorry that I kept the truth from you about what happened to my mother. It wasn't that I was trying to deceive you.' Lucy knew that the confession Debra had just made in front of her sergeant meant that she was left with some real explaining to do, but she didn't really know where to start. There had been so many times that she'd come close to walking into her boss's office and telling him everything. She'd rehearsed everything that she wanted to say a hundred times over. Only she'd never had the courage to go through with it. And as much as she had never meant for the truth to come out like this, now that it was out, she could be honest with him. As she looked Morgan in the eye, she could feel tears forming, betraying her just when she needed to try and keep everything together and salvage the mess that she was in.

'The reason that I didn't declare my mother's murder when I applied for the job was because I didn't want it to be on my record. I didn't want my colleagues to know and have an opinion about it. Because, trust me, my mother's murder has tainted my whole life. It's always hung over me...' Lucy said, furiously wiping away the stray tears that made their way down her cheeks. 'I've never been able to move on from it. I mean, I don't think you can, can you? Move on from something like that. No matter what happens, it's always there in the back of your mind.' Lucy hoped that Morgan would understand why she had never confided in him. She hadn't lied, but she hadn't told the truth. Which was just as bad as far as she was concerned. She'd been trying to live a lie, even if her intentions had been good.

'Christ, her murder was the reason why I chose to do this job. It sounds so stupid when I say it like that. That I wanted to catch the bad guys! Because the police never caught him,' Lucy said, praying that DS Morgan would understand and still hold firm in his belief that she was up for this job. It was all she'd wanted to do, since she was little. And in some ways it helped to heal the pain inside her, knowing that some people were being brought to justice, even if her mother's murderer hadn't been.

'When I first started out in the force I didn't want to come into the job and be seen as another victim. The job's hard enough as it is, Sarge, you know that, without throwing into the mix that I'd witnessed my mother being murdered as a child. I just couldn't face it. People gently treading around me, being careful what they said and did. Stopping mid-joke in case the punchline offended me. You know how officers talk about the fucked-up things that we have to deal with day-to-day. The humour is there to keep us all going, but people would have been different with me if they'd known what I'd been through and I just didn't want that. I wanted a fair go at this, and I wanted to be treated as an equal.'

Now that she'd voiced the truth out loud, she felt relieved. It was as if a huge weight that she hadn't even been aware that she'd been carrying had been lifted from her. But the ball was in Morgan's court now. Lucy just hoped that he understood.

'I should have been straight with you though, Sarge, I realise that now. I should never have gone to her flat. And I certainly shouldn't have voiced my personal life to Debra Jennings. I just wanted her to see that I'm not that different to her, not really. And I wanted to help her. Genuinely. She just got to me, assuming that I live this perfect life, that I've never experienced real pain or loss. But it won't ever happen again. I'm so sorry, Sarge!' She was prepared for him to be angry, but she wasn't prepared for what he said next.

'I should have been straight with you, too, Lucy. I already knew.'

'You knew?' Lucy said, barely able to get the words out. She shook her head, trying to make sense of the tangled mess of thoughts inside her head. 'About my mother? Oh my god. Is this why you gave me the job? Out of sympathy? You moved me over to CID and offered to mentor me because you felt sorry for me? Because the one thing I don't want from anyone is sympathy.'

'No! Of course not. I only realised recently,' Morgan said, realising that Lucy had the wrong end of the stick now. 'Lucy, I joined the force probably before you were born and like yourself, I was a PC first, then I ended up working as a DC under my own sergeant about five years into the job. And one of the first cases that I was sent out on with him was a murder investigation over at the Griffin Estate.'

Lucy shook her head disbelievingly. Her boss couldn't be telling her what she thought he was saying. It was too much of a coincidence to be true.

'Your mother, Jennifer Murphy…' DS Morgan paused as if it was painful even to say the woman's name out loud. 'Her murder has haunted me for much of my career.' He'd known that if this conversation ever came to light, it would be a very difficult one. And now that he had the opportunity to broach the subject, DS Morgan thought that it was better to be honest with Lucy.

'In fact, it still haunts me to this very day.'

Reaching down into his desk drawer, DS Morgan pulled out a file and placed it down on the desk. And even before Lucy read the name emblazoned on the front cover she knew what it was. Her mother's file. A cold case now. Buried away and forgotten. Only, clearly that wasn't the case for DS Morgan.

'It pains me that we didn't catch him. It weighs heavily on my mind, as I'm sure it does to everyone involved in the investigation at the time,' he said. 'It was a horrific crime, and the fact that you witnessed it, as such a child...' DS Morgan shook his head, his voice filled with emotion. 'I vowed that I would catch your mother's killer, Lucy. And I couldn't. I didn't. And for that, I'm very, very sorry.'

Fighting back her fresh tears Lucy nodded. She could see DS Morgan's obvious pain. She could see how much her mother's murder had truly affected him, and being a police officer herself now, she knew how it could. Some cases grabbed you and pulled you in. Some people you just couldn't let go of.

'How did you work it out, then? If you didn't know it was me when I started working for you?'

'I didn't make the connection until a couple of months back. But since we began working together there was something niggling inside my head. Something familiar about you and I just couldn't work out what it was. Jesus, you were just five years old when it happened, and I think I only set eyes on you once by chance when you were in the station with one of the children's psychiatrists. But then, do you remember when your nan went missing from her carer a few weeks back, the day you said you found her in the park?'

Lucy nodded.

'You mentioned your nan by name. Winnie. And it just struck a chord with me. I mean there couldn't be that many Winnies that lived near the Griffin Estate. And the more I thought about it, I realised that the Winnie Murphy I remembered would be about the same age as your nan now, and that you would be twenty-five… Christ the years creep up, don't they?' DS Morgan shrugged. 'Hey, it's what we do, isn't it? Try and piece every part of the jigsaw together until everything fits just so?'

The revelation was almost too much for Lucy to take in. She could feel her heart beating erratically inside her chest. Adrenaline surged through her.

'I read through the cold case again.' He nodded down at the file. 'And then I just knew. It all fell into place. Your nan had made a witness statement back then, too. Her name and details were all in there.'

'Does anyone else know?' Lucy said, dreading the thought that her colleagues had all secretly known the truth about the past all this time. She couldn't bear the thought of them all talking about her behind her back.

'No.' Morgan shook his head. 'And they don't need to know, not if you don't want them to. This conversation doesn't need to leave these four walls, Lucy. You can trust me on that.'

Lucy nodded, not doubting her boss for a second. In the few months that she'd worked alongside her sergeant, Lucy had seen first-hand how the man lived by his integrity. She knew that if he said something, he really meant it. She could trust him.

She wondered if she should tell him about the dream she'd had. That she was certain that she could remember her mother's killer's face. Only she was still second guessing herself if she could trust what she'd seen.

Today wasn't the day.

'You know, this is going to sound crazy, but part of me is glad that you know now,' Lucy said, with the realisation that she meant it too. She really was glad that the truth was out there. And it meant more to her that it was spoken aloud with Morgan because her mother's death had clearly affected him too. Lucy felt as if they had a stronger connection now.

'You did get this job very much on your own merit, Lucy. My offer of mentoring you was purely down to your impressive resume and excellent police work so far.'

Lucy felt the tension that had previously been in the room melt away. Until she remembered her outburst with Debra Jennings.

'What about Debra?'

Morgan pursed his mouth. 'Well, all I can suggest is that if you really do want to keep your past under wraps, you might want to be a bit more choosey about who you share your story with in future. Your private life should always remain private when you're on the job. It's too much of a risk letting members of the public know personal information about you.'

'God, I'm sorry, Sarge. I messed it all up, didn't I?' Lucy shook her head. 'I shouldn't have gone round there off duty. And I shouldn't have said what I said. She just pushed my buttons. Assuming that I didn't come from her world. That I didn't know pain…'

'You're right, you shouldn't have just turned up like that. You could have jeopardised the entire operation,' Morgan said, before sitting back in his chair and grinning. 'But I think that by you doing and saying what you did and opening up to Debra, that you managed to push through a few barriers.'

Lucy raised her eyebrows questioningly.

'She wants to get him. And she's adamant that she can get enough information to put him away for good. Because she really believes that's the only way she'll be able to break free of him, and I have to say, I tend to agree with her. You don't just walk away from men like Gerard. He's threatened her life before, and the life of her children, and I think he has the mentality to go through with it.'

'Is it wise for her to be feeding information back to us about him then? Won't that put her in even more danger if he finds out? She's already in a pretty vulnerable position.'

Morgan nodded in agreement. 'She can't be our informer, you're right. She won't be able to feed anything back to us. Gerard would get suspicious, he'd work it out. She knows that. But as far as she's concerned her life's already at risk.' Morgan shrugged. 'Normally, I wouldn't even entertain considering this, but I believe it's the only way that we'll be able to get to the man and take him off the streets for good, and Debra's adamant about doing it, with or without our help.'

Debra didn't strike Lucy as someone who would just give up without some kind of a fight and Lucy could only admire that in her.

'Where is she now?'

'She's gone home. She did the breathalyser test and it came back clear. No alcohol in her system. Gerard will believe her story about police harassment and I'll have to smooth things over with the arresting officer so that he knows he did a good job in bringing her in. Despite us not getting a result on this occasion.'

'And what about what she was saying about Gerard having someone on the inside? Do you think that's true? That he's got one of our officers on the payroll?'

'I don't know. But we can't take any chances, just in case. For now, we are the only ones that know the real truth behind her visit here today, and I suggest we keep it that way.'

Morgan shifted forward in his seat, keeping his voice low, his tone deadly serious. 'And Lucy, what I'm about to say now doesn't leave this room either, okay? We need to treat this matter with absolute confidentiality. I'm not even going to discuss it with the rest of the team. This is strictly between us.'

Lucy narrowed her eyes in anticipation of what her boss was about to say.

'I think that Debra is capable of getting us the information – in fact I think she's our only way to get near the man full stop. But in order to do so, and more importantly, in order to ensure her safety, she's going to need some help. A lot of help.'

He locked eyes with Lucy and hoped that he wasn't about to make a huge mistake.

'If we are going to completely eliminate the risk of putting Debra in any further danger, then we're going to need to send someone in with her. Undercover.'

Lucy stared at her boss then, guessing where the conversation was heading. 'You're not seriously going to consider what she suggested?'

DS Morgan gave Lucy a wry grin then in answer to her question.

'And after that little speech of yours, Debra Jennings has insisted that it be you.'

# CHAPTER TWENTY-THREE

Staring down the balcony of the seventh floor, Paul nodded to Gerard that the coast was clear. It had gone midnight and there didn't seem to be anyone about. Paul wanted to get their little visit to Jamie Nash over and done with as quickly as possible. But to Paul's dismay, Gerard didn't seem to be sticking with the plan.

'We'll do this my way,' Gerard instructed, holding his arm up to block the way as Paul stepped forward to knock. Gerard indicated for Paul to move back out of the way. Then, before he even had time to register what was happening, let alone protest, he watched in disbelief as Gerard charged his full sixteen stone at the door, splintering it from its hinges as it smashed against the wall behind it.

'So much for us keeping a low profile,' Paul said sarcastically, following Gerard inside the flat with growing trepidation. This wasn't the time to have a ruck with each other. They had more pressing matters to deal with, like sorting out this new kid that had taken over Jax Priestly's role in running one of their county lines. Only the boy was taking the piss it seemed. Word had got back to them both that this kid – Jamie Nash – had been creaming money off their profit and was ignoring Gerard's and Paul's orders to stop selling. Intent on making his own money off the back of gear he'd nicked from them, he was mugging Gerard and Paul off and that wasn't a good look.

Paul had agreed that they needed to have words with the kid, and Gerard had insisted that he wanted to do it personally, determined to teach the kid a lesson that he wasn't going to forget anytime soon. Though as soon as Paul had seen Gerard, he knew that his friend was as high as a kite and when Gerard was in this state, his temper could go from nought to one hundred in just seconds. Which didn't bode well for the young lad they were paying a visit to tonight. Jamie Nash was about to find out just how much deep shit he was in.

'It's all right, lads! It ain't the Old Bill,' Gerard said, charging into the lounge where Jamie and a couple of his boys were sitting, stoned out of their faces by the smell of the weed that lingered in the haze-filled air. The only light in the room came from the Xbox that they'd been playing. Seeing the look of horror that flashed across all of their faces, it was all Gerard could do not to laugh.

'Gerard? I weren't expecting you, mate. Is everything okay?' Jamie said, peering past the man and seeing the chunks of the door on the hallway floor. He was starting to wish that it was the police standing here instead. Because everything about Gerard's demeanour right now, as he stood over them all with a menacing look on his face, told Jamie that something bad was about to happen.

'Mate?' Gerard sneered, twisting his face up at the boy, full of disgust at the blatant disrespect this kid had for him.

'We've done as you said. We've been lying low.' Jamie felt as if he should apologise for the fact that they were all sitting in a smoke-filled room and lazing around playing on the Xbox. 'We thought we'd have a session, you know. Only because we had no work.'

'You lot can leave. Go on, clear out of here.' Gerard addressed the other boys, but all the while his eyes didn't leave Jamie's. Jamie wouldn't be going anywhere.

'You see that?' he went on, as the other boys grabbed their belongings without so much as a word, and quickly piled out of the room. 'They couldn't get out of the flat fast enough.' Gerard shook his head. 'It's all too common these days though, isn't it? There's no allegiance, no loyalty. It's every man for themselves in this game.'

Jamie felt sick as he realised that his little game was up, and that Gerard knew what he had been up to. He glanced at the battered front door that now hung from its hinges, wondering if he could make it if he ran. But Gerard was one step ahead of him.

'Oh no you don't.' Gerard shut the lounge door.

'I don't know what this is about. I don't know what I've supposed to have done, Gerard, mate?' Jamie began. He knew his words were useless but trying to talk himself out of this reprisal was all he had left. The look of fury on Gerard's face told him to shut up before he dug himself into an even deeper hole. He sank down onto the sofa behind him, his stomach bubbling with a sickly anticipation of what was to come.

Gerard continued. 'This is the problem, Jamie. We ain't mates. And I ain't a mug. Though I've heard that you think you can treat me like one.' He laughed mirthlessly. 'Wasn't this enough for you? The money, the status? We let you step in and run your own line. Do your own drops. Be in charge of your own lads. Only clearly it wasn't enough if this is how you think you can repay us?'

Paul had been searching through the cabinet where Jamie hid his stash and now he held up a handful of the baggies that Jamie had been dealing on the sly, confirming what they already knew to be true. Jamie Nash was disrespecting them both.

'I mean we've got to hand it to you! Ten out of ten for fucking using your initiative, I'll give you that. You must have bollocks made of steel.'

The boy eyed the two men, wondering now that Gerard was smiling whether the mood had lightened somewhat, and maybe

Gerard was just going to have a go at him and there was still a way that he could turn this around after all.

'It wasn't like that, Gerard. I wasn't stealing from you. Not really. You still got your money. Every single penny. I just used my initiative to make myself a little bit more…' Jamie said, though even as he said the words, he knew how stupid he sounded. 'I'm in some shit with some people at the moment, deep shit, and I really needed the money.'

'Oh, I'd say you're in the deepest shit with some people right now, Jamie lad!' No one disrespected him. Especially not some jumped up little hood rat who thought he could have one over on him. Gerard was too long in the tooth for all that shit. He was dealing with some real hard men in his line of work. Suppliers, dealers, real criminals. Gerard sneered. Reaching inside his jacket, he pulled out the hammer that he'd been concealing in his coat lining.

Paul bristled, alarm bells sounding in his head. 'Gerard, we said a few words,' he said, putting a warning hand on his mate's arm. He knew that this kid deserved a kicking at the very least, and Paul had been prepared to give that to him, but neither of them had mentioned a hammer.

But before Paul could talk sense into him, Gerard made a grab for the boy. A sickening clunk of metal smashing into skull filled the room. Blood splattered up the walls as Gerard continued to beat Jamie into nothing more than a bloody pulp.

Paul's only comfort was that the first blow of the hammer had taken the boy down, knocking him unconscious. Jamie Nash would never have felt the next almighty blows that killed him. And that was a small mercy.

# CHAPTER TWENTY-FOUR

'I hear rumour has it that Debra Jennings was pulled in for drink driving on the school run yesterday? Seriously, some people shouldn't be allowed to give birth,' DC Holder said, eyeing Lucy, who was so engrossed in reading over the paperwork in front of her that she hadn't seen her colleague make his way over to her desk.

He noted how quickly she shoved the papers back inside the file now that he was standing beside her.

'Yeah, well I expect that got everyone's tongues wagging,' Lucy said with a shrug, not wanting to draw too much attention to the incident, as she played it down. DS Morgan had insisted that if they were going to go ahead with an undercover operation that they weren't even going to enlighten the team about it. And that included Holder. Not yet anyway. 'Though as it turns out she hadn't touched a drop. She passed the breathalyser and was free to go home.'

'So, the arresting officer made a mistake? She wasn't charged?' Holder said, narrowing his eyes. They all knew how badly their sergeant wanted Gerard Jennings, but deliberately targeting his wife with false allegations would only jeopardise their chances of actually catching the man red-handed. Mistakes like this would only alert Gerard that he was on their radar. That they were watching him.

'The officer had reason to believe that she was driving under the influence. He said she was driving erratically. "She was all over the road": his words. Though, I guess that's just women's driving for you though, huh!' Lucy said with a tight grin, playing on an old gripe she held with her fellow co-worker for previous comments he'd made about her own driving when she'd first joined CID.

'Hey, I'm the last one to cast aspersions on women driving,' Holder said, holding his hands up playfully, as if to declare a truce.

'I bet she wasn't happy about being dragged in here?' he said, lingering around the desk, despite Lucy continuing to complete the last of her paperwork, so that she could finish for the day and get off home. He didn't seem to take the hint that she didn't want to talk about Debra Jennings.

The less she said to Holder the better, because Lucy knew that the chances were, he'd be able to read her if she was keeping something back from him. They were detective constables. That's what they did for a living.

'Wasn't happy would be the understatement of the year. She gave us a right mouthful about harassing her, and threatened to get a solicitor and start legal proceedings against us if we pull her in again under false allegations.'

'You dealt with her? Bit of a menial task for CID, wasn't it?' Holder said raising his eyes questioningly.

'Yeah, myself and DS Morgan had to smooth things over. Like I said, she was threatening all sorts and we've got surveillance on Gerard, so we didn't want that jeopardised.' Lucy placed the file she'd been looking at in her desk drawer and stood up. 'Right, that's me done here. I'm just going to pop in and see the sarge before I leave for the weekend.'

'You must seriously be in Morgan's good books for him to grant you with a whole weekend off. Especially seeing as we're in the middle of a murder investigation.'

'The investigation's running cold. We haven't got much to go on.' Lucy shrugged. 'Besides, you lot obviously do such a good job without me that I'm clearly not needed.' Lucy shot her colleague a sweet smile to disguise her irritation. Holder always seemed to have some kind of gripe with her; he always seemed as if he was permanently disgruntled. Well Lucy didn't have time for his melodramatics today.

'See you next week!'

DC Holder nodded in agreement, watching as Lucy went into DS Morgan's office and closed the door behind her. DS Morgan had his back to the window, but Holder could tell that the conversation was serious by the stern look of concentration on Lucy's face as she listened to their boss.

Holder had already read the report on Debra Jennings and everything that Lucy had just told him only confirmed it word for word.

Only something still didn't ring true. Lucy was acting on edge about something.

Opening the desk drawer, Holder eyed the file that Lucy had tucked inside.

Operation Shipley. Narrowing his eyes, Holder turned to the first page and quickly scanned the information. It was a cold case that had happened twenty years ago. A murder investigation. Not wanting to get caught snooping, Holder made a mental note of the Op's name before shutting the drawer.

Casting one last look at his boss and DS Murphy before he left the office, Holder had a feeling he was missing something. Or rather, something was going on and he was deliberately being left out of the loop.

\*

'The detective superintendent is in charge of all intelligence and Ops, and he's just okayed it, Lucy. Looks like you are going undercover,' DS Morgan said, making sure that the door was shut and that no one in the office could overhear them.

'But, and this is a big but, this Op stays only between us. No one on the team can know about it for now. Obviously, this isn't normal procedure. We'd never normally place you undercover on your own patch, but we both know that this is an opportunity that we can't afford to miss. We haven't been able to get anywhere near Gerard Jennings up until now. The DSI only agreed to it because he knows that you are our only option.'

'I know, Sarge,' Lucy agreed. 'Debra's dropped it in our laps. But I won't let you down.'

'We're going to need a tight cover story for you,' DS Morgan said, 'otherwise you'll arouse suspicions before you've even started.'

'I thought I could say that I'm a mother with a child in Logan's nursery. That was my cover when I went over to her flat the other night. We're the same age, so it could work. And I could say that I just recently moved here. That I'm trying to get away from my ex,' Lucy said, not bothering to hide the fact that ever since the idea of her going undercover had been suggested, she'd thought about nothing else. 'That way, worse case, if Gerard gets suspicious and tries to dig up any information on my fake name and he doesn't find anything, he'll think that I'm trying to keep a low profile. My story will look more convincing.'

'That could work, but won't he get suspicious about not seeing you with a child?' DS Morgan wasn't convinced.

'He wouldn't need to see me with a child.' Lucy shook her head. 'If I'm around Debra during the day, it will be because my son is at nursery. Or if it's the evening, I can make out that I've got a babysitter.'

'Hmm. It could work. I mean, it's not very PC I know, but I think the fact that you're a female undercover operative will give you a huge natural advantage. If Gerard thinks you're one of the mums from the school who's befriended Debra, he certainly wouldn't see you as any kind of threat. But you'll need to keep it simple.

Believable. The best cover story in the world won't help you one bit if you aren't given the opportunity to tell it. Gerard and his people will be sussing you out on first sight, before you've even had the opportunity to open your mouth. So make sure you live your story.'

'You're not planning on having me in there for long, are you, Sarge? We're just going to sound things out for now. I mean, realistically, we'll be depending more on Debra to get us the info anyway. I'll mainly just be the go-between. The middle man.' Lucy shrugged. 'Because it's doubtful that Gerard would let anything slip around a complete stranger, no matter how invisible I may be to him,' she said, warming to the idea now that her boss seemed to be in favour of it.

'Hopefully, we'll get what we need quickly,' DS Morgan said, being honest with his young colleague. He didn't want to make Lucy feel as if she was being forced into doing something that she wasn't comfortable doing. 'You'll have to take time off away from the team. This weekend has already been agreed as you know, and I'll change the rota for you next week too.'

This was a high-risk covert operation. Lucy was putting herself out on a limb agreeing to any of it. DS Morgan knew that he was taking a huge gamble, but he also knew that if this paid off the way he thought it might, Lucy would help to put away Gerard Jennings for years.

'If you feel uncomfortable at any point, or if for any reason you want out, you just say the word and we'll call the whole thing off. Nothing's more important to me as you being safe, Lucy. You don't have to agree with anything that you're not happy to partake in.'

'Sarge, I wouldn't be sitting here right now, if I didn't want to go through with this,' Lucy quickly interrupted. Part of her felt terrified at going ahead with their plan. What would Gerard do to her if he realised her real identity?

'We can put a safeguard in place for you. A plan B, if you like,' Morgan said, as if reading Lucy's thoughts, as he slid the phone across the desk. 'I've added Debra's number to it, and a few other fake contacts. You can add my number under the title of a family member. If you need to get out, you call me on that number,' DS Morgan said, trying to read Lucy's expression, to make sure that his officer was comfortable with what she was about to do.

'The only text messages sent from it must be from the character of your cover story. You do not send any names, or any kind of intelligence. This is purely a way for you to have direct communication with Debra, and for you to get help from me, if you need it. It's part of your cover; if Gerard or any of his men get their hands on it, it could be your lifeline. So make sure you keep it that way. We don't want any trail leading back to you.'

'Seriously, Sarge. I'm good for this. I won't let you down and if there's even the slightest sign of trouble or suspicion towards me from Gerard or any of his men, I promise you, you'll be the first person who knows so that you can pull me from the Op completely. I know the risks if I do this, Sarge.' Lucy thought back to the look of fear she'd seen on Debra's face when she'd come here today, risking everything to ask for their help.

This was the perfect opportunity to step up, and really make a difference to their lives. Getting Gerard Jennings at the end of it all would be the icing on the cake as far as she was concerned.

'But I also know the risks if I don't do anything at all.'

She had to do this, for Debra and her boys' sakes if nothing else.

DS Morgan nodded, understanding the context to Lucy's words. Confident that the officer would give the job everything she had.

'Now, we've just got to come up with a different look for you. To make sure that you're not recognised by anyone. A wig, some plain clothes. You just need to blend in, and not draw any attention to yourself.'

Lucy smiled then. 'Oh, don't you worry, Sarge. I'm already one step ahead of you on that one.'

# CHAPTER TWENTY-FIVE

'Are you sure you want me to chop all your lovely hair off, Lucy?' Melissa Holten said, standing behind Lucy with a pair of scissors at the ready in one hand and a handful of Lucy's freshly dyed hair in the other. 'It's such a big change, you might end up regretting it. What if we go a little shorter this time round, and then got for a short pixie cut once you've got used to that? It might be better to do it gradually.'

'No honestly, just go for it!' Lucy said, hoping she sounded confident enough to persuade Melissa. 'I just fancy something different. A complete change.'

'Well, this is as different as it gets for you, seeing as you only ever let me give you a trim. Short and fiery red is going to be a change all right!' Melissa laughed. She'd been doing Lucy's and Winnie's hair for years, coming out to them both regularly, though Lucy had always insisted on keeping her long dark hair mostly unchanged.

'You haven't broken up with a boyfriend, have you? Cause I always get that. First the boyfriend goes, then the hair...' Melissa laughed. 'And trust me, you'll get over the fella a lot quicker than you'll get over the loss of your hair. Your hair might take ages to grow back.'

'Nope. There's no boyfriend.' Lucy shrugged. 'I'm just bored of it, and I want something really different. Even if I hate it, it will grow back eventually,' she said with a finality that even Melissa wasn't going to argue with.

'Okay then, well if you're one hundred per cent sure about this, here goes.' She made the first chop with the scissors. 'No going back now!'

Lucy couldn't agree more, watching as the long lock of her newly dyed red hair fell to the floor. She pushed down the deep pang of regret that she instantly felt forming in the pit of her stomach as Melissa continued to snip away. She'd committed to helping Debra Jennings and she meant it, too. Which meant if she was going to go through with this undercover Op, she was going to do it properly.

Getting someone in on the inside, amongst Gerard's men, had proved near on impossible. Gerard was too shrewd and paranoid to let anyone into his firm that he didn't trust implicitly. No one could get close to the man. But getting close to Debra Jennings would prove a whole different ball game, especially if she was on their side, like she'd claimed to be. It wasn't strict procedure and they were taking a huge risk that could lead to massive retributions higher up in the force if they messed this up. Lucy knew that they really only had one good shot at this.

First impressions would count for everything and there was no way that Lucy was going to set herself up for being in Gerard's and his associates' company only to have someone recognise her from making a previous arrest on the estate when she was back in uniform. Going by the name Laura, with a new look to help her guarantee not having her cover blown, was the only way.

'How's your nan doing?' Melissa asked, bending down and keeping her eye level to the sharp blunt line of hair that sat even at the back of Lucy's neck now, as she cut away the last few wispy edges.

'She's good!' Lucy said, glad to have her thoughts of Gerard and his men interrupted and to focus back on her nan again. 'She's been loving staying at Treetops. Me and Vivian have been to see her every day.'

'She's started sleeping over, hasn't she? Will she be there now for good?'

'She's just doing a few nights here and there to get used to it. They'll be dropping her back here any minute, so you might get to see her before you leave. We'll have the afternoon together before she goes back again tonight.'

'Oh, that will be nice. I love your nan.' Melissa smiled as she brushed Lucy's hair into a short, cropped pixie cut. 'She cracks me up with all her funny stories and she's so honest, isn't she? You gotta love that. Not caring what anyone thinks. It must be so liberating to just say whatever you feel.'

'Liberating? Yep, that's my nan!' Lucy grinned, rolling her eyes up. She knew from experience that wasn't always such a good trait. Especially these days when her nan didn't seem to enforce any kind of tact before she opened her mouth.

'Right, there you go! How's that for you?' Melissa said, placing the brush down and stepping back as she held a smaller mirror to the back of Lucy's head. 'You know what, I wasn't sure at first, when you suggested it. But you can actually pull it off. The red really brings out the blue in your eyes. It looks really lovely.'

Looking back at her reflection in the mirror, Lucy took a few minutes to let herself adjust to the new, dramatically different look before smiling despite herself. Melissa was right. It didn't look too bad. And it certainly made her blue eyes stand out and her complexion look even rosier. Lucy could live with it for now.

'A little bit of make-up and you could look like a right vixen!' Melissa giggled as she started to pack her hairdressing kit away. 'You'll be fighting off the men before you know it.'

'Oh, I very much doubt that. Besides, I haven't got time for men. I'm too busy working.' As if on cue, her new phone beeped with a text message. Lucy knew who the sender was: the phone had been set up to look as if it was Lucy's genuine phone, only Debra was the only real contact on it. Lucy did a double-take as she read the text.

Debra was inviting her to her first job. A party tomorrow night, at the Red Fox pub, to celebrate Gerard's thirty-fifth birthday. Talk about being thrown in at the deep end. Still, she figured, it would be the perfect opportunity to show her face. Gerard would be so busy with all his guests, that his focus wouldn't be solely on her. Lucy could ease her way in with no issues.

'Oh, looks like your nan's back!' Melissa said, grabbing her kit bag, hearing the minibus pulling up outside. 'She probably won't recognise you now.' Melissa grinned, not realising the awkwardness of her statement until it was too late.

'Shit! Sorry, Lucy. What a stupid thing for me to say, I didn't mean because she's ill… I meant the hair… Of course she'll recognise you.'

'Don't be sorry! And you're probably right. Short red hair will be the last thing she'd be expecting to see. Come on, I'll walk you out. I can bet my life that if she doesn't like it she'll be quick enough to tell us, too!' Lucy laughed.

She walked Melissa to the front door and stood out on the step, watching as Winnie was helped off the bus by one of the nurses.

'Hi Winnie!' Melissa said, greeting the woman warmly with an embrace as Winnie approached them. 'Lucy said that I'm going to come to see you next week and do your hair. What do you think of Lucy's new hairdo? Suits her, doesn't it?'

'Oh Jesus, Lucy, I thought you were a friend of Melissa's for a minute. I didn't recognise you,' Winnie said, eyeing her granddaughter's hair dubiously. She shook her head and wrinkled her nose up, the expression on her face making no disguise of the fact that she didn't like Lucy's new look one bit. 'You look like one of those lesbians from the TV. Whatever possessed you?'

'Nan!' Lucy said, rolling her eyes and shaking her head at her nan's sharp tongue. 'You can't say things like that.'

'Course I can, dear. I can say what I like. I hope you didn't pay her to do that to your hair. If you did, I'd be asking for a refund sharpish. If anything, she should be paying you.'

'Oh dear. You don't like it then.' It was Melissa's turn to laugh then, not offended in the slightest. 'Seriously Lucy, your nan's a card, love her. I hope I'm half as outspoken when I get to her age. I'll leave you both too it. See you next week, Winnie!'

'You will indeed, Melissa. But I'll just be having my usual. Won't I, Lucy? I can't let that one loose on me, with one of her fancy creations. I don't think my heart would stand it.'

'NAN!' Lucy said, waving Melissa off before taking her nan by the arm and leading her into the house.

# CHAPTER TWENTY-SIX

'You sure you don't want a drink tonight, Debra? It might help take the edge off things? You could probably do with one…' Kiera eyed her best mate, sitting there in the booth of the pub sipping on a Coke. Her face still showed the signs of her beating, though Debra had done a good job of trying to cover up the bruising with some make-up. If Kiera hadn't known that Debra had been in hospital this week, she'd never have realised what the woman had endured or what a brave front she must be putting on tonight. Sitting here, in the Red Fox pub, pretending everything was perfect as she played the role of the dutiful wife just as Gerard expected of her. Kiera wasn't sure if she could have done it.

'No. Honestly, I'm just not feeling it,' Debra said, with a shrug. 'I'm just going to stay a few hours and then get home to the boys.'

Kiera nodded knowingly. 'You are a better woman than me, Debs! If I was married to him, I'd be a raging alcoholic!' she whispered, hoping to at least get Debra to crack a smile as she nodded over to where Gerard was standing over at the bar, surrounded by a group of his mates, downing shots and playing up to his audience loudly, making out he was the big I-am, in typical Gerard fashion.

After the week from hell her friend had endured, it was no surprise that Debra wasn't herself. Sitting here in the pub tonight, surrounded by all these fake fuckers celebrating Gerard's birthday, as if the man was some kind of God, was probably the last place Debra wanted to be, but Kiera knew that she didn't have any choice in the matter. Gerard was all about keeping up appearances. Debra would have to be seen to be doing her bit. Which was exactly what Kiera was doing too. She was only here to give Debra some moral support. But the last thing she'd been expecting tonight was to be introduced to Debra's new friend.

'So, Laura, Debra says that you met at nursery?' Kiera sipped her wine, eyeing Debra's new friend with curiosity over the top of her glass as she came back from the toilet and took a seat at the table. In truth, Kiera had had her nose well and truly put out of joint by the surprise guest who had joined them tonight. A woman who, until tonight, Kiera had never heard of. Kiera had known Debra for years, and she knew how guarded she could be, how she never let anyone in, and always just kept herself to herself. But it was strange that Kiera had never even heard her mention any other friends, seeing as they spoke almost every day.

Not only that, but Kiera had barely heard a word from Debra since she'd come out of hospital, and she'd assumed that that had been because Gerard was on Debra's case the whole time and doing his usual, not letting the woman out of his sight. Divide and conquer was one of the man's usual tactics, and he knew damn well that five minutes alone with her mate and Kiera would be advising Debra to take her chances, and her kids, and leave the man. But maybe that hadn't been the reason that she hadn't heard from her friend in the last few days at all. Maybe it was really because Debra had this new mate to confide in now.

'You've got a little boy?'

'Yeah, my son's name is Danny. He's just turned three. He took a real shine to Logan on his first day of nursery. They've been inseparable ever since. Haven't they, Debra?' Lucy smiled over at Debra, who had already warned her that if anyone was going to be suspicious of their sudden friendship, it would be Kiera.

Kiera would be none the wiser about anything to do with Logan's nursey school, Debra had promised her. Her daughter Maisie was older, in Mason's class, so as long as they were careful, Kiera would never realise that Lucy's story was completely fabricated. Especially as the plan was that, given some luck, Lucy wouldn't be on the scene for long. But they were proving to have their work cut out convincing Kiera to accept Lucy tonight. And even more so, as it appeared the woman had taken an instant dislike to Lucy on sight.

'Oh God, yeah! Danny's all Logan talks about from the minute he opens his eyes. Best little buddies, they are,' Debra said, backing up Lucy's story.

Kiera raised her eyes, still recalling how Debra and this Laura had been so deep in conversation when she'd arrived that they hadn't even seen her. Yet as soon as she'd joined them at the table, they'd both immediately shut up mid-sentence, as if they were talking about something or someone that they didn't want to include her in. She'd seen the guilty expressions on their faces and the fleeting, almost imperceptible, look they'd shared and wondered for a minute if perhaps they'd been talking about her. Because since she'd sat down she'd been picking up on some weird vibes. But then a small part of her knew she was just acting jealous and petty. Her nose was out of joint, because she and Debra had been friends for years. Up until now it had only been the two of them, and now Debra had another friend, it was probably natural that Kiera would feel instantly left out. Maybe Debra would feel the same if it was the other way around?

Still, Kiera was determined to make an effort to appear friendly to Laura now, because the truth was, she was curious about the woman. Especially seeing as Debra had invited her to Gerard's birthday party. And it wasn't as if Debra would want to show her husband off. If anything, Debra normally wanted the people around her to avoid the man. Something didn't sit right with Kiera. Something about this Laura felt all wrong.

'Where is he tonight then? At home with his dad?' Kiera asked, trying to sound casual as she sussed the girl out. She was attractive in an understated way. Dressed down, in casual jeans and black vest top as if she wasn't out for attention or trying to impress anyone. Short, cropped red hair and glasses. She looked as if she just wanted to blend in. Which was ironic really, as in a room full of girls with their faces plastered in heavy make-up and their arses barely covered by their short dresses, that only had the opposite effect and set Laura apart.

And Kiera had caught the odd few admiring glances that had been thrown Laura's way from some of the men standing at the bar with Gerard. She'd even caught her Micky on the table behind them giving the girl a once-over, which again only fuelled her initial feeling of dislike. Bloody men were so obvious. Though to be fair to Laura, she didn't seem comfortable with the attention she was receiving. It wasn't as if she seemed out to cause any drama or gain any kind of special treatment. In fact if anything, Kiera thought, watching Laura shift in her seat and constantly glance around the room, she looked as if she really didn't want to be here. She watched as Laura occasionally caught someone's eye, and as soon as she did, she quickly diverted her gaze back on her drink or to the floor. Her energy was out. Her body language seemed stilted, false. As if she was on edge about something, or nervous. But what could she have to be nervous about?

Though she figured Gerard's reputation would have, of course, preceded him. Being in that man's company while he got completely bladdered, would be enough to put most of the people in here on edge.

'Let's just say that the father of my little boy wasn't a very nice man. That's why I moved here. To get away from him,' Lucy said, trying to concentrate her hardest on sticking to the script.

She'd rehearsed these lines a thousand times last night. Though concentrating on anything right now was proving nigh on impossible. Lucy was starting to second guess herself now, wondering how she ever thought she could pull this off. To sit here so brazenly, so publicly, drinking with Gerard Jennings's wife in the Red Fox pub, surrounded by some of London's most notorious criminals. Remembering her boss's advice, she made a mental note to try and relax, and play it cooler, otherwise she was going to give the game away before it had even begun.

'My ex was violent. He used to knock me about. I needed a fresh start. So I moved here,' Lucy said with a shrug. She was hoping for Kiera's sympathy, but she didn't want to come across as if she was playing the victim. She just wanted Kiera to give her a break. Keep your story short and sweet, she remembered her sergeant's warning. The devil might be in the detail, but don't give too much away. Because all it takes is one slip up, and you'll end up hanging yourself.

'Don't take this the wrong way, Laura, but you probably couldn't have picked a worse place to call your sanctuary. Come here for a fresh start? Most of us are dying to get out of this dump at the first opportunity we get!' Kiera laughed then, making light of her comment even though it was very much the truth. 'Whereabouts do you live?'

'Jesus, Kiera!' Debra butted in, half joking. 'Is this a conversation or an interrogation? You've done nothing but quiz Laura since you sat down.' She hoped Kiera would take the hint and ease off on Lucy a bit. Debra knew her friend only too well. Kiera could be like a dog with a bone if something didn't sit right with her. And the fact that she was quizzing Lucy with such a steely look on her face didn't bode well.

'Sorry! I'm just curious that's all. You've never mentioned Laura to me before, and I don't really know anything about her,' Kiera shot back. The dig towards her mate was well and truly intended.

'It's fine, Debra. Honestly. Kiera's only making conversation.' Lucy smiled warmly at Kiera, letting the woman know that she wasn't here to come between them. 'Well, I'm not technically on the estate, I'm renting a bedsit over at Jubilee Gardens,' Lucy lied, pretending that she was oblivious that the street she'd just named that ran down beside the cemetery was actually no better than the Griffin Estate; in fact, if anything the place was notoriously worse. But it made sense that if Lucy had just moved here, on her own with a kid in tow, that she'd only be able to afford a rundown little bedsit. 'It's a shit hole, but I've made it my own.' Lucy shrugged, hoping that Kiera believed her. 'To be completely honest with you, I'm just happy I can close the front door and know that me and my son are safe. Anyway, it's hardly news, is it? It happens all the time. Most men are just arseholes!'

'I'll drink to that!' Debra grinned, raising her glass of Coke in the air. Kiera nodded in understanding. It was a tale as old as time as far as she was concerned, especially round these parts, and it would explain why the girl seemed so shifty and on edge. Maybe she was worried about her ex finding her. Kiera felt a pang of guilt for being so quick to judge the girl. It was true Debra didn't easily make friends but maybe she'd seen that this Laura genuinely needed a break. Maybe she'd invited her here tonight because she felt sorry for her. And in fairness, Debra was pretty much in the same boat. Maybe these two did have something in common other than just their kids at nursery. And if seeing this Laura being able to break free on her own and start again helped Debra gather the courage to maybe think about getting out too, then Kiera was all for it.

'Who wants another drink?' she offered, willing to start again and give Laura a fair chance. A peace offering of sorts, which Lucy accepted wholeheartedly.

'Let me get this one, yeah?' Lucy insisted standing up and looking at Debra. 'Are you sure you can't be tempted with a small glass of wine?'

'Go on then,' Debra said, smiling at Kiera, to let her know that she had finally broken her down.

Making her way towards the bar, Lucy made a point of squeezing in behind Gerard and his mates.

Holding out her money she waited her turn to be served, hoping to catch a few snippets of something that she could report back to her sergeant later.

She knew that DS Morgan would be feeling just as on edge as she was right now. He'd taken a risk allowing her to go through with this job, and as much as Lucy was nervous about being here right now, she knew that he'd be feeling exactly the same. He'd be waiting anxiously to hear from her tonight so that he knew that she was safe. It might be his head on the chopping block at work if she messed this job up, but it was Lucy who was gambling tonight, with her own life.

# CHAPTER TWENTY-SEVEN

'Stick another one in there will you, Jimmy.' Gerard Jennings beamed, slamming his glass down on the bar top, and relishing with delight how the landlord flinched at his order.

'The place is heaving!' Gerard said proudly, casting an approving eye across the busy pub. Pleased to see that the Red Fox was already packed to the rafters, so much so that there was barely any floor space left, and every table and chair in the place was occupied.

'It's a great turnout, Gerard,' Jimmy said in agreement, having already spotted a few big faces from London's underworld in the room. Though unlike Gerard, he wasn't so foolish to think that most of the people here tonight might be here under the guise of helping Gerard celebrate his birthday. Half of them were just playing the game. They weren't friends of Gerard's. Not really. They were here because they had to be, a bit like himself, tolerating Gerard, for fear of the reprisals if they didn't come. Gerard wasn't a popular man by any account, because popularity wasn't bought by fear and intimidation; it was earned by respect and admiration. And they were two things that Gerard Jennings had never quite managed to master. Still, as long as they kept drinking all the alcohol and Gerard settled the tab tomorrow, Jimmy wasn't about to complain.

'Oh, here he is! Give us a pint for Paul too,' Gerard said, beaming as he caught Paul's eye as his friend walked across the pub towards him.

''Bout time, fella! Here, Jimmy, give us a couple of whiskey chasers too, will you? Paul's got some catching up to do,' he added, seeing the angsty look on Paul's face and choosing purposely to ignore it. He knew that Paul was still furious with him for the other night, but as far as Gerard was concerned it was done. Jamie Nash had been dealt with. Paul needed to let it go, but the look on his face told Gerard the man had no intention of doing that.

'Nah, I'm good with just a pint, Gerard,' Paul said, waving Jimmy off, making a point to turn down the offer of shots.

'You took your time, didn't you? Where have you been?'

'Where have I been?' Paul said incredulously, leaning in towards Gerard, so that they couldn't be heard by anyone nearby.

'I've been in bed, Gerard. I'm knackered, no thanks to your fucking psychotic episode the other night, me and a couple of the other lads spent the best part of last night and most of today cleaning up the mess you made. Scrubbing claret and brain matter off the walls of that lad's flat before having to dispose of the poor kid's body. For fuck's sake, Gerard, what were you thinking? He was seventeen!' Paul spat through gritted teeth, feeling the anger surging inside him once more as the memory of Gerard annihilating the boy with a hammer whirled around inside his mind.

'It doesn't matter how old the kid was, he was mugging us off. Mugging me off. And it was common knowledge. As far as I'm concerned, he had it coming,' Gerard said, knocking back both the shots that Jimmy had placed down on the bar and enjoying the heat of the liquid burning through him. This was his night, his party and he was determined that he was going to have a good time despite Paul's bad mood.

'Are you having a laugh, Gerard? The kid didn't deserve to have his head caved in with a hammer. You said you were going to give the lad a warning! I was expecting a few strong words to keep the boy in line, and a couple of digs with your fists, old school style. The fact that you went there tooled up meant that you planned it,' Paul said, finally letting on what was really bothering him. Gerard had planned the horrific attack all along. He'd had his own agenda for going to Jamie Nash's flat the other night and he hadn't thought to give Paul the heads-up about it. He'd acted on his temper, his fury getting the better of him, and hadn't thought about the aftermath or the consequences of killing that boy. It was happening more and more lately. Gerard acting out on a whim, depending on his mood. And Paul knew why. The drugs were getting to him. He was taking more and more to reach the highs he once had, and the gear didn't mix well with his volatile temper. He was paranoid enough without it. Gerard was becoming more and more of a liability as the days went on, and Paul needed to constantly rein him in. Though, sometimes, like last night, he couldn't even manage that. And so he'd been left to pick up the pieces once more and make sure that this shit didn't come back to them.

'You might not agree with what I did, but I ain't going to be made to feel guilty about it. And it's done now. The lesson has been learned. No other fucker is going be so stupid as to follow in Jamie Nash's footsteps once they've heard how they'll be dealt with if they're caught out. None of them would dare!'

Paul couldn't argue with that. 'But that's just it, Gerard. People are already talking. And you know that we can't afford for there to be any comeback about this. If the Old Bill get wind of it, they'll be led straight back to you. To us. We were supposed to be laying low. You could have caused us untold aggro.'

Paul had heard the rumours that were already rife around the Griffin Estate about Jamie Nash's sudden disappearance. Of course people were talking – how could they not after Gerard had made such a grand entrance? Kicking the front door off its hinges, which Paul and his mates had had to replace. Gerard always had to make a point of being seen and heard. Of wanting to make public examples of anyone who crossed him, and despite their frantic clean up last night and the most part of today, the man's actions had added fuel to the already smouldering fire.

'People will always chat shit! So what? No one can prove anything. Like you said, you cleaned it up, yeah? So, who's to say the lad didn't just do a runner in the middle of the night, because he'd got word that I had the hump with him and he couldn't handle the fallout? That's the rumour that needs to be put out there, Paul. So you see that it is, yeah,' Gerard said with finality, the conversation over for now.

'Now will you lighten the fuck up, man, and have a couple of shots with me. It's my fucking birthday. Surely that's something worth celebrating, you miserable sod!' Gerard said, not taking no for an answer, raising his hand and summoning Jimmy back down the bar to fill up the shot glasses.

Paul didn't argue this time. Instead he accepted the drink. He had a feeling he was going to need something to help him take the edge off having to spend the evening with Gerard, lording it up, oblivious of the shit storm he kept creating for them all. And Paul couldn't shake the feeling of dread that he could feel swarming deep inside his gut. A premonition of sorts, that there was far worse to come. Gerard was out of control. He wasn't listening to Paul any more. He wasn't listening to anyone. That he hadn't shown an ounce of remorse murdering a young lad, for battering the boy's body until it was unrecognisable – a body that was now submerged beneath the dark, murky waters of the Thames, while Gerard stood here sinking shots without a care in the world – told Paul everything that he'd been suspecting for a while now. Gerard Jennings was a law unto himself, which made him an extremely dangerous man.

# CHAPTER TWENTY-EIGHT

Cursing to herself as she tried to get the lighter to work, Kiera gave it a hard shake before sparking it once more in a bid to light up her cigarette, to no avail. About to go back inside the pub and borrow one, she was pleased when the back door opened, the harsh pub light and pulsing beat of the music spilling out into the dimly lit garden, hoping that someone had come out to join her on a quest for a cigarette too. She bristled as she saw it was Paul Denman walking towards her. He was the last person she'd been hoping to bump into tonight, out here on her own. Actually, make that the second last, after Gerard, of course.

'Please tell me you've got a light on you?' Kiera said, doing what she always did and acting indifferent to Paul's company. She knew that by acting so detached that she then appeared standoffish, unemotional, when inside she felt the exact opposite.

'You back on the fags then? I thought you gave up!' Paul grinned as he stepped forward. His hands cupped hers and she concentrated on the flame as it licked the end of the cigarette, turning it from grey to a bright orange, making a point not to look up and meet Paul's gaze that she knew was resting on her.

She nodded, unable to shake the familiar anger that Paul always managed to stir from somewhere deep inside her. Which was stupid after all this time, all these years, but she couldn't help it. She was still angry. Angry at herself for settling with Micky. Dependable, boring Micky. She'd chosen stability and normality over a life of chaos with Paul. The only good thing that had come from it all was Maisie. Kiera loved her daughter fiercely and wouldn't change for the world all that had happened since her daughter had been born. Though sometimes she'd quietly wondered to herself about how Paul would have been as a father. If the three of them would have worked as a family. But then she reminded herself of Paul's biggest downfall: the fact that he was Gerard Jennings's number one, and Kiera would never succumb to that way of life. Paul had told her that one day he would get out of this life. That he'd leave it all behind him. If she'd only take a chance on him. Only Kiera hadn't taken him for his word.

Paul had been born into this life. It was ingrained inside him, just as it was with Gerard.

Maybe Micky was gormless and happy to just plod along in life, working as a delivery driver on a fairly average wage, but at least his living was an honest one. As least she could trust that the bills were paid without anyone losing any blood. She blew a long flume of smoke from her mouth, hoping that the combination of smoke and tobacco would mask the heady musky scent of Paul's aftershave that lingered in the air between them both. The smell for ever ingrained in her olfactory memory, bringing her mind back to the two of them entwined together in bed, skin on skin. The smell of him all over her.

'Thanks!' She stepped backwards, consciously or unconsciously putting some space between them, aware that being in such close proximity to Paul was a dangerous act in itself. For her at least. Especially now that she was feeling the effects of all the wine she'd drunk kick in. She needed to keep her guard up. She'd never show him how she really felt.

'You all right?' he asked, smiling at her as if he could see right through her and read her thoughts. She nodded, trying to look casual, but really trying to read the man right back. Trying to work out if he was playing the same game that she was and pretending that whatever was once between them was no more. Because it had been something all-consuming. And Kiera had never felt anything like it before or since. You didn't just forget that kind of feeling. She shook her head then, instantly dismissing the thought. Christ, he was a man. He probably moved on to his next conquest and hadn't given her another thought. It had been seven years ago, after all. A lifetime ago now, before Micky. Before Maisie.

'What?' Paul said, eyeing Kiera as she frowned and shook her head, guessing that like most people inside the pub, she'd had too much to drink.

'How can you still be friends with him? You know what he did to her, don't you?'

'I do now, yes. But he played it down. At first.' Paul had known that this was coming. Kiera had always been so outspoken, so forthright in her opinions and views. He liked that about her. She didn't play games and he always knew where he stood. At least he thought he did. 'He made out it was something else. A fall. An argument. He didn't go into details, but yes, I know what really happened.'

'Do you? Do you know that I found Mason and Logan clinging to her as she lay unconscious on the kitchen floor? That that bastard kicked the baby from her stomach? Come on, Paul. Don't you think enough is enough! What if he kills her next time? Because it will happen, if someone doesn't rein him in. You need to stop him.'

'I'm not his keeper, Kiera. What happens in their marriage is down to them. It's got nothing to do with me.'

'He listens to you, Paul. Can't you talk to him? Warn him off somehow? I'm worried about her, Paul. Like genuinely worried. She's not herself. I'm worried that she's going to do something stupid,' Kiera said, and judging by the way that Paul clenched his jaw so rigidly in the way he always used to do when he was riled, she'd clearly hit a nerve.

Riled with her for daring to speak up? Riled with Gerard for what he'd done? Kiera didn't care what was causing him to look so annoyed, as long as she got through to him somehow. She knew from experience that the truth was always a bitter pill to swallow, but someone had to speak up, for Debra's sake, if nothing else.

'You're wrong, Kiera. Gerard doesn't listen to anyone. Not even me,' Paul spat, acutely aware that no one else on the planet would ever dare to call him out the way that Kiera was right now, because no one else would get away with it. But he knew that this was just Kiera's way. That she only meant well by voicing her concerns. And he also knew the reason she was stirring so much anger inside him was because she was only speaking the truth. Gerard did need reining in.

Next time he might kill Debra. Because he was more than capable of doing it, wasn't he? When he really lost it. The other night with that young Jamie Nash lad had taught him that.

'Look, I'll speak to him. Again,' Paul conceded, wanting Kiera to know that he had already at least tried. 'How's she doing?' he said, changing the subject. He'd been genuinely concerned about Debra, too. The two times he'd been over at Gerard's flat this week, the woman had barely even acknowledged him. And he'd felt that part of her had blamed him too. Just as Kiera did. Guilty by association. Paul hated that more than anything, because he respected Debra. She was a good woman, and Gerard took nothing but advantage of her.

'I don't know,' Kiera said honestly. She'd been worried sick all week that Debra's head wasn't in the right place. 'I knocked most days and rang her. Only until tonight, she'd all but gone into hiding. I was worried sick that she'd do something stupid.

Like hurt herself. But she wouldn't do that, would she? Because of the boys. She wouldn't put them through that.'

'Course she wouldn't,' Paul said with a certainty that he didn't feel, and Kiera could sense it.

'She's just not herself. Something's changed in her. She's, I dunno… acting different tonight.' Though even as Kiera said the words she knew that she shouldn't expect anything else. Of course Debra was acting different. She'd just suffered a miscarriage. She was angry and grieving.

'I thought that maybe Gerard was deliberately trying to keep her away from me. But she seems so busy with this new best mate of hers.' Kiera regretted the words as soon as they left her mouth and she caught the smirk on Paul's face.

'The redhead?' He'd spotted the woman himself and figured that she must be one of Debra's friends. She'd been sitting with Debra and Kiera for the entire night so far.

'Yep. That's the one. I know how petty I sound, believe me.' She shrugged, trying to make light of her feelings, hating herself now for sounding so childlike. They were grown women after all and Debra could be friends with whomever she wanted. She didn't have to justify herself to anyone. But Kiera couldn't shake the feeling that there was something going on. Something that she wasn't privy to.

'They met at nursery. Logan and Laura's little boy, Danny, are mates. They're in the same class,' Kiera said, breathing out a trail of smoke and shaking her head. 'I just think it's strange that's all, that Debra's never mentioned her to me. I mean, we speak every single day. You'd think she'd have dropped her name in… It's like she's purposely keeping things from me.'

'Well, I don't know. Maybe she just didn't think to mention her. Or maybe,' Paul said teasingly, 'she did keep her from you, because she knew that you wouldn't like her?' He laughed then and rolled his eyes. Knowing that was more likely the case. Debra would have guessed that Kiera wouldn't like this new friendship that didn't include her, and judging by Kiera's sullen expression right now, she'd been spot on. Paul didn't want to get drawn into Kiera's dramas. He had enough of his own melodramatics to tend to right now. Feuding women were the least of his worries tonight.

'It's not that I don't like her. It's just there's something not right about her. I dunno, she's odd. I can't put my finger on it.' Kiera shivered as the cold night air swept over her. She finished the last few drags of her cigarette before stubbing it out. 'Anyway, whatever. Debra's out, and she's having a few drinks and trying to enjoy herself. I guess I can't ask for anything more than that. Christ knows, she deserves a night off putting up with him.' Kiera raised her eyebrow, almost challenging him to say otherwise about his so-called best friend. Which only made Paul laugh at her boldness.

'I'm going back in,' she said, ending the conversation as abruptly as it started. 'Catch you around.'

Paul nodded, watching Kiera as she made her way back inside the pub. The pang of regret and loss at losing the woman to a deadbeat like Micky still galled him. But he knew that Kiera didn't feel the same about him. She'd moved on it seemed. She was happier without him. He needed to do the same, too.

He thought about Debra. Kiera was right. He'd been watching Debra earlier and he'd seen the difference in her too: sitting in a booth with Kiera and another mate and knocking back the wine like there was no tomorrow. Slurring her speech and almost falling over when she got up from her chair to go to the toilet, it was as if she was only there in body, not in spirit. The haunted look on her face of a woman brought to her lowest ebb. It pained him that she had avoided all eye contact with him too, making a point to not say hello to him, as if he was just as bad as Gerard.

But Debra was wrong. There was one thing that Paul could never condone and that was any man who thought it was okay to use a woman as a punch bag. He'd promised Kiera he'd have a word with Gerard again, and he was a man of his word; he would. And all he could do was hope that this time the man really listened. Because otherwise they were going to have a huge problem.

# CHAPTER TWENTY-NINE

'You all right, Laura?' Debra asked as Lucy came back from the bar and placed the tray of drinks down on the table. Though she could see by the strained look on Lucy's face that she wasn't herself. If she was up at the bar all that time, then chances were she'd managed to listen in and hear what Gerard and Paul were talking about. And chances were whatever it was, wasn't good. Which was the whole point of Debra inviting her here tonight. So she'd be hidden in plain sight, unsuspected by Gerard and his mates of who she really was. And alcohol loosened tongues, so it was inevitable that Lucy might hear or see something that might give her the tip-off they needed.

'You were ages up there.'

'Yeah, sorry. They didn't have any Chardonnay left. The landlord sent one of the barmaids down to have a look in the cellar for some more,' Lucy said, not mentioning that she'd really deliberately sent the barmaid on a wild goose chase to look for a particular bottle of drink that she'd guessed they wouldn't have, in the hope of buying herself some more time at the bar so she could home in on Gerard's conversation.

'Everyone's drinking the place dry!' Lucy smiled, throwing Debra a cautious look as Debra picked up her glass of wine and downed it in one.

'Whoa, steady on!' Kiera laughed. 'You'll have yours finished before Laura's even had a chance to sit her bum back down on the chair. Tell you what, to save us being up and down at the bar all night, I'm going to pop to the ladies and then I'll grab us a couple of bottles on the way back. Because if there is a shortage on wine tonight, I will not be happy!'

'Not for me, thanks. I've got a bit of a headache coming on,' Lucy said, shooting a look at Debra and hoping the woman would take her hint and follow suit. Lucy had only ordered herself a drink so that she'd blend in. It was a party and it was Saturday night, after all. But she had every intention of only sticking to the two. She was making this the last one. Waiting until Kiera had walked off across the pub towards the toilets, leaving the two woman alone, she leaned in to Debra.

'We're not supposed to be getting drunk!' she said tightly, keeping her expression neutral and her voice low so as not to draw any attention to themselves. 'We both need to keep our wits about us and stay on the ball. We can't afford to get drunk and mess this up. We agreed.'

'A few glasses isn't going to hurt anyone though, is it?' Debra said shrugging her shoulders before shaking her head. 'I can't do this, Lucy. I can't just sit here and pretend that everything's okay. Look at him,' Debra spat, no longer listening to Lucy. She was too busy staring over towards the bar to where Gerard stood laughing manically at one of his own jokes, the men around him all dutifully joining in, regardless of whether or not what Gerard had said was funny.

'Standing there, laughing and joking around as if he hasn't got a care in the world.' Shaking her head, her words loaded with venom, Debra knocked back the last of her wine and slammed the glass down on the table.

'Debra. We can't do this. Not here. Not now,' Lucy said, clasping her hand over Debra's to try and help bring the woman's fractious mood back down. She could see the pain behind Debra's eyes, the tears that formed as she stared blankly ahead and Lucy knew that she was still thinking about the baby that she'd lost.

'He has no conscience, do you know that? He does whatever he pleases, to whomever he pleases and nobody ever dares to even so much as question him, let alone stop him. Look at him. Does that look like a man that killed his own child, that murdered his own baby? Does that look like a man who gives a shit?' Picking up Kiera's glass, Debra finished the rest of her drink too, her face flushed red with rage as she watched her husband acting so normal, so indifferent and oblivious to the pain that she was in.

'He thinks he's unstoppable,' Debra declared. 'He's completely oblivious to how many people hate him. How many people wish him dead. How I want him dead.' Debra's jaw was clenched so tightly now that her voice shook with emotion.

'You don't mean that,' Lucy said quietly. She understood Debra's surge of emotion but Lucy needed to try and keep her level-headed. Drinking was just going to heighten everything the woman was feeling and it would put them both and the operation in jeopardy.

'I do mean it! I hate him. He got some young girl from around the estate pregnant.' Debra finally admitted what was really eating away at her tonight. 'I saw her the other day when I was out with the boys. She was wheeling a buggy around the shop and she kept on staring at me. I thought that she was following me, that maybe she knew me and she had something she wanted to say. So when I got a chance, I told her how lovely her little boy was. And he really was. I looked down at him and I was shocked at how alike to Mason and Logan he looked at that age. And then I saw it on her face. Who she was. Who the child was. Christ, she looked barely out of school. A kid really. And the baby could only have been a few weeks old. That's the real reason why I came to see you the next day, because I knew that if I stayed any longer,

I'd end up killing him. I'd end up doing time for that scumbag. Breeding kids with kids, and all the while he took my baby away.'

'You came to us because you're better than that,' Lucy said, squeezing the woman's hand. 'I know it doesn't feel like it yet, but you are fighting this. You are fighting him. And you will win. You'll get your justice. The right way.'

Debra laughed. 'Justice is too good for him. I want him to suffer. I want him to pay.'

'And he will. I promise you that. But we will do this the right way. And then you can focus on Mason and Logan. You can have your lives back. That's all that really matters, Debra. You mustn't lose sight of that.'

Taking a slow deep breath, Debra nodded. 'I know you're right. Deep down, I do. But watching him, seeing him act so normal, so unaffected by what he's done, it makes my blood boil. And I wonder what other things I don't know about. What he's really capable of. Because I don't know that man at all.'

Lucy relaxed a little as Debra calmed down. 'We'll get him, Debra. You'll have your day. Soon. I promise.' Then nodding down at the glass she added, 'And please, go easy on that lot.'

'Here we go, ladies. Two bottles of Pinot and a bag of salt and vinegar crisps each, don't say I don't spoil us.' Kiera smiled as she placed the ice bucket down on the table. 'Though, I've just eyed up the buffet, Debs, and the food looks unreal. Bang goes my diet, huh! Oh look, there goes my Micky, straight over to the food. I swear that man only thinks about his stomach, and I can guarantee that he won't bring anything over here for me. I have to fend for myself with that one,' Kiera said, half joking as she nodded over to where Micky was loading up a plate high with food.

'Wow, he really does like his food,' Lucy laughed, watching as the man stuffed a whole pork pie in his mouth, clearly in his element. She scanned the room, still on edge about being recognised by someone, though she knew that the chances of that happening were almost none. She looked completely different now with her cropped red hair, and her fake glasses.

Staring over towards the bar, she met eyes with Gerard and for a few deadly seconds she almost felt her heart stop as their eyes locked. But then as quickly as he'd looked over at her, he'd looked away. She didn't even factor on the man's radar. Tonight had been the hard part really.

The moment where she'd swapped places from looking from the outside to looking in. She was inside now, well and truly. Who'd have thought it?

Lucy watched Paul as he bent his head down, talking to someone intensely now, deep in conversation. Lucy couldn't see the other man's face but she could see from Paul's expression that the conversation was serious. She knew that Paul was Gerard's right-hand man and that the two men were best friends as well as business partners. But Lucy had heard the anger in the man's voice earlier when he'd spoken about how Gerard had acted alone and put them both in jeopardy by murdering a young lad by the name of Jamie Nash. She'd heard the exhaustion in Paul's tone, and wondered if his patience was also wearing thin. Maybe he'd had enough of the man, too. Paul moved to the side then, stepping back so Lucy could see who he was talking to. She dropped her glass.

'Shit, Laura. Don't waste it. There's a wine shortage, remember? Debs, get her a straw! She'll have to slurp it up.' Kiera giggled, eyeing the spillage all over the table.

But Laura wasn't laughing with her. She was still looking over at the bar. Her face paled to almost translucent as she recognised the man who Paul had been speaking to. It was DC Ben Holder.

# CHAPTER THIRTY

'How did I get so dunk. Dunk.' Debra Jennings giggled before correcting herself. 'I mean drunk. Druuunk!' She grabbed hold of Lucy and Kiera tightly, as the two women desperately fought to hold Debra upright and keep her from falling through the open front door of her flat.

She felt a bit sick now, and her head was spinning.

'Do you think someone spiked my drink? I don't feel too well…'

'No.' Lucy laughed. 'I think it might have been the two bottles of Pinot Grigio that you put away tonight! Not to mention the tray of shots. So much for only having the one glass!' Lucy said lightly, not letting on that she was annoyed with Debra for getting so drunk tonight. There was no point getting into it now anyway, Debra was barely coherent. She was just glad that she'd been able to get Debra and Kiera to agree to leaving early. After spotting Holder, Lucy hadn't been able to get out of that pub quickly enough. Though she'd been forced to sit with her back to her colleague while Kiera and Debra had insisted on drinking the wine that Kiera had bought first.

To say that she would have been compromised if he'd have spotted her was an understatement.

And she couldn't even begin to get her head around what he was doing there. But she knew one thing for certain, it wasn't good.

Though right now, she needed to concentrate on looking after Debra.

'Oh, shit!' Kiera cursed loudly then as Debra slipped from her grasp as they made their way along the hallway.

Both of the women struggled under Debra's weight, not strong enough or quick enough to catch her as she took a tumble over the doormat inside the flat. Lucy winced at Debra's botched attempts at steadying herself, as she stuck her arm out before she hit the wall, and slid awkwardly down into a heap on the floor.

'Debra? Are you okay?' Sophie, the babysitter said, running into the hallway to see what all the noise and commotion was, unable to hide the expression of shock on her face, as she took in the sight of Debra sprawled out on the floor, her make-up streaked down her face as she giggled to herself.

'Oh my god, are you drunk?' Sophie's initial concern quickly changed to laughter as she realised what was going on. Sophie was only fifteen, and she lived in the flat just along the balcony from Debra and Gerard and had often babysat for them both. They always paid her well, and the extra money she made came in handy. But normally it was Gerard who caused a scene, not Debra.

Debra was always so sensible and composed. 'I've never seen you drunk before.'

'She's not drunk. She's dunk,' Kiera quipped, hiccuping as she corrected the girl, not too far behind Debra in the drunk stakes. 'Come on, Debs. Up you get, mate,' Kiera insisted, trying her hardest to hoist her friend back up on to her feet, only Debra had gone a dead weight now.

Slumped on the floor, with no energy to stand back up, she held out her hand, but only ended up pulling Kiera down on top of her.

'God, I wish I'd had more than just the two drinks now!' Lucy grinned, shaking her head as she watched the two paralytic women writhing around the floor in hysterics.

'Sshh! You two are going to wake Mason and Logan up if you're not quiet,' Lucy whispered, trying to help both women back up and guide them into the lounge, with the help of Sophie now.

Which was still no easy mission as the two women kept falling about the place laughing at nothing in particular and making it difficult for them. Finally, they managed to get Debra into the lounge and lead her over to the sofa, where she promptly draped herself across it, as Kiera slumped down in the armchair opposite.

'Can you pay Sophie for me, Lucy? There's money in my bag,' Debra managed to mumble, closing her eyes and looking as if she was ready to pass out.

'Wow! I've never seen Debra so drunk before. Is she going to be okay?' Sophie said, eyeing Debra as if she had two heads.

'She'll be fine. She just had a little too much wine and needs to sleep it off,' Lucy said then, trying to play it down, as she took a twenty pound note from Debra's handbag and paid the girl, and saying goodbye as Sophie let herself out.

'Lucy?' Kiera said, sitting down on the chair opposite Lucy, and watching as Lucy turned her head towards her. Then narrowing her eyes as Lucy visibly flinched, realising too late her mistake. Though Lucy quickly tried to redeem herself, by pretending that she hadn't heard it.

'What's that?'

'She just called you Lucy!' Kiera said, not ready to let the comment go now that she'd seen the ashen look on Lucy's face.

'Are you sure?' Lucy laughed. 'That's not what I heard. No offence, Kiera, but haven't you also done the best part of two bottles tonight? I think you're hearing things,' Lucy said, putting on a fake cheery laugh as she shrugged Kiera's comment off. Praying that Kiera took what she said as true, that she'd be too drunk to question it.

'I dunno, maybe she did say Laura?' Kiera shrugged, realising that the wine was no longer agreeing with her now either. The room was starting to spin and she needed to go and lie down. 'Oh God, I don't feel too good…'

'Go home!' Lucy said, with a smile. 'Honestly, I can put sleeping beauty to bed and stay for a bit in case the boys wake up. I don't need to rush off home. My sitter is sleeping over. Saves her having to walk home on her own so late,' Lucy lied; there was no babysitter, there was no child.

'No!' Kiera said with a firm shake of the head. 'I may be drunk but I'm not completely off my head. I'll stay. Trust me, you do not want to be here on your own when Gerard gets home. He won't like you being here in his house. He doesn't even like me here,' Kiera slurred, keeping her voice down now as she looked over to where her friend lay, soundly asleep on the sofa. 'The man is a monster. 'Wow! I've never seen Debra so drunk before. Is she going to be okay?' Sophie said, eyeing Debra and letting her know just how much danger Debra was in. 'He's told her if she ever thinks about leaving her that he'll do it. Worse than that, he threatened the same of Mason and Logan too. You're lucky you got out while you could. Not everyone can.'

Lucy nodded sadly in agreement.

'I think Debra felt sorry for me,' Lucy said. 'Because by the sounds of it, she's in a pretty similar boat with Gerard.'

Kiera got it then, what Debra could see in the girl. After spending the evening with Laura, she realised that she'd been too quick to judge her. She was a nice girl. And maybe that was exactly it. Maybe Debra needed someone around her who had been in the same situation as she was in, and who'd managed to get out.

'Listen, I'm sorry about being a bit of a cow earlier.'

Lucy laughed then and shook her head.

'You weren't a cow. You were just looking out for your mate,' she said dismissively, not letting Kiera say anything more on the matter. She knew that after tonight they'd be fine. That Kiera would accept her. It was mission accomplished as far as she was concerned.

'Oh, God! I've just remembered, Maisie's got ballet first thing. God, why do we do this to ourselves?'

Kiera looked up at the clock on the wall.

'Right then, come on, help me get her into bed, and then you get yourself off home,' Lucy said, this time not taking no for an answer. 'The second Gerard walks through the door, I'll leave.'

Feeling too sick and tired to argue, Kiera nodded in agreement before standing up and doing as Lucy asked.

'Right I'll grab her arms, you get her legs. Hopefully, we can make it to the bedroom.'

Placing Debra down on the bed, Lucy walked Kiera to the front door.

'Thanks for tonight,' Kiera said sincerely. 'I know she's in a bit of a state now, but it's been a long time since I've seen Debra let her hair down like that.'

'Well, that was down to both of us,' Lucy said with a smile, before they both said good night, and Lucy shut the front door.

She was standing in Gerard Jennings's hallway. In Gerard Jennings's home. This was really happening. She'd made it this far. Now all she had to do was play her role convincingly and make sure that she didn't get caught out in the process.

*

'I want my mummy!' Logan cried, bristling at the sight of the stranger sitting in his lounge.

'You must be Logan? It's okay, darling, I'm a friend of your mummy. My name is L-Laura,' Lucy said, eyeing the small child and guessing that he was the youngest of the two children, as she tried to console him. 'Mummy's in bed asleep, as she's ever so tired. Do you want me to show you?'

Logan nodded, allowing Lucy to hold his hand and lead him into Debra's bedroom.

'She's fast asleep, isn't she?' Lucy whispered to the little boy as they both stared at Debra sprawled out on the bed, gently snoring.

'How about I make you a nice glass of warm milk and we go back to bed? We can see mummy in the morning,' Lucy said, seeing Logan shiver as he was out of his own bed, his tears subsiding now that he'd seen that his mummy was safe. Lucy wondered just how much the two boys had suffered this week, following Debra's attack. It clearly played on their minds. Logan was only three years old, yet he wouldn't have settled tonight unless he'd known his mummy was okay. Leading the boy into the kitchen, Lucy warmed some milk up in the microwave before taking him back to bed.

'Here you go, darling,' she said now, her voice a mere whisper, as she tucked Logan in and gave him the cup to sip from as she looked over to the older child, Mason's bed and saw him sleeping soundly.

'Will you read me a story, Laura?' Logan said, passing her the cup back before snuggling back down in his bed.

'Course I will, sweetheart.' The child was barely able to keep his eyes open as it was. She knew it wouldn't take long until he fell back to sleep. And she'd almost finished reading the first page when she heard drunken voices and the sound of the front door close loudly.

Logan opened his eyes and sat back up in the bed, a worried look on his face which said it all.

'Daddy's back.'

Making her way to the kitchen with Logan in her arms, Lucy braced herself to speak to Gerard directly. But to admit that she was more than a little anxious right now was an understatement. Reaching the door, she saw it was closed and she could hear two voices on the other side. Placing her fingers on her lips to tell Logan to stay quiet she listened, panicking for a few seconds that it might be Holder. Then her cover would be blown completely. She didn't have to wait long to realise that the only two voices she could hear were Gerard's and Paul's. She recognised the same angry tones she'd heard earlier. They were talking about the murder. Lucy thought for a few seconds that it was about Jamie Nash. Only she heard Gerard say Bobbie Carter's name.

Bingo, she had him.

Getting her phone out, Lucy was just about to press record and try and tape the conversation when the kitchen door opened abruptly, causing her to drop her phone.

'Who the fuck are you?' Gerard asked, eyeing the woman standing in his hallway, holding his son.

'Sorry, er, I'm Laura,' Lucy said, handing Logan over to Gerard before swooping down and retrieving her phone from where it lay on the hallway floor. 'I'm a friend of Debs. Debra's,' she stuttered nervously as Gerard's eyes burned through her. *Get it together, Lucy! You've come this far!*

'She's in a bad way, I'm afraid. I had to put her to bed. And this one woke up wanting his mummy.' Lucy smiled at Logan now, glad when the child smiled back calmly, confirming her story was in fact true.

'And now that you're home, I should get back home too. Can you tell Debra that I said thanks for tonight?' Lucy said, trying to hold herself together and steady her heartbeat as she spoke, putting on the act of her life, because she knew that if Gerard suspected her even for so much as a second it would be game over. Then, as an afterthought, she added, 'And happy birthday once again. I hope you had a good night.'

Gerard watched as Lucy left, closing the front door after her. Then he turned back to Paul and raised his eyebrows suspiciously.

'You know her?' He'd seen her talking to Debra in the pub, and assumed she was a mate, but she wasn't a mate that he'd ever seen at the flat. And Gerard would remember if he had. The girl looked the type he'd remember.

'She's one of the mothers from the nursery apparently.' Paul shrugged his shoulders, not really interested in pandering to Gerard and his usual paranoia that everyone in the world was against him and secretly out to get him. 'Your little mate Danny's mum, isn't she, Logan?'

But then Logan shook his head, unsure what Paul was talking about.

'You know. Danny from nursery? Your friend?'

'I don't have a friend called Danny,' the small boy said, with a yawn, shivering now with the cold. He wanted to go back to bed. 'My friends are Blake and Harrison,' he said, then sensed his father stiffen at his reply and instantly realised that he'd said something wrong. His daddy seemed angry.

'Does that lady go to your school, Logan? Have you seen her speaking to Mummy? Do you know her?'

'I didn't see her before; she made me some warm milk when I crieded,' Logan said, worried that his daddy thought he might be telling lies. He'd done something to make his daddy mad now, only Logan didn't know what. 'She was nice to me. She read me a story,' he said, sobbing again now. 'I want to go back to bed. I want Mummy.'

'Come on, mate!' Paul said then, holding out his arms and hoping that Gerard would let him take him. Not wanting to see the poor kid get upset.

'She was snooping,' Gerard said, with certainty, preoccupied with his thoughts as he handed the child over. 'When I opened the kitchen door just then, she was standing there listening in to what we were saying.' Gerard narrowed his eyes. 'She was doing it at the pub too.' He remembered the redhead that had been standing behind them at the bar for ages waiting to be served.

'I'm going to put this one back to bed,' Paul said, sensing Gerard's shift in mood now too, and not wanting to see Logan upset. They'd carry on this conversation when the child was tucked up back in his bed.

Only when Paul came back a few minutes later to finish the conversation where they'd left off, Gerard was gone.

# CHAPTER THIRTY-ONE

Lucy was shaking, she realised, quickening her pace as she made her way back through the grounds of the estate. And it wasn't from the cold night air that whipped wildly around, it was from the terror that she'd felt inside of her at having to stand in front of Gerard Jennings, look him in the eyes and barefaced lie. She'd come so close to completely blowing her cover tonight. She winced at the memory of Gerard opening the kitchen door and almost catching her recording their conversation with her phone. What would have happened to her then? Would he have caved her head in, just as he had with Jamie Nash? Would she have ended up in the Thames just like Bobbie Carter? She shuddered again at the thought and felt another wave of nausea sweep over her.

She'd known that going undercover posed a huge risk when she'd agreed to it, but it wasn't until tonight, when she'd heard Gerard talk so flippantly, so casually about killing a seventeen-year-old boy, that she'd realised just how dangerous and unhinged the man actually was. Though she guessed now she'd seen first-hand that Holder was working for Gerard on the sly, that he was their weak link, she knew that tonight had been her only chance to get anything on the man. As much as DC Holder had pissed her off when she'd first moved over to CID, and sometimes acted as if he was put out by her presence, she'd actually quite liked him. How had she got him so wrong?

Double-crossing them all by feeding Gerard with information behind his colleagues' backs?

DS Morgan would be just as disgusted and disappointed as she was. Tonight had been full of revelations, and none of them had been good. DS Morgan would pull her from the Op once she told him. And rightly so. They had too much at stake to carry on. She wasn't only thinking of herself. She was thinking of Debra and her boys too. Lucy shook her head.

Pulling her jacket up around her ears to keep the cold chill from her neck, she couldn't help but give a tiny smile at the gesture, despite her fractious mood. It was a die-hard habit her nan had ingrained in her when Lucy had been small. She could still hear Winnie's voice inside her head.

*Wrap up, Lucy. Jesus girl, it's so cold out there the wind could cut you in half, and then quarters.*

Her nan's funny sayings always made Lucy smile. Even while some of them had sounded like complete and utter nonsense, Lucy had always found a strange sense of comfort in them. She missed her nan so much. More so tonight, when she knew that she was going home to an empty house, instead of a friendly face and a much-needed chat.

She missed the way that things used to be, when her nan was well. Because since she was just five, Winnie had been like a mother to Lucy. She'd brought her up and Lucy had fond memories of them at home together eating a meal that her nan had cooked. Boiled bacon, cabbage and spuds. The times that Lucy had moaned about her food! The irony was she'd give anything to have her nan cook it for her now, before they'd both snuggle up and watch a movie. It was never long until Lucy lost her patience with her nan, because Winnie always managed to talk her way through every film they watched, guessing the next line or the main plot, or telling

Lucy some useless bit of gossip she'd read or heard about one of the actors. She smiled again, her thoughts a welcome distraction as she made her way through the dimly lit row of garages.

Everything used to feel so much easier when she was younger. Sometimes now she felt as if she had the whole world on her shoulders. Hearing a can scrape across the pathway behind her, Lucy stopped dead before turning, her eyes fixed on the pathway that she'd just walked down, convinced that she'd just heard someone walking behind her. But there was nobody there.

Hearing the noise again, she breathed a sigh of relief as she watched an empty can roll on the floor as the wind took it. She rolled her eyes. She'd scared herself over some litter.

Though it paid to be alert, she reasoned, keeping her wits about her as she continued making her way towards the alleyway at the end of the garages. The truth was, she was never really off duty. Because she never really felt safe. Not just now, being undercover. But every day of her normal life too. She wondered sometimes if everyone felt like that? If it was a sign of the times that you had to always look over your shoulder, and always be slightly suspicious? Or was she like that, more so, because of what had happened to her mum?

She figured that it was a combination of the two. And she couldn't help but feel a flurry of relief when she made her way through the other end of the alleyway and out on to her nan's street.

It was funny really, how the small residential street was only a few streets away from the Griffin Estate, but it instantly felt like a world away. She saw her nan's house up ahead, lit up by streetlights. Exhausted now from the night's events, she was looking forward to getting into bed tonight and trying to get some sleep. Try being the operative word. She was already dreading her breakfast meeting with DS Morgan in the morning. She'd already texted him to tell him that she was on her way home and that she'd give him a full breakdown of her evening's findings tomorrow. He wasn't going to be happy at all with what she had to tell him. Twisting the key in the lock of the door, Lucy went inside. Completely unaware that someone had been watching her from the shadows the whole way home.

# CHAPTER THIRTY-TWO

'All right, all right! I'm coming. For Christ's sake,' Ben Holder shouted, padding down the stairs, dressed in only his boxer shorts, still half asleep.

He felt as if he'd only just closed his eyes when the loud banging from the front door had woken him up. Which in a way was a godsend because he was on earlier today and it was almost six a.m. He was due on shift in less than an hour and couldn't afford to be late. Though after last night's antics he was currently nursing the mother of all hangovers, and he'd give his left testicle right now to just be able to crawl back into bed and stay there all day.

He just wanted the banging to stop. The noise was so loud it felt as if it was penetrating his brain. But he was also filled with trepidation at who was standing on the other side of the door. Because whoever they were sounded thoroughly pissed off and they clearly had no intention of going away anytime soon.

'Gerard?' Ben exclaimed, pulling the door open and eyeing the man as if he was imagining him. The last person that he'd expected to see standing on his doorstep this morning, or any morning in fact, was Gerard Jennings. And the man looked extremely pissed off.

'Paul! What's up, mate? I wasn't expecting you,' Ben said, trying to conceal the small sigh of relief that escaped him as he spotted Paul standing close behind Gerard.

Going by the thunderous expression on Gerard's face, something was clearly up, but at least if Paul was here, it meant that Gerard would be kept under some kind of control.

'Come on in,' Ben muttered sarcastically under his breath, as Gerard did exactly that and charged into his flat without waiting for his invite. Paul followed closely behind.

Closing the front door behind them, Ben cleared his throat, buying himself some time to work out what was going on as he tried to mask the fear that rapidly spread through him. Convinced that he hadn't purposely pissed the man off in any way.

He tried his hardest to recall what had happened last night. But thanks to the copious amount of shots that Gerard had insisted he neck, his memory was vague and his head was still pounding. He hadn't intended to get so drunk at the party, he'd wanted to keep his wits about him. He hadn't been working with Paul and Gerard for that long, but it was still long enough to know that he had to keep his guard up around the men. Gerard was volatile. One wrong word, one wrong look and the man would come down on you like a tonne of bricks. But equally Ben hadn't wanted to piss him off. It had been Gerard's birthday and he wanted all his men to celebrate the occasion properly with him. Despite Ben's protests at having work today, Gerard had a persuasive way about him, and singling Ben out – purposely because he was a copper no doubt. Gerard had been showing off to his men, that he could do and say what he liked to him – so much so that they'd all laughed as if their mission had been accomplished when Ben had skulked off to be violently sick in the pub toilets. And come to think of it now, he had no recollection of how he got home. Had he said or done something he shouldn't have? Something that would royally piss Gerard off enough for the man to turn up at his flat first thing the very next morning?

'We've got a problem?' Gerard said, clearly riled about something. 'I think there's a grass amongst us.'

'A grass?' Holder said, rubbing his forehead trying to make sense of Gerard's fury.

'Yeah! Someone is digging around in my shit who shouldn't be and I want to know why?'

'Who?'

'Some nosey cow going by the name of Laura, supposedly. She was snooping around my flat last night and I caught her red-handed trying to listen in to one of our conversations. She fed me some bullshit story about her living over on Jubilee Gardens. So when she left, I followed her home. It pays to question everything and everyone, doesn't it? And guess what, my instincts were right and the bitch was lying. She lives the other side of the Griffin Estate on West Street. I need you to run a check on an address for me so I can find out who she really is.'

"Sure. Of course. I can do that,' Holder said relieved that he wasn't the one on the receiving end of Gerard's vicious temper. He'd happily oblige if it meant he was to remain in the man's good books.

'I'll have to go to the station to get access to the information though. All our searches are automatically logged on the system but I'm sure that I can think of something that won't make anyone suspicious. What's the address?'

'Number twelve West Street.'

'Are you sure?' Holder said, narrowing his eyes at the familiar address without thinking about the repercussions of his initial reaction. He wasn't a hundred per cent on form yet due to the alcohol that was still playing havoc in his system. By the time he'd realised his mistake in not playing his reaction down, it was too late.

'Why? Do you know it?' Gerard said, suspicious now that Holder had recognised the address and had immediately started acting cagey.

'No, I mean... I'm not sure...' Ben started backtracking. Desperately trying to talk his way out of an awkward situation before he made things even worse. Though his sentence was cut short as Gerard grabbed him roughly by the scruff of his neck and launched the man along the hallway.

Looming over him as he landed in a heap on the wooden flooring, before grabbing him again, this time by a fist full of his hair as he dragged him roughly back on to his feet again.

'What do you mean you're not sure? Is the address familiar to you or not? And don't fucking lie to me, Holder. I'm not in the fucking mood,' Gerard said, his tone dripping with menace.

'Look, Gerard, I don't know what the fuck's going on, but there must be some kind of a mistake.' Ben screamed out in pain, holding his hands up and begging Gerard to release him from his hold. Which the man did, leaving Ben's scalp burning from where Gerard had ripped away a patch of his hair.

'You said the woman's name is Laura, only, one of my colleagues lives at that address. I had to drop a file off to her after my shift one day. But it's not Laura, her name is Lucy. Lucy Murphy.'

'One of your lot?' Gerard eyed Holder then, waiting for him to enlighten him some more.

'Yeah. She joined CID about three months ago. She lives with her nan, though I think the old girl is in a nursing home now. It can't be Lucy. Why would she be in your flat? How did she get in?' Holder said, convinced that this was just one big misunderstanding.

Convinced that there would be some kind of explanation as to prove Lucy's innocent in all of this, Holder was certain there was no way that Lucy would have been anywhere near Gerard Jennings, let alone inside his flat.

'She was at the party last night. A mate of Debra's supposedly. The devious bitch is obviously playing her too.'

'She was at the party? Shit! What if she saw me? She'll know that I've been working for you both.' Holder had spent months trying to cover his tracks and stay off everyone's radar as he went back and forth between the force and Gerard Jennings.

And one drunken night of letting his guard down could have completely blown everything.

'You really expect me to believe that you didn't know? Bull! Are you in on this too? Pretending to be working from me, but really you and your lot are trying to properly stitch me up? Don't play fucking stupid with me, Holder. Now we can do this the hard way or the easy way. But you are going to tell me everything you know,' Gerard said, pulling a hammer out from the inside of his coat pocket.

'Woah! What the fuck, Gerard?' Holder said, seeing the weapon and recognising the intent in Gerard's glare. The man would use it on him, he was certain of that.

'Gerard. We said we were just going to have a chat,' Paul said, stepping forward and shooting a warning look to his mate. This time he wasn't willing to just stand back and let Gerard loose with a hammer. Especially not on a copper.

They'd end up living out the rest of their days behind bars, and Paul wasn't willing to have his own life gambled away just because of Gerard's vicious temper and him acting out on a whim.

'A chat? What's a chat going to do, huh? We should have been having a chat before all of this, shouldn't we? The prick is on our payroll to feed us with intelligence? Well where's the fucking heads-up that one of your coppers is undercover and spying on me? That she's at my fucking birthday party. And in my fucking house, with my fucking wife!' Gerard bellowed now. Incensed at the liberties the police were taking in order to get to him. They'd stop at nothing to stitch him up for anything they could pin on him. Well Gerard had no intention of going down without a fight.

'You have my word, Gerard. This is all news to me. I don't know what you're talking about,' Holder said, his eyes darting from Gerard's to Paul's in a bid to get the two men to believe him. 'If Lucy saw me last night then this will be over for me. I'll lose everything. Fuck!' It was Holder's turn to show his angst now, as he began pacing the flat. Thinking out loud as he walked frantically back and forth trying to work out what he should do. Thinking back then to all of Lucy and Morgan's cosy, little meetings lately. And the stilted conversation that he'd had with Lucy in the office the other day.

'Shit!' Holder said. 'They are purposely keeping me out of the loop on this one. I thought something was up, the other day, when Debra was pulled in for drink driving. I questioned why my sergeant and DC Murphy were in the interview room with her. CID don't get involved with drink driving offences usually. But Lucy had fed me some story about them having to help smooth things over, because Debra was threatening to kick off, claimed the police were harassing her.'

'They were harassing her. She hadn't been drinking. Of course she hadn't.' Gerard shrugged. 'Your lots' sole purpose lately is to make my life as difficult as possible. First you force me to shut everything down, then you start spying on me, and then, to top it all off, you humiliate my wife while she's on the school run,' Gerard spat, before screwing his face up then at the realisation that if what Holder was saying was true, Lucy had been in the interview room with Debra the other day. Which meant Debra knew that she was a copper. She must be part of all of this too.

Holder watched as Gerard put the hammer back in his pocket, a look of genuine shock flashing across his face that his wife would stoop so low as to work with the police to try and destroy him.

'Debra was in on this all along,' he said. 'The realisation of his wife's betrayal almost made him doubt the words as they left his mouth. 'Lucy wasn't having her over. She was working with Debra. That lying conniving wife of mine tried to set me up!'

# CHAPTER THIRTY-THREE

Walking up the steps of the Riverview coffee shop on Lambeth Pier, Lucy spotted DS Morgan already sitting waiting for her at a table just to the right of the entrance, taking in the stunning views of the Thames as he nursed the cup of coffee in front of him.

'I'll have a black coffee, please. Two sugars.' Lucy smiled politely at the passing waitress before greeting her sergeant and sitting down opposite him.

'Heavy night?' Morgan said, eyeing his young colleague dubiously. Lucy looked pale and there were dark circles under her eyes. 'You look as if you haven't slept a wink.'

'I haven't,' Lucy said with a shrug. 'And I can't even go back to bed today, I'm picking up Nan shortly. She's home with me for the night. Still, I'm not going to complain. I miss her so much when she's not at home.' Lucy smiled. 'Wow, this place is a gem! London's best kept secret. I've never even heard of it.' She eyed the breathtaking scenic view of the Thames that stretched out from either side of the small bohemian coffee shop perched in the prime location of the Embankment, overlooking the Palace of Westminster. The place was a tourist trap, bustling with customers, but she guessed that was exactly why DS Morgan had suggested meeting here today in the first place. So that they could blend in amongst the crowds, far away from any prying eyes and ears of people they might know, and more importantly, well away from their colleagues back at the station. Because DS

Morgan knew from Lucy's text message he'd received last night that whatever Lucy had to report back to him today was delicate and the information had to be treated as such.

'So, how did it go last night?'

'I'm not going to lie, Sarge, it was awful,' Lucy said honestly. 'I nearly lost my nerve halfway through the evening. The place was packed and Gerard and his mates were so loud and raucous, I was terrified that someone would recognise me. Despite the new hair!'

As if only just noting the short red style, DS Morgan smiled. 'It suits you.'

Lucy rolled her eyes, though she knew that the sacrifice of a new hairstyle was a small price to pay if it meant keeping her identity unknown.

'One of Debra's mates gave me a hard time to start off with, quizzing me on where I've come from and asking a lot of questions. I got the impression that she didn't believe me, and it just set me on edge. I felt out of my depth.'

DS Morgan nodded, before taking a sip of his coffee. 'I was worried that that might be the case.' He had been anxious that Lucy might be jumping into something with both feet tied, not knowing exactly what she was really dealing with here. DS Morgan had taken a huge risk agreeing to let the operation go ahead. It had been a big ask and one that DS Morgan would never have even entertained, except that Lucy had been so insistent that she could pull off going undercover. He knew that she wanted to prove herself and to show him that she could do this, so he had given her the chance. Now though, he was wondering if he'd been right to be cautious all along.

'If you're not comfortable we can pull you from the Op? It would be damage limitation. I don't want you to feel as if you are in immediate danger either. If you think it's too dangerous, we'll cut our losses and stop.' Morgan paused as the waitress came over and placed the coffee down in front of Lucy.

'Can I get you both anything to eat? English Breakfast? Pastries?'

Lucy shook her head, unable to stomach anything other than coffee this morning. She waited until the waitress had walked off before she replied to Morgan.

'I think you're probably going to have to pull me anyway, Sarge,' Lucy said reluctantly, taking a big swig of her coffee, hoping a hit of caffeine would give her some much-needed energy after her sleepless night last night. 'I overheard a conversation between Gerard Jennings and Paul Denman at the bar last night about a seventeen-year-old called Jamie Nash. Gerard's men have put the word out that the boy's done a runner, so I doubt he's even been reported as missing. But he's dead, Sarge. Jennings killed him. I heard Paul Denman having a go at Jennings about it. Jennings acted alone by the sounds of it.' Lucy frowned. 'I also heard Jennings mention Bobbie Carter's name, though I only caught a snippet of the conversation, because I didn't want to draw any attention to myself.' She winced, recalling how she'd nearly blown her cover at the end of the night, when Gerard had almost caught her listening in on his conversation. She'd save that snippet for her boss for another time. 'But there's something else, Sarge!'

'Worse than a possible murder?' Morgan said, sensing the apprehension in Lucy's voice and wondering where she was going with this.

'Do you remember when Debra told us that she thought Gerard might have some of our officers working for him?'

DS Morgan raised his eyebrows. He could sense by Lucy's tone that he wasn't going to like what she was about to say one bit.

'I saw an officer in the bar last night, talking with Gerard and Paul. They looked as if they were having a pretty intense conversation and I saw the three of them go outside.' Lucy paused, not wanting to be the one to break this news to her boss. She was still trying to get her own head around the revelation herself. 'It turns out that Gerard's contact is closer to home than we realised, Sarge. It's DC Ben Holder.'

'DC Holder? Are you sure?' Morgan repeated, shifting uncomfortably in his chair, though he knew that Lucy wouldn't make that kind of accusation unless she was certain.

'He didn't see me; I got out of there pronto,' Lucy said with certainty, knowing what her boss was going to say next. That her position might have been compromised. That Gerard Jennings might already be on to her.

Morgan nodded, relieved to hear that at least. Though the last thing he'd expected to hear today was that one of his own trusted team was working on the sly for Gerard Jennings and feeding the man information. This changed everything. Their unit was compromised. Lucy was compromised. They couldn't carry on with their undercover operation.

# CHAPTER THIRTY-FOUR

'Come in, Lucy. I thought we could have a little chat before you take your nan home.' Nurse Hamilton smiled brightly at the young woman, leading her into the office.

'Is everything okay?' Lucy asked, immediately suspecting that her nan had been causing more trouble amongst the other residents again.

'Yes and no,' Nurse Hamilton said, offering Lucy a seat. 'Your nan has been suffering from night terrors. I wasn't sure if she did when she was at home, but I think perhaps with this being such a big change for her, staying here overnight sometimes, that it has magnified them.'

'Yeah, she sometimes has them. Only I didn't realise they were affecting her so much,' Lucy said, trying to take in what the nurse was telling her and feeling heartbroken that her nan was suffering, and that the transition to staying here more permanently wasn't going as smoothly as she'd hoped it would. 'Are they getting worse do you think?' she asked, knowing that she was plagued with nightmares herself. She had been all her life, since her mother had been killed, but she'd never really discussed them with anyone else. She'd just learned to live with them.

Only the one she'd had the other night was much more than just a bad dream.

She'd recalled her mother's murderer's face.

And she still didn't know what to do about it. If there was anything she could do about it?

'I don't want you to worry about it,' the nurse continued, interrupting Lucy's train of thought. 'It's perfectly normal and actually extremely common, especially with the big changes moving into a residential home can bring. And trust me, I've seen much worse than what your nan's experiencing.' Nurse Hamilton paused as if trying to find the right words before she continued. 'A few nights ago, she had a bad dream about your mum. She woke up very distressed saying that your mum was trapped. And last night I found her wandering the corridor, looking for help. Which isn't that strange in itself – it's normal for patients to revert back to childhood times, wanting their parents or to be back in their childhood home. They remember the feeling of safety it brought them. And that's what they crave. A safe place, so they go looking for one.' She paused again, this time for a little longer, clearly trying to broach the subject as gently and tactfully as she could.

'But last night, your nan was in a really bad way. She was convinced that there had been a man in her room. Obviously, there hadn't been. We have a locked door policy here at Treetops. Only staff hold the skeleton keys to the rooms, and the residents only have their own. As you know, other patients can't gain access once the bedroom doors are closed. So there's no way anyone could get in. But I thought I better bring it to your attention so that you can keep an eye on her once you get her back home.'

'Thank you,' Lucy said feeling sad then, aware that Winnie had a tendency to go off wandering when her mind started playing tricks on her. Lucy couldn't even begin to imagine the confusion and distress she felt when the same feelings took her in the middle of the night, when everything felt so much more sinister and magnified.

'Your nan was very distressed for a long time afterwards, but I managed to calm her down and sat with her for a while until she went back to sleep.'

'Do you think it's all too soon for her or too quick?' Lucy said, feeling wracked with guilt. 'Maybe this wasn't the right thing to do? She might be better off at home with me? Full-time.'

'No, Lucy. It is the right thing. She'll never be ready. And you'll never be ready. It's not too soon. Other than the nightmares, she's doing really well. She's interacting with the other residents and she's developing her own routine. And sure, she's having some teething problems, but that's to be expected. It's a big change for you all.'

Lucy nodded then, just glad that Nurse Hamilton had stayed with her until she'd gone back to sleep. That made her feel a little better. To know that her nan wasn't left on her own to just get on with it. She just wished that it wasn't so difficult. That just for once things would slot into place.

'So do you think it's a good idea for me to take her home with me for the night still? Or should I leave her here?' Lucy said, not wanting to confuse her nan any further.

'Take her home, Lucy. Though she could probably do with a little afternoon nap at some point. She's exhausted. So she may be very tired and irritable today. We can assess the situation as we go, but I think a day at home with her granddaughter will be just the tonic your nan needs. I just wanted you to be aware of the situation so that you can keep an eye on her while she's back in your care.' The nurse stood back up and showed Lucy out of the office.

# CHAPTER THIRTY-FIVE

'It's nice to be home again, hey, Nan!' Lucy said, placing a hot cup of tea down on the table in front of her nan, before busying herself making the woman some breakfast. 'How do you fancy your eggs, scrambled or fried?'

'Oh I'm not really that hungry, Lucy. Scrambled I guess,' Winnie said, casting another odd glance Lucy's way. Which she'd been doing from the moment that Lucy had picked her up from Treetops Care Home and helped her into the car. 'Have you done something different to yourself, Lucy? You look... strange.'

'Oh, blimey! Thanks, Nan.' Lucy laughed. 'It's my hair. You remember when you came home for a few hours on Friday. You saw it then.'

'Ohh I don't like it, Lucy. It makes you look like one of those lesbians from the TV...'

'I know, Nan! You already said,' Lucy said, whisking the egg mixture faster in the frying pan as she tried her hardest to hold her tongue.

'Still, it will grow back, won't it?' Winnie said, oblivious to her bluntness or of any offence she may have caused. 'Or worst case, you can wear a hat, or borrow one of my lovely silk scarves.' Winnie beamed at her granddaughter then, as if suddenly seeing her before her.

'I love you my Lucy-loo. You know that, don't you?'

'Ahh, of course I do, Nan. And I love you, too,' Lucy said, making her way around the breakfast bar and wrapping her arms around her little old nan. The frailty of the woman in her arms instantly shocked her. She felt so tiny and vulnerable. It pained Lucy so much that in such a short space of time, her nan had morphed into a shadow of the fiery strong woman she had been before.

It was Lucy's time to care for her nan now. The roles had reversed somehow, almost overnight.

'Right, now. Let's get some food into you,' Lucy said, aware that she didn't want to get upset in front of her nan and confuse the woman further. She put on a fake grin. 'If we're going to be spending an action-packed day together, were going to need all our energy,' she said, steering herself back around the counter to the cooker, dishing the eggs onto a plate and adding a slice of toast that had just popped up from the toaster. Lucy placed the plate down in front of the woman. 'I thought we could take a drive down to Brighton and sit on the beach together, Nan. Like we used to do, years ago when I was little. We can get some of those donuts that you like?'

'Oh I don't think I'm fit for much action today, Lucy,' Winnie said honestly as she yawned for what felt like the hundredth time today.

'You not been sleeping too well, Nan?' Though Lucy knew that was an understatement.

She'd been shocked at how exhausted her nan looked when she'd first set eyes on her this morning. Her skin looked blotchy and thin and her eyes dark and sunken. The sparkle that had once been there, gone.

'Nurse Hamilton told me you've been having really bad nightmares, Nan. That they've made you sleepwalk.'

'Nightmares? Have I been having nightmares? Oh, I don't remember,' Winnie said, a pained look on her face as she tried so hard to focus on her thoughts.

'Nurse Hamilton said that you dreamt about Mum? That you were trying to help her, Nan. And the other night you thought there was a man in your room?'

'Oh, did I? I can't recall… Oh, yes. I think I do. But I don't remember the dream only that Nurse Hamilton came in and brought me a nice cup of tea.'

'Well, if you have any nightmares again, you just have to try really hard to remember, Nan, they're not real. They can't hurt you. They are only bad dreams.'

'I don't want this, Lucy,' Winnie said, pushing the food around on the plate absently now, uninterested in eating it. Lucy could tell that her nan was having one of her bad days. That she was struggling more so than usual. Nurse Hamilton had been right about tiredness taking its toll on her.

'I know, Nan. Why don't you go and have a little nap, and instead of us going out later on, I'll see if Vivian fancies joining us. We can have afternoon tea in the garden?'

'Oh, that sounds lovely, Lucy,' Winnie said, smiling at last. Before giving in to yet another dramatic yawn. 'Yes, a nap would be nice.'

'Come on then, sleeping beauty, let's get you upstairs and into bed.' Lucy smiled, leading her nan out of the room. She'd give Vivian a call and see if she was free, and then maybe she'd get a quick nap while her nan slept too. Winnie had only been home for less than an hour and already Lucy felt exhausted trying to keep up with her. She had a feeling she was going to need all the energy she could get today.

# CHAPTER THIRTY-SIX

She thought she was dreaming. She could hear Gerard's voice roaring at her, shouting her name angrily, the sound pulling her from her blurry drink-hazed sleep. The pain in her head came quickly then. *Slap.* She was wide awake. Gerard was standing over her, a handful of hair wrapped around his fist as he dragged her from the bed, ripping a chunk of it from her scalp as he did so.

'Gerard! Stop! What's going on? What's happening?' Debra screeched, unable to tolerate the pain as he slammed her down on the floor, her body still not fully recovered from the last beating the man dished out to her.

'Are you going to tell me about your mate then?' Gerard said, glaring at her furiously.

'My mate?' Debra said, cowering on the bedroom floor now. 'Who? Laura?' Though even as she said Laura's name she knew that the game was up. That Gerard knew. She desperately tried to rack her mind and remember what had happened last night at Gerard's party. How could he know? How did he find out?

The night was a blur and she couldn't even remember how she got home, let alone getting into bed. She had no recollection of when she last saw Lucy. She didn't have time to think of anything smart to say. Her head was too fuzzy and pounding too hard to think anyway. All she could do was lie in a bid to buy herself some time, and pray that she could somehow get away with it. Because if Gerard knew that she'd set him up, he'd kill her. And he'd kill Mason and Logan.

'Or Lucy! Isn't that the real name she fucking goes by?!'
Gerard knew.

'Lucy? What are you talking about?' Debra said, feeling her heartbeat quicken. 'Her name's Laura, and I don't know where she is. She must have left. And so did Kiera.'

'She's a fucking copper!' Gerard roared, his temper getting the better of him, grabbing Debra by a chunk of her hair again and hoisting her up onto her feet. He dragged her out into the lounge and threw her roughly down on to the sofa before pacing the room, his veins surging from the rush of coke he'd just snorted, his temper colossal as he continued to bellow at her loudly, calling her every name under the sun and telling her what he was going to do to her.

Debra thought of her boys. Cowering in their bedroom as she knew they would be. Because Gerard's outburst would have woken them by now. He would have woken half the Griffin Estate. Mason and Logan would be terrified. She had to try and calm him down.

'Gerard, I swear on the boys' lives, I promise you, I don't know what the fuck you're talking about.'

They were only words she told herself. Empty words that meant nothing, but she said them if it meant that she could guarantee her sons' safety. Gerard knew she'd never swear on her boys' lives and lie, and right now, she had no other option. She had to make him believe her, any way that she could.

'How do you know her then?' Gerard said, wanting Debra to dig herself into a deeper hole. She was lying to him. There would be no coming back from this now.

'From the nursery.' She spotted the vein in Gerard's temple pulse as he locked his jaw. A tell-tale sign that he'd spotted her lie. She quickly tried to cover her tracks, wondering if this was how he found out. Did Logan say something? Had Gerard been quizzing him?

'Her son has got special needs. He has a different teacher to Logan.' She shrugged, trying to appear casual though inside her anxiety was building rapidly and she was acutely aware of how much danger she was in. If Gerard worked out that she was lying, he'd kill her. 'I don't really know her that well. She's only just moved around here. She's trying to make a break from her ex.' Debra shook her head, doing her best impression of looking completely perplexed at what was going on. Which was partly how she really felt.

'Look. If you don't believe me. See for yourself,' Debra said scrambling around inside her purse for her mobile before passing it over, safe in the knowledge that Lucy's new number was only ever to be used strictly in character.

Lucy had insisted upon that, so that if Gerard ever got suspicious and looked, it would only clarify their cover story.

Gerard scrolled to the messages. A couple of short conversations about school, and the party last night. Nothing revealing. No sign of foul play. He nodded, tucking her phone into his trousers pocket for safe keeping.

Then he smiled as she breathed a sigh of relief. Physically relaxing then as she mistakenly thought Gerard believed her. Only he was about to wipe the smile from her face.

Because he still didn't believe her.

'If you don't know her that well, why did you invite her last night?' Gerard demanded.

'I felt sorry for her. She doesn't know anyone around here. I don't understand what's going on, Gerard? Why did you call her Lucy? What's going on?' Debra rubbed her head. Instantly sober now, every part of her body was on alert. She had to stay focused. Guarded. She needed to stay in role.

'Because I fucking followed her home last night. I caught her out last night trying to listen in on my conversation with

Paul. She was loitering around in the hallway with Logan. He woke up, snivelling about something. While you were lying in your pit, passed out drunk,' Gerard sneered, before Debra asked him, as he knew she would. 'He said he'd never seen her before last night and he didn't know her little boy. It didn't add up, so I followed her home. And I was right to be suspicious. She's a copper, Debra. She's undercover.'

'Oh my god,' Debra said, looking shocked, all the while holding Gerard's gaze as his dark brown eyes stared right through her. She knew that he was reading her body language, cross-examining her expression, looking for evidence of her lies. She wasn't going to give it to him.

Not if her life depended on it, which it very much did.

'Fuck!' he shouted, slamming his fist into the wall. 'She's played you good and proper Debra. Pretending to help you so that they can get to me. You stupid fucking cow. The police will say anything to make you believe them. You think that they won't take Mason and Logan away from you too, after all this? You've played right into their hands.' Gerard started pacing the room again then, incensed at the audacity of police that they thought they could impinge on his life in such a way. 'They're scum. The lowest of the low, using my kids and my wife to get to me,' he mumbled to himself, the coke heightening his paranoia as it always did.

Debra felt her chest constrict then, barely able to breathe as she second guessed herself.

Lucy wasn't like that. She'd told her that she'd help her and she'd meant it. Hadn't she?

'What did you tell her?' he said, stopping still in the middle of the room and scowling at his wife. Because Debra was an easy target. He'd ensured that himself by putting her in hospital and making her lose the baby. She had acted like she hated him the past few days since she'd been out. She would have given Lucy exactly what she wanted.

'She must have asked you about me?' Gerard said, standing over her once more and looking menacing.

'She didn't, you can ask Kiera. We only met up last night at the party. And we just had a laugh. Had a few drinks. She spoke about her life more than anything…' The alcohol she'd consumed was still clouding her brain. Her pounding head wasn't helping either. But she had to think quickly, to throw him off the track. She narrowed her eyes then as if the truth had suddenly dawned on her. 'Maybe that was her plan all along? To befriend me. That must have been what last night was all about. Talking all about herself, and her sob story about her ex, so that she could get me to trust her.'

'Stop lying! You kept our baby from me on purpose,' Gerard started. His voice steady now, calmer. So it seemed. 'And ever since you've come out of hospital, you've been different. Withdrawn. But I guess that's to be expected.' He'd gone too far this time, he figured. What with her losing the baby. He'd made her snap. 'I'm guessing that this is what you had planned all along?' Gerard laughed then, despite himself. Trust nobody. Not your mates, not your associates and certainly not your wife.

'Well, I told you what would happen if you ever went against me. If you betrayed me, Debra. And you have betrayed me. Now you're going to pay the price,' Gerard said then, when he saw the look of horror spread across her face as she realised that Gerard wasn't as gullible as she'd hoped he'd be.

That he was on to her. It was over.

'Now let's start this conversation again, shall we. From the beginning.'

# CHAPTER THIRTY-SEVEN

Waking, Winnie lay still in her bed. Someone was in the room with her; she could sense them. Behind her, standing by the bedroom door, watching her. She wasn't sure what woke her and alerted her to them being in the room, but she could feel the menace lingering in the air as she focused on the wall in front of her, trying to adjust her eyesight to the darkened room. She was too scared to look. Too terrified to even turn her head or sit up and switch the lamp on. Even if she were braver, her entire body had betrayed her and gone rigid with fear.

She could feel her heart pounding erratically inside her chest, and each tiny downy hair on her arms stand to attention; the surface of her skin prickled with goosebumps. She felt so paralysed with dread that she could barely breathe. She gulped down a lungful of air then, as she felt the surge of adrenaline rush around her body, heightening the eerie sensation that something rotten and evil was contained inside these four walls with her.

You're just dreaming, she told herself, desperate to coax herself back from her night terrors that she was currently trapped in. Desperate to convince herself that it was true, that that was all this was. Another bad nightmare again. She needed to wake up. Nurse Hamilton would be here soon, with her warm smile and her endless chatter. She would bring her some hot tea and they would sit together by the window and take in the view of the sunrise together, just as they always did when Winnie had one of her nightmares.

Only staring down at the duvet cover that wrapped around her body, she realised she wasn't at Treetops. She was back at home. With Lucy. And no matter how much she tried to convince herself that her nightmares weren't real, she knew deep down that this felt different. It wasn't like the bad dreams she'd endured that left her mind even more vague and fuzzy than she usually felt. This time she was wide awake and her fear was real. Winnie couldn't just lie here and hide from the demons that were tormenting her. She needed to face her fears and show her demons that she wasn't scared any more. That as long as they kept on coming for her, she'd keep fighting them off. She was Winnie Murphy. And despite her predicament of late, she was tough as old boots. She forced herself to turn her head.

She immediately regretted her actions as the confusion on her face quickly turned to utter horror, as she saw the man's silhouette taking up the whole of the closed door behind him, as a rare flash of light flooded into the room, as the curtains moved rhythmically in time with the midday breeze.

The window. That was how he'd got in, she realised, as she felt the cool rush of air all around her. That was what had woken her. The cooler temperature, laced with imminent danger.

'Who are you? What do you want?' Winnie managed to say through the darkness of the room, surprised that she'd even managed to find her own voice. She could feel the tears streaming down her face, and she was aware of what she'd been reduced to. A quivering wreck of a woman, alone and scared in her bed, at the mercy of this stranger who had somehow got into her room.

The man didn't answer. Instead he slowly drew his finger up to his mouth, and placed it on his lips, telling Winnie to stay quiet. She could see a flash of what looked like madness dance behind the man's eyes. And it was all she could do not to let out a scream.

# CHAPTER THIRTY-EIGHT

'Oh, Vivian! You shouldn't have,' Lucy said, leading Vivian through the house and into the kitchen.

'You might be right, Lucy. I can't see where I'm going,' Vivian joked, her arms laden with flowers and chocolates for Winnie.

'Seriously, Vivian. You spoil her. You know that, don't you? Just seeing you is enough! She loved your visits.'

'Oh, don't be silly. Besides, I like treating her. I know you shouldn't have favourite patients,' Vivian mocked a whisper now, 'but your nan is mine. Don't tell her that, though, she'll have me jumping through hoops for her if she realises I've got such a soft spot for her.'

Lucy couldn't help but laugh then. Vivian had only been in the house for less than two minutes and already she'd managed to lift Lucy's mood better than it had been all day.

'Oh, Vivian, how we miss you,' she said, giving the woman a hug.

Vivian could sense the emotion in Lucy's words. And she could tell by how tired Lucy looked that she was going through a hard time.

'Are you all right, my darling?' she said, stepping back and holding Lucy's arms so that she could take a good look at her, seeing the tears that threatened. Lucy didn't even need to speak. Vivian already had her answer.

'Oh, darling what's the matter? Is your nan okay? Are you okay? You look shattered,' Vivian said, immediately concerned.

'I'm fine now you're here.' Lucy could see by the stern look of disbelief on Vivian's face, that she didn't appreciate her playing down whatever it was that was troubling her. She wanted to know that they were both okay, and Lucy at least owed her some honesty.

'Actually, I'm not okay. Oh, Vivian. It's just everything. There's some stuff going on at work. It's complicated, but I'm taking a few days off,' Lucy said, knowing that it was never wise to discuss her cases, especially something as complex as this one, no matter how much she trusted Vivian. 'And while it's so lovely having Nan back home with me for the night, she's not been herself today at all. She's been having nightmares apparently. They found her wandering the corridors late one night, and then last night she was convinced that there was a man in her room.'

Seeing the horror on Vivian's face, she added: 'She is hallucinating. Nurse Hamilton thinks she might be suffering from night terrors. It's obviously unsettled her because she's barely made any sense today, and she hasn't wanted to speak to me about it. Every time I bring it up, she makes out that she can't really remember her bad dreams. Oh, what if I've made a mistake, Vivian? What if putting her in the home wasn't the right thing to do?'

'Lucy, you absolutely haven't made a mistake at all, darling. You just have to be patient with her. I know it's hard and I know how you struggled with the decision. But I have to say, I'm impressed with the place, she seems happy there and I think it will do her the world of good. And Nurse Hamilton has the patience of a saint. You need someone like that when you're dealing with your nan's condition.'

Lucy nodded. Deep down she knew that Vivian was right.

'And maybe she seems worse today because she's picking up on your mood? You look exhausted, Lucy. A few days off will do you the world of good. It will do you both the world of good.'

'You're right. I know. I am exhausted. Though I managed to have a quick power nap before you arrived,' Lucy said, instantly feeling better after Vivian's little pep talk. The woman always was the voice of reason when it came to her worrying about her nan. 'In fact, Nan's still in bed, but she'll kill me if I don't wake her and let her know you're here. She was so excited when I said I'd invite you over for afternoon tea. She insisted on using all her best china and a tablecloth. You'd honestly think she was expecting the queen,' Lucy said, rolling her eyes up playfully.

'Well, she's not a silly woman…' Vivian said, holding her hand up and gesturing a royal wave as if to claim her new title.

'Shall I go up and wake her?' Vivian asked.

'Yes, she'd love that.'

'Here, let me carry out some of the plates for you, first.' Beaming she eyed the plates of food that Lucy had gone to the trouble of preparing, as Lucy picked up a tray with the teapot and cups. 'Oh, I say!' Vivian giggled, putting on her best posh voice. 'Scones and cream, how rather splendid.'

'Only the best for Her Royal Highness Queen Vivian…' Lucy played along, leading the woman out into the back garden.

'I have to say, the house is awfully quiet; normally I can hear Winnie before I see her.'

'Knowing Nan, if she was up, she'd have probably been busy pinning Union Jack flags to the fence in anticipation of your arrival, or laying out the red carpet for you,' Lucy quipped back, as the two women set the trays of food down on the patio table. 'In fact, you never know what you might find when you go up and wake her!'

'Neither will she. I hope I'm a pleasant surprise for her.' Vivian grinned and went back inside and upstairs towards Winnie's bedroom. She knocked loudly, waiting a few moments before she opened the door.

'Is she okay?' Lucy said coming up the stairs and walking into the bedroom behind Vivian. Seeing the unmade bed, Lucy ran to the bathroom and her bedroom, only to find both rooms empty. Her nan was nowhere to be seen.

Vivian pursed her mouth.

'Oh no, Lucy! She's done it again, hasn't she? She's gone wandering off on one of her adventures. Hopefully, she won't have gone far.' They ran back down the stairs and out on to the street in a bid to find Winnie. Lucy scanned the length of the road in both directions, only there was no sign of her.

# CHAPTER THIRTY-NINE

Debra kicked at the cupboard door once more, before collapsing on the small floor space under the staircase behind her. Her efforts to break out were pointless. She was trapped in here. Nothing that she did would make the door budge. Gerard had locked it, and she guessed by the sound of the furniture she'd heard being scraped along the hallway floor earlier before he'd left, that he'd barricaded the door too just to be on the safe side. Because he knew that she'd be like the antichrist, the second that he told her he was taking Mason and Logan.

And he was right. Seeing red, she'd gone for him, clawing at his face and his arms, screeching like a wild animal, no longer caring what her reprisal would be for speaking back to the man. Because there was nothing left that he could punish her with. She couldn't let him take the boys.

Because she knew what that meant. He was going to punish her now, in the worst possible way.

So she had fought with all of her being, only Gerard was bigger, stronger. Lifting her off her feet, he had carried her here to the cupboard and shoved her roughly inside. And she'd fallen backwards, into the wall, banging her head. The pain so sharp and immobilising that she was surprised that she hadn't passed out. Instead her body slid lifelessly down the brickwork, and she lay staring up at Gerard from the floor. Dazed and scared at what he was going to do to her next.

And it was as if she was seeing him suddenly for the very first time. This big mountain of a man that she'd stupidly married. Staring down at her, his face completely devoid of emotion. His eyes blank. He didn't care if she was in pain; he didn't care if he hurt her.

'You bastard,' she spat, aware that she'd wasted the last six years of her life with a man she'd didn't even like, let alone love. A man she was now more than certain was capable of murder. A man who was capable of murdering his own children if it meant punishing her.

'Don't take them, Gerard. Please. They haven't done anything wrong. They're just two innocent little boys. Look at their faces, Gerard. Look at them, they look just like you. They are your sons…' Debra was crying. Openly pleading with Gerard, begging him not to go through with his threat to hurt her babies, because he knew that would cause her the most pain in the world. It would destroy her. And that's exactly what he wanted to do.

'Please, Gerard, if you are angry. Take me. Hurt me,' Debra had screamed. Knowing that it was her last chance to try and fight back, she had leapt from the floor and ran at the man. Only Gerard had already anticipated her next move, and after the bang to her head from the fall she'd just endured, she wasn't as fast on her feet as she believed.

He'd laughed when he'd slammed the door in her face. She shook her head now as she recalled the sickening, callous sound; he had actually laughed. She'd lost track of time now, but she guessed she'd been locked inside the cupboard for hours.

Desperately trying to break the door down, only nothing she tried had worked.

She was wasting time. She needed to find a way out.

Crawling to the back of the cupboard she swept her hand into the crawl space, not caring about the thick mass of cobwebs that entangled themselves around her skin. Spiders were the least of her worries right now as she desperately searched for something, anything, to help her break the door down. But there was nothing of any use. An old hoover that didn't work properly that they'd dumped in here and forgotten about. A few of Mason's and Logan's toys. Picking up the little tatty blue bear with only one eye, Debra smiled, despite herself. Mason had loved this bear with all of his heart. Refusing to part with it, despite Gerard's insistence that the thing was a 'filthy rag' that he shouldn't be carrying around with him. Debra had said that she would buy Mason a new one, the exact same bear. But Mason had said that he didn't want a new teddy, a cleaner one. He only wanted his one. So Debra had made a secret deal with Mason to hide the bear from his father, tucking it away in the back of the cupboard for safe keeping, and for a while, it had pleased Mason, to know that his precious bear was safe from his dad's reach. As time had gone on, Mason had forgotten all about the bear and it had stayed here in the cupboard ever since.

She thought about her children then. Knowing how scared Mason and Logan would be right now. How they hated being alone with their father. Even more so now that they'd watched him hurt their mother. That their father had taken them away. Gerard would be fractious and unpredictable.

They'd sense the real danger that they were in. She could just see Mason now, being the best big brother and comforting Logan, just like he always did, and Logan, the softer, more gentle of the two boys, would be crying. For her.

Eyeing the old, redundant radiator on the back wall, Debra stared at the ancient iron pipework that ran down the side of it. One end of the pipe flattened into a sharp flat edge where it had been sheared off by the last plumber, who had disconnected it. She turned and examined the cupboard door. Her eyes going to the small slither of light that ran along the hinged edge. She'd been doing this all wrong. Trying to break out from the bolted side of the door. If she could fit the iron bar inside the other side, she might be able to pop the hinges off and prise the door open. She yanked at the bar, wrenching it with all her strength, her hand gripping it so tightly that her knuckles turned a bright white. She flew backwards into a heap as the pipe finally came away from the wall. She set to work. Mason and Logan needed her. She had to get to her children.

# CHAPTER FORTY

Hearing the hammering at her front door, Kiera woke from where she lay on the sofa.

'How long's that banging been going on for?' Kiera asked Maisie, who was sitting with her eyes glued to the TV screen, purposely ignoring it.

'I don't know. A minute.' The child shrugged, not moving her gaze from the screen.

Kiera knew that Maisie was sulking, and she felt bad then. She was still so hungover from last night that she'd made Maisie miss her ballet class this morning. Instead she'd plonked herself and Maisie down on the sofa, in a bid to try and stop the room from spinning every time she stood up. Only she must have dozed off. Poor Maisie had been sat in front of the TV all morning, but she was a good girl for sticking to their rules and never answering the front door, unless Kiera expressly told her she could. And by the sounds of it, someone really wanted her to answer it. Whoever it was sounded as if they were going to break the door down. Making her way to the door, Kiera was far from impressed.

'For Christ's sake, Micky!' she yelled, assuming it could only be her husband who would bang so impatiently like that. 'What have I said to you, take your bloody key... You'd forget your bloody head if it wasn't attached... Oh, Debra! What's happened? Are you okay?' Opening the door, Kiera stopped in her tracks, seeing Debra frantically crying, remnants of her make-up from last night smeared down her face, and her hair all clumped to one side. Kiera narrowed her eyes.

'Has that bastard hit you again? That's it, Debs, I know you don't want me to get involved, but Jesus Christ, he's going to end up killing you. When's it going to stop?' Kiera said, stepping aside and letting Debra in, thinking that Debra wanted some sanctuary away from the man.

'No, it's not that,' Debra said, pacing the kitchen, visibly distressed. 'I kept something from you, Kiera,' she went on, unsure where to even start with explaining to her friend what had gone on. 'Laura… her real name is Lucy. She's a detective constable.'

Kiera opened her mouth to speak, only she didn't seem capable of any words.

'I'm sorry that I didn't tell you. Trust me, if it wasn't such a risk, I would have told you. You know I would. We tell each other everything. But it was too risky, so I lied, and I'm sorry. Lucy was undercover. She was going to help me and the boys get out. But Gerard's found out about her, and I think he's gone after her and I don't know what to do.'

'Gerard knows that she's a copper? Shit!' Kiera said, realising what Debra was telling her. 'Who's she working with? Do you have anyone you can contact?'

'Her detective sergeant helped set everything up. DS Morgan, I could call him,' Debra said, looking nervous.

Kiera narrowed her eyes, wondering why that hadn't been Debra's first thought. Why she hadn't picked up the phone and called him. Instead she'd come here.

'What is it, Debra? What are you not telling me?'

'He left ages ago…' Debra finally admitted. She'd been pacing the flat frantically on her own, debating what to do for the best. It was selfish of her but she had her own motives to keep her mouth shut. For the sake of her boys. But her conscience had got the better of her. Lucy had put her neck on the line to help her out; Debra owed her the same. Lucy was in danger. She couldn't let Gerard do what she suspected he was about to do.

'He's taken the boys with him, Kiera. So that I wouldn't speak out. He's using them as leverage. He told me, if anyone comes looking for him, if I tell anyone, he'll kill them after he's killed her.'

'Fuck,' Kiera said. This had gone too far already. There was no telling what Gerard might do. 'I'm going to call Paul. He'll know what to do. He's the only one that Gerard will listen to. Maybe we don't need to tell the police just yet.'

Debra was crying now. All she could think about was how scared Mason and Logan must be right now. How Gerard didn't give a shit about those boys, and how he'd always just used them to get to her. She'd never hated anyone more than she hated him.

Kiera grabbed her phone and dialled Paul's number.

'It's going to be okay, Debs. You can still keep your promise. The boys will be just fine. Paul will fix everything, I know he will.'

# CHAPTER FORTY-ONE

'Right, here we are. In you get,' Gerard said, holding the back door of the car open for Winnie.

'Oh, a gentleman! You don't get many of them nowadays.'

Gerard rolled his eyes as the old bird climbed in. So far, Winnie Murphy was making things far too easy for him. Ever the opportunist, he'd climbed in through the bedroom window at the side of the house, out of direct sight of any of the neighbours. He hadn't expected to find the old lady in there sleeping in the middle of the day. Only she'd woken, and he'd registered the terrified look on her face when she'd caught sight of him standing in her bedroom. But he hadn't come here for her, he'd come here for Lucy. So he needed to get the old woman to stay quiet and not alert her. Willing to use the woman's fear against her, and threaten her into keeping her mouth shut, he quickly found that he hadn't had to. Because the old woman had started talking nonsense. Babbling away as if she knew him. As if he wasn't some stranger who'd just crawled in through her window uninvited.

Gerard wasn't sure if the woman's ramblings were from fear or confusion, but she started putting her own narrative to the story of why he was actually in her house, in her bedroom. She seemed a bit deranged and not all there in the head. Still, Gerard had happily gone along with it all, in a bid to keep the woman calm and to stop her from shouting out and alerting that Lucy bitch that he was here. Inside her house.

'Yeah, that's right. I'm your taxi driver, I've come to collect you, Winnie. To take you for a nice day out.'

'Brighton? We're going to Brighton!' Winnie had squealed, the look of confusion on her face melting away, replaced with pure excitement. 'Ooh, I better get dressed into something more suitable…' she'd said, looking around the room for something to wear on her outing.

Gerard nodded, before slipping out of the room. Looking for Lucy. Sneaking as quietly as he could along the landing, he kept his huge frame pushed close up against the wall as he listened out for any noise in the house. Assuming that Lucy would be downstairs, but the house was in complete silence and he wondered if she was out in the garden.

Though as he reached the next bedroom, the door ajar, he peered in and saw a figure lying in bed, noting the tell-tale cropped red hair. It was her. He watched as the blanket covering her rose and fell with each deep breath. Sleeping so deeply. Nice for some, he thought. It must be exhausting being such a treacherous bitch. Plotting to happily ruin his whole life, destroy everything that he'd worked for, yet here she was, sleeping like a baby, as if she didn't have her own conscience.

He'd thought about dragging her out of her bed and smashing her head repeatedly off the floor. Or sticking a knife in her while she slept. But none of it seemed fitting enough. Because Gerard wanted her to pay for trying to fuck him over. For having the nerve, the barefaced cheek, to come into his home and conspire with his wife against him. He hated coppers almost as much as he hated grasses. And he hated this copper most of all.

'How do I look?' Winnie said, unaware of the murderous thoughts in the man's head aimed at her granddaughter, as she stepped out of her room dressed in a leopard print hat on her head and a pink polka dot scarf around her neck.

Gerard nodded his approval, speechless, wondering if the woman was taking the mick. She was still wearing her yellow nightie, though she didn't seem to realise, and the hat and scarf only made her look as ridiculous as she was acting.

'You look a million bucks,' he said, keeping his voice down now so that they wouldn't wake Lucy.

He'd had an idea. A change of plan if you like.

'Shall we get going? We don't want to be late,' Gerard had said, taking the woman by the arm and leading her out to the car. So that she wouldn't have time to think about Lucy lying asleep in her bedroom. Child's play.

'Oh, and who are these two little darlings?' Winnie said, beaming at her fellow passengers, sitting in the back seat of the car next to her as she climbed in. 'My name is Winnie. Nice to meet you,' Winnie said, holding out her hand to greet both of the boys.

Gerard rolled his eyes as he ran round to the driver's side, convinced now that the old dear was a sandwich short of a picnic, that was for sure. Not questioning for a second why her 'taxi driver' would have his children in the car with him. He climbed into the driver's seat.

'I'm Logan, he's Mason but he's grumpy,' Logan said, basking in the woman's friendly smile as he playfully shook her hand, while side-eyeing his brother to check his approval.

Though Mason hadn't uttered a word since they'd left home.

'Well, what handsome boys you are,' Winne said. 'Are they your sons?'

'Yes, I hope you don't mind. I had to bring them to work with me.'

'Oh, how lovely. Of course I don't mind.'

Clicking the child lock button down so she couldn't get out while they were driving, Gerard started up the engine.

'Right then, where are we off to?' Gerard asked, playing along. Though he knew exactly where he was going to take Winnie and the boys. There was a house they used over in Putney. They cleared it out a few weeks ago now. No one would know where to find him there.

'Can we go home?' Mason said, still thinking about his mother. He didn't want to go anywhere with his father. He just wanted his mum.

'Oh, no. We're going to Brighton, aren't we? To the seaside,' Winnie said, closing her eyes now, and imagining she was breathing in the sea air, the rare glimpse of a memory bringing tears of joy to her eyes.

'We used to sit on pebbles and eat fish and chips. And they have those lovely warm donuts there. You know the ones that are coated in sugar. We used to play a game where we'd have to eat a whole donut without once licking our lips. Oh the mess we made…' She laughed then. 'Would you boys like to do that? To eat all the donuts but not lick all the sugar off our lips?'

'But we can lick a little bit of sugar off at the end?' Logan said, not sure that he could make such a promise and keep it.

'Every last bit!' Winnie laughed then, excitedly, remembering the trip that Lucy had promised her earlier in the day. 'Oh, no,' she said suddenly, her tone tinged with apprehension as a feeling of doubt crept in. 'We can't go. Lucy said she cancelled the trip. Vivian's coming instead. We're going to have afternoon tea in the garden.'

She looked down as she spoke and frowned, wondering why she was still dressed in her yellow nightie. And why she was in a taxi without Lucy.

'Oh, well, you see, I shouldn't be telling you this, Winnie. It's top secret. But Lucy is actually surprising you,' Gerard lied as he continued to drive, with no intention to stop and appease the woman. She couldn't get out now, even if she wanted to. Though Gerard wasn't going to spell that out for her. 'She's going to meet you there. At the beach. Vivian is going to be with her.'

'Oh, they are already there?' Winnie said, the fleeting confusion gone again as she looked down at Mason and Logan and relaxed once more. She was being silly. Of course she was. She tried to ignore the feeling of doubt that crept in that something bad was happening, something she couldn't quite understand. She looked down at Mason and Logan and shot the boys another friendly smile.

'Do you know the song "The Wheels on the Bus"?' Winnie said, as Logan nodded in the hope of impressing the woman, reciting the first verse as if to prove to her he did. It was his favourite song; they sang it at nursery. Mason didn't sing. Instead he gave his brother a tiny dig in the ribs for being so happy and quick to forget about their mum.

But Mason hadn't forgotten. He'd heard his daddy shouting again, and his mummy crying. And he'd seen his daddy lock his mummy in a cupboard. He glared at his father with disdain in the rear-view mirror. And he didn't believe his dad's lies, that they were going to the beach. Because his dad wasn't nice, no matter how much he was pretending to be to Winnie. There was something else going on, only Mason didn't know what. All he did know was that he wanted to get out of this car and away from his dad as soon as he could. The only thing he wanted was his mum.

# CHAPTER FORTY-TWO

Gerard stared at his phone as Paul's name flashed up on the screen. Bending down to the kitchen counter, he snorted another thick line of coke before tipping his head back and laughing out loud in elation. Pure and uncut. This shit was the best. And they had stood to run the London streets with it, and make an absolute killing. Only his cunt of a wife had well and truly put paid to that now. High as a proverbial kite, Gerard psyched himself up for the next part of his plan as he paced the kitchen, purposely ignoring the irritating sound of his phone as it continued to vibrate across the kitchen counter.

As the phone went silent, he relaxed, taking a deep lungful of breath. Only it rang again, immediately. And Gerard couldn't help but grin as Paul's name flash up once more. He was a stubborn bastard. Just as obstinate and tenacious as Gerard was. Once Paul got something in his head, he didn't let up. It was one of the things that Gerard liked the most about him, because it had always been the one thing that had proved to Gerard that really they were one and the same. Like brothers.

That their minds worked in the same way. Only today that quality in his friend was as annoying as fuck.

'Gerard, mate. I don't know what the fuck is going on. But you need to tell me where you are?' Paul asked, when Gerard finally answered his call, debating on telling Paul to do one and launching his phone against the wall. Only he thought it only fair to hear Paul out and see what he wanted. Though he could already guess by the panicked strain in Paul's voice on the other end of the receiver that Paul was sounding him out. He was checking up on him. He knew. Which only meant one thing.

'I take it that bitch managed to claw her way out of that cupboard that I locked her in! I should have finished her off.' Gerard smirked, though the smugness he felt from knowing how deranged she would have been, that he'd taken her two precious sons, was short-lived, when he realised that by now, she'd probably got straight on the phone to all her new copper mates, telling tales on him again.

'Where are Mason and Logan? Are they okay?'

'Paul, do me a favour yeah, keep your nose out of this one. They are my kids. And this is my business. Business that should have been kept between me and my untrustworthy, grassing, conniving bitch of a wife. She did this. Not me. This is all her fault.' He'd come this far now. There was no going back. Nothing Paul could say would stop him.

'What's her fault? Shit, Gerard, please tell me you haven't done anything to those boys?' Paul shouted, afraid now that what Kiera had told him was true. Gerard had threatened Debra with killing their two boys. He had told her he was going to punish her. That he was going to make her pay. Maybe he was too late.

'They're only kids, Gerard. They're probably scared right now. And I know you didn't mean what you said to Debra. I know you wouldn't hurt those boys of yours…'

But even as he said the words out loud, he wasn't sure. Gerard had become ruthless and unpredictable of late. His coke habit was out of control. And as much as Paul didn't believe that Gerard would stoop that low, to that level of depravity, part of him had doubts.

'Is that what you know, is it, Paul?' Gerard said, incensed then as he realised what Paul was trying to do to him. He was trying to pacify him. He was trying to get Gerard to calm down. To talk him out of his original plan. 'You're taking that bitch's side, aren't you?' Gerard said, almost disappointed. Though he should have known that he couldn't trust any of them. Not Debra, not Paul.

Everyone was out to get him. They all wanted to destroy his life.

'Gerard, please! I know you're angry and you have every right to be. I get it. I really do. But do not take it out on those two boys, Gerard. That's not who you are. That's not who we are,' Paul said, pleading with his friend. 'Tell me where you are, and I'll help you. We can stop this. We can put everything right. Me and you, Gerard. Just like it's always been.'

'You think I can come back from this?' Gerard spat. Angry once more, riled now as the surge of the drugs in his system amped up all his emotions. 'That copper probably knows all about Bobbie Carter and Jamie Nash, and all of the others. Of course she does. Snooping bitch. And no thanks to my grass of a wife. Going behind my back and telling the plod all my business. And what? I'm supposed to just sit back and let her rip my whole life away from me? We spent a lifetime working our arses off to get to where we are today. And we were almost fucking there, Paul. Almost at the top of the chain. We were making real names for ourselves. And cutting out our main suppliers would have changed everything, completely. Only Debra had to go and spoil it, didn't she?' Gerard was quiet then for a few seconds and Paul could hear the sound of him glugging down a drink. Whisky, he guessed. The man was drunk and stoned and out of his mind by the sounds of it.

He wasn't thinking straight. He wasn't thinking at all.

'This is her revenge. Her reason for betraying me. All because she lost some poxy baby. Which, let's be real. It wasn't even a proper baby. She was only a few months gone. All this fuss for something the size of a fucking tangerine. And she didn't even want it! She'd told me as much. How she never wanted to bring another child of mine into the world. Well she'll get her wish now. She's about to find out what it's really like to lose her kids.'

'Is that Lucy?' A voice called out from the background.

'Shut it!' Gerard replied, stomping into the lounge, where Mason, Logan and Winnie were sitting huddled on the sofa together. Their hands and feet tied. Unable to move. He should have taped their mouths shut too, so he didn't have to listen to their moaning and whimpering.

'I don't want to hear another peep from any of you,' Gerard shouted, throwing his phone down on the floor, before grabbing the roll of thick gaffer tape and taking it to wrap it around each of their faces, ignoring the pleading looks in his children's faces as they looked up at him, pleading to him with their eyes not to hurt them. Completely detached, Gerard acted like he couldn't even see them. As if his own kids were nothing more than strangers.

Paul heard a door slam, and heavy breathing and he knew that Gerard had the phone back to his ear once more.

'Gerard, mate. What the fuck are you doing? Why are the boys crying like that? What did you do to them? And who's the woman?' Paul said, feeling sick at the thought that Gerard might actually go through with his threats.

Paul was desperately trying to get through to him, only yet again, he wasn't listening.

'I've taken some collateral damage from the copper. I've got her old gran here,' Gerard said casually, as if admitting to an insignificant crime like pinching someone's handbag, or nicking a pair of trainers from a store.

As if an elderly woman's life meant nothing to him.

'Why?' Paul said, unable to hide his confusion. 'Why the fuck have you done that?'

The phone went silent. He could hear Gerard moving. He sounded like he was outside now.

Paul pressed his phone to his ear, searching for anything that might give him a clue on the man's location.

'Gerard. Speak to me. Tell me what you are planning to do. This is me you're talking to. Not the filth. Not Debra. Me, Paul, your mate. Your brother. We've been in this together from the very start. You and me, mate. You can trust me, Gerard, You know you can.'

There was a loud creak of metal, as if an old metal shutter or door had just been opened followed by a few seconds of silence. Paul pushed his ear to the phone and concentrated on the background noise. Birds chirping. Gerard was outside. The sudden sounds of church bells, not too far off in the distance. The metal creaked loudly again and then a door slammed. He guessed that Gerard was back inside.

'Tell me where you are, Gerard. I'll help you. I'll get Holder and we'll both come and help you. He's got contacts. He'll be able to cut you some kind of deal. We'll fix all of this. It's not too late.'

Gerard finally spoke.

'You tell them from me, Debra and that copper Lucy, that I didn't do this. This one's on them. They did this.'

'They did what?' Paul said, his voice filled with panic then, as he felt a pit of dread form in his stomach. 'Gerard, what are you going to do? Where are you?'

Gerard hung up. He stared down to the Jerry can of petrol that he'd placed at his feet, having just retrieved it from the garage at the side of the house, before pursing his mouth. He didn't want Paul to talk him out of this one. He needed to do this. He needed to show them all that he was a force to be reckoned with. That if you were foolish enough to betray him, he would destroy you. And that's exactly what he intended to do to both Debra and

Lucy. To hit them both where it truly hurt. To tear both of their hearts out. They'd never recover from this. First of all, he was going to do one more big fat line of cocaine. Then he was going to set the fucking house on fire.

# CHAPTER FORTY-THREE

'Sorry to disturb you, Sarge, but we've got a big problem,' DC Holder said, walking in to DS Morgan's office and shutting the door behind him.

'We do?' Morgan said, eyeing the officer warily.

Holder looked shifty this morning, more so than usual, and Morgan noted that the shirt he was wearing was creased, his hair un-brushed. The man was clearly looking worse for wear after attending Gerard Jennings's birthday party last night. Though, of course, Holder hadn't mentioned his dirty secret.

'What kind of a problem?' Even from this distance behind his desk, Morgan could see that the man had clearly had a heavy night. Taking in the paleness of the man's skin, tinged with a sickly green from too much alcohol. As well as the film of perspiration and beads of sweat forming across the man's forehead. He was jittery and anxious looking. Which was exactly what Morgan wanted.

Only not quite yet. Morgan had a meeting set up with the DSI later to discuss the new intel that he'd received from Lucy about DC Holder working with Gerard and his men. Morgan was keeping quiet for now. But Holder was spot on, they had a huge problem, only the man didn't know the half of it.

'Holder?' Morgan said, sensing the man's reluctance to confess whatever he'd come in here to say. Morgan fought to keep his expression and body language neutral; the last thing he wanted to do before he'd sought advice on how to handle this delicate situation, was to give the game away and alert Holder that his superiors were on to him.

Allegations of serious corruption involving officers in the force was a sensitive matter and should be treated as such. Someone much higher up the chain of command than Morgan would be dealing with Holder once this all came to light, but for now, Morgan knew he had a duty to do things by the book. And that meant he had no other choice but play it cool, and pretend that he had no knowledge of Holder's extra-curricular activities with Jennings and his men.

'I can't tell you how I know this, but you need to trust me, Sarge. I've received intelligence that Gerard Jennings has gone on the warpath looking for Lucy Murphy,' Holder said, unsure where to even start.

'Why would he be looking for Lucy?' DS Morgan asked, his hackles instantly raised that Holder had any knowledge of Lucy's involvement with Gerard. Though at the same time a tiny part of him wondered if this was some kind of a ploy. Lucy had seen Holder last night at Gerard Jennings's party. Who was to say that Holder hadn't seen her there too, and that this was his way of raising questions to find out more on the covert operation that Lucy was involved in? So that he could gather more information to feed back to Gerard.

'He believes she's been working undercover, Sarge. He's found out her address…' Then almost unable to say the next part out loud, Holder coughed to clear his throat. 'I've just received a phone call to say that he's abducted Winnie Murphy and I have reason to believe that her life may be in danger. He's got his two children with him, too, Sarge. Mason and Logan Jennings.'

Seeing the genuine concern on the officer's face and hearing the urgency in the man's tone, Morgan knew that the threat was real. And that meant that time was of the essence.

'Get a unit to Lucy's house, now!' DS Morgan instructed, as he picked up the phone and dialled Lucy's mobile, surprised and relieved to hear Lucy's voice sound so casual at the other end.

'Lucy? Are you okay?'

'Well, no, not at this particular moment in time, Sarge,' Lucy said, narrowing her eyes and wondering why her sergeant sounded so concerned about what she was doing, after he'd told her to take some time off. 'My nan's gone walkabouts again. Only this time, she's really done a vanishing act, because myself and Vivian have been searching for almost an hour now and she's not in any of the usual places. The residential home is hoping that she might be making her way back there, but so far, I've heard nothing. I don't know what to do. So I guess I'm just going to have to keep on looking.'

'When did she go missing, Lucy? How long ago?'

'I'm not sure. Within the last hour and a half? We both had an afternoon nap. Only briefly, but when I woke up she was gone. This wandering off has become a habit of hers,' Lucy said, sensing something else was going on, now that her sergeant had gone quiet. 'Is everything all right, Sarge? Do you know something?' Lucy said worried then, as it dawned on her that this wasn't just a courtesy call after all.

'Lucy, where are you?'

'I'm at the park, Sarge. Over on Wandsworth Common. I thought that she might come here; it's where I found her the last time.'

'Lucy I need you to get home. Now.' Morgan cut her dead. 'I'm going to send an officer over to stay with you.'

'To stay with me? Why? Sarge? What's going on?'

'Gerard knows, Lucy. He knows that you've been working undercover.'

'What's that got to do with my nan?' Lucy began, filled with utter terror then, as she realised that her nan hadn't just gone wandering off this time. 'Oh my God. He's got her, hasn't he?'

'I believe so.' DS Morgan answered honestly. Playing down what he knew to be true in a bid to keep Lucy calm.

'No! He can't have taken her. How?'

But even as she said it, she knew instantly that was exactly what had happened. Gerard was going to seek his revenge on her through her nan. Thinking back to last night, Lucy closed her eyes as she realised how foolish she had been to actually believe that she'd managed to trick the man. Her cover had been blown. She'd underestimated Gerard Jennings. Even in his drunken state after the party, he'd picked up that something was wrong and been suspicious of her. He must have followed her home.

'I need to find her, Sarge. The man's an animal, there's no telling what he will do to her.'

'No, Lucy. Get home, please. Let me deal with this one. Promise me, you'll do that and I'll get her home safely to you,' DS Morgan said then, putting the phone down and hoping that Lucy would listen to him and not do anything stupid. And more importantly that he could keep his own promise. His officer's safety and the safety of her family had been compromised. He needed to fix this and fast.

Morgan stormed into the main office and gathered the team around for a quick update.

'I want every officer out there looking for Gerard Jennings and Winnie Murphy. We are looking at a possible kidnapping of Mason and Logan Jennings and Winnie Murphy. An officer has been deployed to Lucy's address. We need someone to get over to Debra Jennings flat too, and pronto.' Morgan looked to Holder for reassurance that his instructions to send units out had been executed. Only as his eyes searched the room, he realised that the officer was gone.

'Where's DC Holder?'

'I don't know, Sarge,' one of the other officers said. 'He was here just a few minutes ago.'

# CHAPTER FORTY-FOUR

Weaving in and out of the busy Sunday afternoon traffic, like a man possessed, Paul Denman kept his eyes fixed on the road as he sped through the red lights on Putney Bridge Road, ignoring the car horn that blared loudly at him as he forced another driver to do an emergency stop. He'd broken every speed limit there was since he'd picked up Holder from the station just a few minutes previously. And Holder could tell by the look of concentration on the man's face that he was on a mission to get to Gerard and his boys as quickly as physically possible. Only the silence in the car now was setting Holder more on edge. Because until just a few minutes ago when Paul had filled him in on what he guessed Gerard intended to do to his own children, Holder hadn't realised just how deranged and dangerous Gerard Jennings actually was.

'I can't believe he could even think about doing anything like this to his own kids,' Holder said, thinking out loud as he tried to make sense of it all. He could feel his heart pounding inside his chest. His palms clammy now with perspiration. These were the type of people that he'd got himself mixed up with. Ruthless, twisted mad men who were capable of murdering their own children if it served a purpose and meant that it would punish their wives in the most depraved way. Just the thought of Gerard's threat made Holder feel sick to his stomach.

'Do you think he'll really go through with it?'

Paul shrugged.

'Not if I've got anything to do with it,' he added, his jaw clenched tightly as he spoke. Gripping the steering wheel harder, he pushed his foot down to the floor. Holder could see the anger coming off the man in waves and he understood why.

Despite Paul's and Gerard's dubious work ethic and obvious criminal activities, Holder was as aware as they all were that there was a code of conduct that these men lived by. An unspoken rule. Women and children were strictly out of bounds. An honour amongst thieves, if you like. Paul was thinking exactly the same.

'Gerard just isn't himself any more. He's paranoid and he's letting the drugs rule his head. It's all he lives for. The gear, the notoriety. The man believes his own hype these days and thinks that he's truly untouchable.' Paul shook his head, unable to get his head around his friend's way of thinking. 'How he thinks he'll get away with this, I do not know. But then that's just it. He ain't thinking straight any more. He's only out for himself, and God help anyone who sets out to try and destroy him, because when he goes down, he's dragging everyone else down with him.'

Holder stayed quiet, sensing the raw emotion in Paul's voice.

'I'm going to have to try and talk some sense into him, talk him down. But I'm going to need you to try and fix this, Holder. With your contacts, maybe you can make some kind of deal.'

'I don't know that my lot are going to be lenient on the man, Paul. Not now there're kids involved.' Then knowing that his loyalty stood with these men, he nodded as he knew he was supposed to. 'But you know I'll do my best... I'm sure we'll figure something out.' Only, as they continued driving both men knew that was a lie. No one could help Gerard now, that was the truth. The man had gone too far.

'We ruled the streets once. I mean, we really ruled them. We were selling our gear to every dealer this side of the Thames and making an absolute fortune. And Gerard, he had it all planned out. He had big dreams, you know. The fancy show house, the fleet of sports cars. Only, it never materialised. He's got money, don't get me wrong. He's got a shit load of money stashed all over the place. Invested in properties and businesses all over London. Yet he always refused to leave that goddamn estate we grew up on. And all right, his flat may look fancy. It's been done up nicely; Debra has got good taste.' Paul pursed his mouth. 'And of course, Gerard's got every useless gadget and gizmo on the market. Always has to look the part to a point. Always has to have something that no one else has got. Yet, still he would never move away from the Griffin Estate. Refused to even entertain it,' Paul said, turning off Putney Bridge Road, and into a small side road. They were almost there now.

'I used to think that he was properly attached to the place, you know. Despite the fact that he didn't have the best childhood, nor great memories of his mum. But I thought, that was it. You know, he wanted to stay in the flat that he'd grown up in. The place he'd spent his whole life. Only, it isn't that at all and I've finally worked it out. The man is still trying to prove himself. All these years later he's still trying to prove that he is the big-I-am. He basks in the fear that he's created. He needs that validity that people are afraid of him, that they are intimidated by him; he thrives off it. That's why he stays. Because to him, it's like being royalty. And it's enough for him. And he's still doing it now. This is his way of not going out without a fight. He's going down and he's going to take those boys and Winnie Murphy down with him. Maximum reprisal. That's Gerard all over.'

Paul sounded sad now. His voice thick with emotion as he realised that actually this wasn't a revelation at all. He'd known this about Gerard for a while now. And it was part of the reason they'd begun to grow apart. Paul had wanted different things. This life, this way of living, it wasn't enough for him. But of course, Gerard revelled in it.

'How much further is it?' Holder said, anxious now as Paul made another turn, driving slower along a residential street.

The truth was they didn't even know if they were going to the right address. They were here on a whim. Paul had suggested this place on only a hunch. But a hunch was enough, because they had nothing else to go on. Paul had said that he'd heard the noise when he'd been on the phone. Of a metal door. A garage perhaps, because it sounded like Gerard had gone outside. Then he'd heard the church bells ringing out for a wedding, and that's when he knew.

St Mary's Church was situated right next to Putney Bridge, overlooking the Thames, and the trap house they owned was nestled in the backstreets behind it. Empty now from where they'd cleared it out after they'd first heard that the police were watching them.

'He's here,' Paul said, relieved that his hunch had paid off, as he came to a stop, turning off the engine and eyeing Gerard's Range Rover that was parked further up across the driveway of the house they owned. They'd found him. Only his solace was short-lived as he saw the plume of thick black smoke billowing out from the downstairs front window.

Holder saw it too.

'Fuck, man! He's really doing this. He's fucking lost it.'

'I think it's fair to say, Gerard lost it a long time ago,' Paul said, running from the car.

'What's the plan?' Holder shouted, quickly following behind, feeling uneasy now. Going into this house, unprepared, when he knew that an elderly woman and children's lives were at risk.

Neither men knew what they would really be walking in to.

'Get in there and get them kids and Winnie out of there. Get them to safety,' Paul said, indicating to Holder to go around the back, as he got his key out of his pocket and went for the front door.

'What about Gerard?'

'Don't worry about Gerard, leave him to me.'

# CHAPTER FORTY-FIVE

He pressed his hand down on the door handle of the lounge. It was time. Only Gerard couldn't go inside. His feet wouldn't budge from where he stood at the doorway. It was as if he was stuck there, on the spot. Unable to move one foot in front of the other. The whole time, his hand gripped the Jerry can, but the doubt had well and truly crept in. He couldn't go through with it. He couldn't go in there and pour a deadly flammable liquid all over the room, knowing that Mason and Logan would be gazing right up at him. That they would be terrified of what their father was going to do to them. He must love the boys in some way, he realised, stalling now. The surreal feeling making him feel uncomfortable for a few seconds. Unprepared.

He needed to stay focused. And detached. Because love, whatever the fuck that was, was only an emotion and it was fleeting and pointless in the grand scheme of things. It didn't mean anything at all, did it? Not really. It only held you back and caused you pain. He thought of his own mother then, how she'd spent all her days picking him apart. Belittling him at every opportunity. Telling him that it was his fault that his father had left them both. He'd loved her: what good had that done him? And then his loving, loyal wife, Debra, that self-righteous bitch. He recalled the genuine hate and disgust that he'd seen in her eyes when she'd looked at him before he'd taken the boys, acting like she was better than him after the lies she'd told him. After betraying him.

He took a deep breath. He needed to concentrate on the job in hand and the bigger picture. He had no choice but to do this now. Christ knows what that copper had gone back and told the police about him, but he already knew that it was over for him now. As soon as the police set their grubby mitts on him, he'd be arrested and those two bitches would make it their mission to make sure that he did life for all of the crimes he'd committed. He'd spend the rest of his days behind bars, sleeping in some four-by-six cell, watching his back for any enemies that he'd made along the way.

And the truth was Gerard had made so many enemies. He was hated. He knew that. And at the very least, tolerated. Though those around him would never dare say that to his face. But fear was the only thing he had left. He wasn't willing to go down without a fight, and if that meant some victims along the way, then so be it. But he was going to leave a path of pain and destruction in his wake. He wasn't going to suffer alone. Debra and that Lucy bitch could pay the price too.

Or maybe he would get away with it. He could do a runner. Leave London and find somewhere else to work from. He could go abroad? He perked up a little then. He'd always fancied Spain. Things could still work out. But whatever happened, he needed to show everyone exactly what he was capable of. So that they think twice before they even think about coming for him.

Backing away from the lounge doorway, Gerard decided to start on the stairs, making his way through the hallway and up the steps, before walking backwards and sloshing the contents from the Jerry can all over the carpet and walls as he went. The heady, intoxicating smell filled the room.

This was his way of staying detached. He'd start the fire here. Small. The rest was down to fate if the fire spread, and anyone got killed. At least that was how he justified it to himself.

Making his way back into the kitchen he took another mouthful of the whisky, but the stench of petrol filled the house now, and overpowered the liquid in his glass. And it didn't give him the buzz he was craving. He needed the buzz. Bringing his head down to the table, he snorted another line of cocaine. Rejoicing in the instant high that he craved. He felt powerful then. He could do this. He would do this. It was time.

Making his way back out into the hallway again, he struck a match, allowing the heat to lick at his fingers while he stared at the flame as it danced so gracefully at the top of the match.

Willing it to get hot so that he was forced to drop it, and when it did, it was mesmerising.

How quickly the fire gathered its momentum. How the thick mass of yellow flames lapped and licked their way over and across every surface, taking out everything in their path. The house filling with smoke. In just minutes the room was on fire. Snapping out of his trance as the smoke pulled down deep in to his lungs, Gerard started coughing. He needed to get out. Only just before he reached the front door to leave, it opened. And Paul walked in.

'What the fuck are you doing here?' Gerard said, caught red-handed as he made a bid to escape via the front door now that the house was quickly filling with smoke. Though he laughed despite himself.

'Fuck me, Paul. You're always one step ahead, aren't you? I didn't tell you where I was.' Gerard was too drunk and stoned to piece together how Paul had found him. He barely remembered the phone call they'd had just over twenty minutes earlier. Everything was a thick, hazy blur now. The air inside this house. The thoughts inside his head.

'You're too smart for your own good,' Gerard said, but he meant it. He could trust Paul. He could depend on the man, because Paul, unlike everyone else, was loyal to the core. And sometimes it was as if they both shared the same thoughts, the same brain. They were on the same page. They wanted the same things. They'd often said over the years that they were like brothers and Gerard felt that right now more than ever.

'I heard the church bells,' Paul said, realising that the fire that had spread up the staircase and most of the upstairs was now alight. The curtains down here on the window next to him had gone up too. The air was dense and full of smoke.

Staring past Gerard's large frame, he saw Holder sneak in through the back door and tiptoe quietly towards the door nearest to him, in a bid to search for Winnie and the boys. Paul needed to keep the man talking. He needed to distract the man so that Holder could get everyone out safely, and he couldn't let Gerard fuck that up too. Which he would, of course. Because everything had to be done his way.

'I figured you might be here. What the fuck is going on, Gerard?' He watched as the fire obliterated what was left of the curtains, the flames growing taller, lapping up towards the ceiling.

'Where are the boys and Winnie?' Paul said, before placing the sleeve of his jacket over his mouth and nose, casting his gaze suspiciously up the stairs. If they were up there, he'd somehow have to fight his way through the already building inferno.

'It's all in hand, Paul. You don't need to worry about any of that. It's been dealt with. We need to leave.'

Gerard was slurring his speech.

Unsteady on his feet, he leant his hand up against the wall as he walked. The smoke around them continued building as he coughed and gasped for air. Still he continued, though.

'We can go to Spain. Just get the next plane out of here and start again.'

'Spain?' Paul said, only he wasn't interested in Gerard's fantasy theories, he was just trying to buy some time for Holder to find Mason, Logan and Winnie and get them all out.

'It ain't a bad idea, Gerard. We've spoke about Spain before. Maybe you're right. Maybe it's time to start again somewhere else.'

'Yeah! We'll be bigger. We'll come back stronger. Those two bitches tried to screw me over. But I won't let them win. I'll show them.'

Paul could see Holder now, opening the back door and guiding Mason, Logan and Winnie out into the garden to safety as quickly and as quietly as he could. It was only as Logan turned his head and saw his father that he started to scream.

'He's there. Daddy's there. He's going to hurted us again.'

Holder couldn't get them out of the door quickly enough, and of course, Gerard was immediately incensed. Realising that Paul had stood here purposely distracting him, while Holder had gone and freed the only real collateral that he had.

'Oi! They are my kids. Do not take my kids!'

Bounding towards the back door, Paul was on him in a heartbeat. They were left all alone.

# CHAPTER FORTY-SIX

Mason and Logan were clinging to Holder tightly. He wrapped his arms around them both as he led them and Winnie away from the burning house and across the road to safety.

'Mind your step, Winnie,' Holder said, as he placed the boys down on the grass verge and offered a hand to Winnie, so that she could step up the kerb and sit down on the grass too.

'That taxi driver is a bad man. I can tell,' Winnie said, nodding knowingly. As if she had a hunch about him and hadn't just experienced his wrath first-hand.

He watched as they all gathered their breath, in shock at their ordeal. Holder bent over, fighting to get his own breath back then as the adrenaline surged through him. They'd got here just in time. If they'd been just a few minutes later, he didn't even want to think about what he would have been walking in to.

'We need to go!' Mason said, his voice laced with panic, as tears slid down his face. Gripping Logan's hand tightly, who was now sobbing uncontrollably, he got back up on his feet as if he was ready to make a run for it. His eyes were fixed on the front door, as if he was anxious that at any second now, it would be wrenched open and his dad would appear and drag them all back inside. 'He'll come and make us go back in there. We need to get away from here. Far away. He'll come for us.'

'He won't, Mason. You're safe now. Uncle Paul is in there. He's going to speak to your dad, and make him see sense. He's not well, Mason. But he won't hurt you, buddy.' Holder saw the boy bite his lip, but he didn't look convinced. And Holder could understand why. 'You're safe now. We won't let anything happen to you. I promise.'

Gerard Jennings was completely unpredictable and today had only proved that. Holder couldn't do this any more. He wouldn't do this any more. Pulling out his mobile phone he dialled DS Morgan.

'Sarge, I've got them. Winnie and the boys, they're safe. But the house is on fire, and Paul Denman and Gerard Jennings are both still inside. You need to get some units down here now. And a fire crew. Pronto.'

He could sense the apprehension in DS Morgan's voice on the other end of the line, as he undoubtedly wondered whose side Holder was really on. Only there wasn't any time to get in to any of that right now. Reciting the address to his superior, Holder put down the phone and eyed the house, waiting for the men to come out. Thick, dense black smoke poured out from where the roof was on fire now too.

# CHAPTER FORTY-SEVEN

Paul punched Gerard square in the face, possibly breaking his hand with the sheer force. Only he didn't care about that. All he cared about was that Gerard was now sprawled out on the floor. Paul straddled him then, and wrapped his hands around Gerard's throat.

'If those kids meant so fucking much to you, you wouldn't be acting like such a sick twisted bastard and be doing this to them,' Paul said, gripping his hold on the man tighter as he registered the shocked look on Gerard's face as he fought to break free. Writhing violently beneath him, Gerard was strong. Paul had to be stronger.

'It's over for you, Gerard. And I can't do this any more. You've messed everything up. That was always your problem, you know. You couldn't appreciate a good thing when you had it. You had to spoil it. Destroy it completely.'

Gerard was wheezing now. His face turning a puce red as he tried to drive some oxygen into his screaming lungs. Only the house was filling up with smoke rapidly. It seemed suddenly darker, as if the sun had gone down in the middle of the day.

'I cringe every time you say that we are like brothers, you know that? Because, I ain't nothing like you, Gerard; because unlike you, I ain't into murdering innocent old women and little kids.'

Paul could feel the intense heat spreading towards him now. He knew didn't have much longer.

'And just for the record, Holder ain't bent. He's been sent in by the Old Bill to get a capture on you. I've known it for a while but instead of turning him in to you, I thought I'd use him to my own advantage. He has no idea that I know. And he trusts me. He trusts the information that I've fed him. It's been going on for months. Way before Bobbie Carter's mutilated body was pulled from the Thames. He knows about Jamie Nash and all the others too. He was coming for you, Gerard, and I was going to sit back and let it happen, "mate"!'

Paul squeezed tighter, purposely expelling the air from the man's body as Gerard fought profusely beneath him, kicking out. But drunk and coked up, he was too disorientated to fight back properly. His reflexes were too slow. And he was choking violently now. Gasping for the last bit of air to keep him alive.

'Spain sounds nice though. You're right. Maybe I'll go there. Start again. Get out of this life. Cause it ain't cracked up to much, Gerard, really! We ain't exactly living the dream. I spent my life clearing up your shit and being treated as if I'm your dogsbody. Well this is my last gift to you, Gerard. The last time I try and clean up your mess. I'll spare you from prison. And I'll save you from yourself.'

Paul stared down at the lifeless body on the floor and for a second he was overcome with the realisation that it really was over now. Gerard was dead. The man wasn't his problem any more. He wasn't anyone's problem. And the only thing that Paul felt was relief.

It was over.

# CHAPTER FORTY-EIGHT

They should be out by now, surely, Holder thought. The fire was too intense. Roaring through the entire building there was no way that anyone inside of it had any chance of survival. The neighbours were out of their doors, standing out in the street and watching the inferno with a mix of horror and fascination. As much as Holder wanted to leave, he knew he had to sit this out and see it through to the end. He needed to wait for his colleagues to arrive and finally hand Gerard Jennings in. Because he wasn't out of the woods just yet, and he couldn't raise any suspicions about his true identity if the two men did come out. His life would be in danger if they realised that he wasn't in fact a bent copper at all.

He'd just been playing the part, for months now. Living two separate lives and flitting between being an officer and a crook. But it had all been for the greater good. Sent in on covert mission to gather intelligence on Gerard Jennings and take the man down. But as of now, it was all over. He just needed his sergeant here, so that he would have backup. Then he could finally end all of this and take Gerard in. They had enough evidence and intelligence on the man to put him away for the rest of his years. Paul Denman too.

Though Holder genuinely felt bad about that, because he'd grown to like the man.

Which was weird when he thought about it, because Paul was just as bad as Gerard in some respects. Only the man did have integrity and spent his life reining Gerard in, and Holder knew that without him, Gerard would have been a loose cannon long before today.

After what felt like an age, Holder finally heard the sirens, as a fleet of squad cards and a fire engine descended on the street. And even after Winnie and the children had been taken back to the station with the family liaison officers, Holder stayed. The fire was out now. The scorched, blackened shell of a house smouldering as if still fighting against the gallons of water that the fire fighters had used to put it out.

He waited as the chief fire officer approached him to give him the news that he knew was coming. Because Gerard Jennings and Paul Denman hadn't got out.

'We've got a body.'

'Just one? There were two people in there?'

'We're still searching, but yeah, it looks as if there was only one person in there. Maybe the other person got out?'

# CHAPTER FORTY-NINE

'I owe you big time. It's my round. In fact, drinks are on me for the next year,' Lucy exclaimed, standing at the bar with Holder and Morgan.

'Whoa, steady on! If it's not the new red hair that's making you unrecognisable, it's going to be the fact that you've actually got your purse out and you're offering to get a round in! Who is the imposter?' Holder laughed as Lucy ordered two pints of beer for her fellow officers and a glass of wine for herself.

'Very funny!' Lucy said, passing the drinks to her two colleagues. 'Though, genuinely, I can't thank you enough for everything you did last week, Holder. Getting my nan and the boys out of that house…' Lucy fought back her tears even now. Her voice thick with emotion every time she talked about what had happened. Part of her still couldn't bear to think what would have happened if Holder hadn't got to that house on time, if he hadn't had gone inside that burning building and led her nan and Debra Jennings's boys to safety.

'You don't need to thank me, Lucy. It's part of the job. You'd do exactly the same, and you know you would. Though I will say, I think a year's worth of drinks is a bit tight. I reckon I could negotiate at least two, seeing as you were so quick to palm me off as "fraternising with the enemy",' Holder said, playfully, as Lucy blushed then, realising how ridiculous it seemed that she'd ever doubted Holder's integrity on the job. Even DS Morgan had to laugh at that, because he'd done exactly the same.

'Well played, Holder. Though I think it's safe to say that you had us both fooled for a while there.'

The covert operation that Holder had been part of had been initiated above DS Morgan by the DSI, who was in charge of Intelligence and Operations. DS Morgan hadn't been informed about a simultaneous operation because of how delicate the Op was, and the stakes at risk if Holder's real intentions got back to Gerard Jennings and his men. Holder was, in fact, not bent. He had been working secretly against the men. And even when Morgan had sent Lucy in, the DSI still didn't shed any light on the Op. And Morgan understood why. It had been a dangerous Op. And everyone involved had everything at stake. Because Gerard, knowing that Holder was a bent copper, meant that he wouldn't necessarily trust him with any damning information. The man had just used him for his own gain. Unaware that he'd been played all along. Whereas Lucy could get close to Gerard through Debra Jennings. She could find out things that Holder couldn't even get close to. It was a two-pronged attack.

It had been paramount that Gerard and his men believed Holder was a bent copper right up until the very end. And they had. They'd paid him considerably well for the past few months, completely unaware of the double bluff and that he had been feeding them false information and intelligence, and only what the force wanted them to hear. Holder had been reporting back to his own superiors the entire time and the money that he'd been receiving as payment for working for Gerard had been paid into the police funds. His integrity should never been in question.

'Oh, yeah! I must have played it well, Sarge. So well that I had you all against me at one point or another. Mr Popular, huh!

Even Gerard thought that I was in on it and wanted to smash my skull in.'

'Too bad that he didn't survive the fire,' Lucy said, not feeling very sympathetic to the man's horrific demise. And knowing that her colleagues felt the same, only they were all too professional to voice it.

But Lucy knew that they thought it, nevertheless. That Gerard Jennings's death had been no real loss. But that, in some ways, it had meant that the man had avoided his justice. He should have gone to prison for everything he had done. He should have been punished for the lives that he had taken. He should have been made to suffer every single day. Instead he'd probably died from smoke inhalation before the fire had finally got to his body. He wouldn't have known anything about it.

'And I doubt we'll ever see Paul Denman again. He must have made it out the back of the house and done a runner. I still can't work out if he knew all along that I was on to him,' Holder said, still trying to figure out when he'd given his game away. 'Or if Paul had just known that it was the end of the road for them all. Whatever it had been that had made the man run, I don't reckon we'll be seeing him again.'

'I'll happily drink to that. And let me just say, Holder, thank fuck you're on our team!'

'Well, either way, whatever his fate, that's two of London's most notorious dealers off our streets. Your lovely nan and Debra Jennings and her kids are safe.' DS Morgan smiled at Lucy, before nodding at Holder. 'So as far as I'm concerned, it's a job well done. Here's to team effort, whether you both like it or not.'

# CHAPTER FIFTY

'You are doing the right thing, Debra! Trust me. God, if I had the chance to pack all my things up and leave this godawful estate, I'd be there in a heartbeat. In fact, I'd let you pack me and Maisie up in the boot so we could go with you.'

Kiera hugged her friend tightly, as they stood next to Debra's car. The boys were sitting in the back seat, waving and making funny faces at Maisie through the window.

'I know I'm doing the right thing really. I need to go, and start fresh. The boys need a new start. Away from here. They've been through so much,' Debra said, sadly. Though the only sadness that she felt was that Gerard's death had been a relatively quick one. The man wouldn't have suffered nearly as much as she would have liked him to.

And both the boys wore their scars heavily from the day that their father took them. It had been almost three weeks since Gerard had perished in the fire. And every single night she'd been woken by either Mason's frantic nightmares, or Logan wetting the bed. Because their father haunted them.

One of the liaison officers at the station had told Debra that the boys would be too young to really understand. That they'd heal given time.

Only they did understand. They knew that their father had attacked their mother in front of them and locked her in a cupboard, and he'd tied them both up and set fire to a house with the intention of killing them both inside of it. And Debra wasn't sure either of them would ever get over it.

'You know that you are the only person I'm going to miss, don't you? You're the only person that I care about.'

Kiera couldn't hold her tears back then.

'Oh Christ, now you've bloody started me off. I should have known not to bother with mascara.' Hugging her friend tightly. 'We'll visit. When you're settled. You're not getting rid of me that easily.'

'What are you going to do?' Debra said, raising her eyes at what she was referring to, so that Maisie wouldn't pick up on the undercurrent of their conversation.

'I don't know,' Kiera said honestly. 'But I know that I have to do something. I can't keep living this way either. Like you said yourself. Life is too short.'

'It is indeed,' Debra said giving her friend's arm a tight squeeze to show her support. 'But you'll work it out. You'll know in your heart what the right thing to do is.'

'There's something that I want you to do, for me, Kiera. Can you take this over to Jodie Edwards's address?' Debra grabbed a thick envelope out from her handbag. 'It's not much really, just some money that Gerard had hidden away. It's the least he owes the girl.'

'Jesus, Debs. You are a bloody saint, girl, anyone else would be ripping the little tart to pieces and dragging her arse all over the estate.'

Debra laughed at Kiera's expression and shook her head.

'She's a kid, Kiera. Another young woman used and manipulated by Gerard. She doesn't deserve to be condemned for that, and neither does her baby. Please? Just drop it off for me. Don't give her any grief.'

Kiera nodded.

'I'm in awe of you, Debs. Do you know that? You always do the right thing. After everything you've been through, you never let this life grind you down.'

'That's because I've no other choice, babe. You see those two in the car, same as you are with Maisie. They are our kids. They deserve better than all of this. And I want them to know right from wrong. I never want them to turn out anything like him. We've got to show them the right way, haven't we?!'

Feeling herself welling up then, Debra gave her friend one last hug before bending down and kissing Maisie goodbye and getting in the car.

'As soon as I get to Cornwall, I'll call you. You can come down. Stay for the week. Stay for the whole of summer!' Debra smiled, fighting back her tears.

'You just try stopping me!'

Watching as Kiera and Maisie made their way back into the Griffin Estate, Debra started the engine. Glancing at herself in the rear-view mirror as she wiped her eyes, she saw a figure running towards the car and wound down the window just as Lucy Murphy tapped on the glass.

'Thank God I caught you before you left,' she said, panting for breath, having run half the way here. 'I just wanted to wish you luck. At your new place.' Lucy smiled in at the two boys before giving Debra a small bag that she'd brought with her. 'I got them some sweeties and some magazines. I figured with the journey and all it might help to keep them occupied. Though I'm guessing maybe all this sugar might actually not be the best idea!'

'Oh, Lucy! You shouldn't have!'

'Well, I'd be lying if I didn't say that my nan had a lot to do with it. She was insistent on me buying up half the sweet shop for them. I think she's got a soft spot for them both.'

'Ahh did you hear that, boys? Winnie and Lucy have got you some sweets and magazines. Say thank you!'

'Thank you!' the boys chorused.

'And thank you once again, Lucy. For everything. I really don't think you'll ever understand how much you did for me. Putting yourself on the line like that.'

'Well, I don't know about that. I mean, I messed up, didn't I? In the end. Thankfully DC Holder was more on the ball.'

'No, Lucy! If I hadn't had you with me, I would never have been brave enough to go through with any of it. You gave me hope that I could find my strength too.'

Lucy smiled, knowing that Debra was referring to her confession about her own mother's murder.

'I'm glad that you're getting out, Debra. And I wish you all, all the best!'

Standing back, Lucy watched as Debra and her boys drove out of the Griffin Estate for the very last time.

# CHAPTER FIFTY-ONE

'Will we go and visit Mason and Logan soon, Mummy?' Maisie said, not able to hide her upset as she and her mummy stepped inside the lift of the Griffin Estate.

'Yeah, of course we will, darling,' Kiera said, as she pressed the button to their floor. 'Maybe we can go for the summer holidays, like Debra said. We can go to the beach and you can swim in the sea.'

'Will there be sharks in the sea, though? Cos, I don't like sharks.'

Kiera laughed. 'No darling, I doubt there'll be any sharks in the sea in Cornwall. It will be far too cold for them.'

'Will Daddy be coming, too? Cos if there were some sharks, he could rescue me.'

'Ohh I don't think Daddy will be able to, darling. He'll probably be too busy working,' Kiera lied, thinking that was the worst idea she'd ever heard. If anyone would need rescuing from bloody sharks it would end up being Micky. The man was a liability in every sense of the word.

Though in fairness to him, he was harmless enough. She was too hard on him. But she knew that would never change. Because he would never really be enough for her.

With Maisie distracted now with the promise of a holiday to see her two best friends, Kiera leant up against the lift wall, and pulled the postcard out of her pocket. It had come through the door this morning. A panoramic view of the stunning Puerto Banús harbour in the Costa del Sol, lit up in all of its glory by a stunning red sunset. She'd known before she'd even picked up the postcard and shoved it inside her dressing gown pocket who it was from.

*Wish you were here.* And a phone number. She smiled. Paul never really had been big on conversation. But then, he didn't need to say anything else. Because for her that had been enough. He'd disappeared from the house fire, and no one had seen anything of the man since. She'd heard rumours that Paul had gone against Gerard in the end. That he'd helped to set him up. Kiera didn't know anything for sure though. All she did know was that he'd been true to his word and he'd got out. He'd got away from this life and he hadn't forgotten about her.

It changed everything. And she hadn't been able to think about anything else all day. Debra was right. Life was too short to live a miserable existence.

As the lift doors pinged open Kiera knew what she had to do. Taking Maisie's hand, she smiled down at her daughter.

'I think that maybe we need a little adventure of our own, Missy. How about we go on our own little holiday?'

# CHAPTER FIFTY-TWO

'Okay, so you bite the donut, but you mustn't lick your lips. No matter what. And I'm watching you both closely and there's nothing wrong with my eyesight, so no cheating!' Winnie said pointedly, explaining the game to the three women as they sat on the stones at Brighton beach.

'Nope. Can't do it,' Vivian laughed, taking a huge bite of the hot donut and instantly licking the layer of sugar from her lips.

'You're out of the game. Disqualified,' Winnie said, taking the game extremely seriously then as she eyed Lucy, defying her granddaughter to come up against her and actually win.

'Come on, Lucy. It's me and you now, girl. You want to lick all that sugar off, don't you?!' She smiled wickedly, before placing a third donut in a row in her mouth. Winnie finished the thing in record time.

'Nan! You're going to end up with chronic indigestion at this rate,' Lucy warned, knowing that her nan was so stubborn and determined to win, she'd happily chomp her way through hundreds of donuts just to prove her point that she would be champion of this game. She was just going to have to let her nan win. Lucy licked her lips.

'Ohh, Lucy's out too! You're a loser too, Lucy!' Vivian winked. 'You're in my club now, sweetheart! Loooosers!'

'Ha! I knew I'd win! I told you I would,' Winne shrieked excitedly.

The sight of the woman acting so triumphantly and self-righteously with a thick line of sugar circling the outside of her mouth and all down her chin only made Lucy and Vivian roar with laughter.

'You look like you've got a moustache, Winnie.'

'How bloody dare you!' Winnie said indignantly as if deeply offended. Her tone was deadly serious for a few seconds before she let out a loud cackle to show the two ladies that she was just messing with them. 'But I'll happily wear it, if it means I'm the winner.'

'Oh, Nan, you really are one of a kind, do you know that?'

'I should think so, Lucy. They don't make them like me anymore,' Winnie said with a wink as she finally gave in and licked the sugar from around her lips in the most unladylike fashion, as if to purposely enforce the point.

Lucy smiled, sitting back and staring out at the deep blue sea that spanned out all the way down towards Brighton Pier.

She went back to the dream she'd had a few weeks back. She was now convinced that she'd finally been able to see the face her mother's murderer in her mind's eye. Only until today she hadn't known what she should do about it. She'd kept it to herself, because she felt her nan had already been through enough. They'd all been through enough.

If there was any chance that they might find her mother's killer, Lucy owed it to herself and her nan to see it through, no matter how much pain it might bring them both to open old wounds.

She'd finally decided.

She was going to talk with DS Morgan the next time she was on shift.

He'd help her.

She watched as her nan pointed at the seagulls and laughed as they swooped down on the stones in front of them, fighting amongst themselves for any scraps of food. The sound of children laughing echoed out from where groups of kids stood in clusters at the water's edge.

Lucy smiled.

Today was a good day.

Thankfully her nan didn't have much recollection of Gerard Jennings kidnapping her. But she did recall that she'd been promised a trip to Brighton, only the bad taxi driver hadn't taken her there. Which was why Lucy had brought her here today. Winnie wanted a trip to Brighton more than anything, and Lucy was happy to oblige. Not only because she'd never hear the end of it if she didn't. But she knew how they all needed this. Herself, Winnie and Vivian. As much as her nan needed the normality of spending some proper time with Lucy, enduring daytrips like this to break up her daily routine of staying at the residential home, Lucy very much needed days like this too.

Because as she sat there with her nan and watched the woman laughing so freely, as she too looked out on to the ocean, Lucy caught sight of that old familiar twinkle in the woman's eyes. And part of her was so grateful for days like these. For all these little things like sitting in the sunshine, eating donuts and putting the world to rights with the two favourite women in her life.

'Hey, earth to Lucy!' Winnie said, placing her hand on her granddaughter's knee and giving it a tight squeeze.

Lucy smiled then at the loving gesture and held on to Winnie's hand tightly. Life was hard. Full of obstacles and setbacks and its regular ups and downs. And all they really had was each other. And today, that was enough. In fact, it was more than enough. It was at times like this, that Lucy felt like one of the luckiest women in the world.

# A LETTER FROM CASEY

Dear Reader,

I want to say a huge thank you for choosing to read *No Fear*. If you enjoyed it, and want to keep up to date with all my latest releases, just sign up at the following link. Your email address will never be shared and you can unsubscribe at any time.

*www.bookouture.com/casey-kelleher*

I'm so thrilled with readers' love for Lucy Murphy and her feisty nan, Winnie. I've really enjoyed bringing them back for a second time, and introducing them to a whole new world of trouble. As always, on the Griffin Estate, you never know quite what you're in for, and amongst some of the darkness (and there is a lot of darkness) there are always characters that shine through, that we as readers long to root for. I truly believe that's why a lot of us read crime, so that we can champion the survivors.

I hope you loved *No Fear* and if you did I would be very grateful if you could write a review. I'd love to hear what you think, and it makes such a difference helping new readers to discover one of my books for the first time.

I love hearing from my readers – your messages and photos of the books always make my day! Please feel free to get in touch on my Facebook page, or through Instagram, Twitter or my website.

Thanks,
Casey Kelleher

  OfficialCaseyKelleher

  @CaseyKelleher

  caseykelleher

  www.caseykelleher.co.uk

# ACKNOWLEDGMENTS

Many thanks to my brilliant editor Therese Keating. It's been an absolute pleasure working alongside you once again on this second Lucy Murphy book! I really appreciate all your hard work and advice. The cover for this one is stunning, and possibly one of my favourites; thank you so much Emma Graves. I'd also like to thank Jan Currie for her fantastic copy-editing and Alison Campbell for her amazing work in bringing the audiobook to life.

Special thanks to Noelle Holten, as always one of the most supportive people in this industry. I'm so blessed, not only to have your friendship but for also having the best PR for my books (and not to mention your corruption with those bloody lethal Long Island cocktails at events). Thanks also to the rest of the Bookouture team, it really is a pleasure to be published with you. Biggest shout out to the Bookouture authors too, that I've been so lucky to meet along the way, for all the giggles, and for keeping me sane! Special mention to Emma Graham Tallon, Alex Kane, Angela Marsons, Helen Phifer, Susi Lynes, and Barbara Copperthwaite.

Huge thanks also to Colin Scott. You are the best!

And to the best book group on Facebook Gangland Governor, formally known as The Notrights. Though, you lot will always be Notrights to me! Thanks for all the support and the laughs along the way!

Special mention to the real-life Lucy Murphy, my bestie, who has always been so super supportive of everything I do. We will get to that gin festival eventually!

Thank you to David Gaylor, Peter James's real-life Roy Grace, for all your help and advice when it came to police procedures. Though as always, creative licence does come into play when writing fiction, so any discrepancies will, of course, be mine.

To all my fantastic readers, thank you so much for all your kind words about my books. You are the very reason I write; without you, none of this would have been possible. I love receiving your feedback and messages, so please do keep them coming!

As always I'd like to thank my extremely supportive friends and family for all the encouragement that they give me along the way. The Coopers, The Kellehers, The Ellises. And to all my lovely friends. Finally, a big thank you to my husband Danny. My rock! Much love to Ben, Danny and Kyle. Not forgetting our two little fur-babies/writer's assistants Sassy and Miska.

x x

Printed in Poland
by Amazon Fulfillment
Poland Sp. z o.o., Wrocław